Every Rose

D1825214

Karen,
I'm so happy
to meet another as
kindred soul such as
yours. Always find the
sweet in the bittersweet.
Love,
Lynetta Halat

LYNETTA HALAT

Published by Lynetta Halat at CreateSpace

Copyright 2013 Lynetta Halat
ISBN 9781483935904

Photo credit: Judy Merrill-Smith
"Rose Among Thorns"

Cover design: Okay Creations

Prologue

I've never liked roses. Well, that's not completely true. I love roses growing, especially unexpectedly, wild. But cut roses, no matter how arranged, repulse me. The actual act of trimming them to force them into a mold, conforming them to what society expects them to be—thornless, almost leafless—to me lifeless—is horrifying, almost sacrilege.

I didn't always hold this particular, admittedly strange, philosophy on roses. Honestly, if I hadn't been the analytical type, I probably never would have explored my feelings on the subject. However, I've just wrapped up my undergraduate experience with a double major—English and history with a pre-law declaration, which means I analyze. Some would call it overanalyzing, but I consider that a misnomer. I've also been experiencing a completely life-altering, for a lack of a better word, "event" that has left me contemplating specifics like roses, tattoos, love, life, existence.

During my summer break before I'm expected at law school, I've decided to test my limits and pen a few words about my recent event. Someone crucial to my very being suggested that I had repressed my urge, my need to create. He was right: I've never experienced anything like my current overwhelming state. It threatens to overcome all that I am. Therefore, I've decided to have a little faith in myself. Am I destined for law school? Or do I yearn for something grander, something unexpected, something unpruned, something wild?

Chapter One
Lesser of Two Evils

"What do you mean you're closing the store for Christmas vacation?! I always work Christmas vacations." I could hear the whining tone of my voice and feel the gears turning, showing me my alternatives. Christmas with my family. Mom pretending. Step-dad drinking. *Yeah, no thanks.*

Elise looks over the top of her glasses to pin me with her gaze, and her words cut to the core. "Of course you have worked every Christmas. Working provides you with the perfect excuse not to go home. It's called avoidance, and it's no good." Before I can respond, she changes gears; and her ever-present infectious smile overtakes her face while her gray-green eyes light up. "My son asked me to go up for the holidays, so I'm closing the store and doing just that."

I feel tears spring to my eyes. It was final then. She would do anything to spend time with her beloved son and grandson. There was no way I could argue her out of it. And if I couldn't work, I couldn't afford to stay here for the break. My options were limited—starve or spend Christmas with my family. Honestly, it was hard to decide.

She probably sees all of these thoughts cross my face, so she pulls me into a side embrace and hugs me tight. "It'll be OK, Lorraina," she assures me. "You love your mamma, and she will be happy to see you. You didn't spend near enough time at home this last year."

Resignedly, I kiss the top of her head and nod mine. It was done. No use in dwelling on the fact. "I hope you have a wonderful time with your family, Ms. Elise. I'm excited that you to get to see Jack and Jasper." I was surprised to hear the ring of truth to my words because this was absolutely the worst possible moment for me to be forced into a visit home. Of late, I'd been plagued with doubts about my choices. I didn't need to get dragged into a bunch of drama and nonsense.

Even though I am miserable about it though, there is no reason to take that out on her. I give her a real hug and a real smile. Elise is the doting, caring version of the mother figure that I've never had. My mom has always been too preoccupied with surviving to show any real interest in me. I can't blame her. She went from one shithead to another, effectively ensuring herself a life of misery and worry. Elise had had the same bad luck with a shithead of another making; however, Elise had gotten out, pursued her dreams, and stayed single.

Unbeknownst to her, I'd been following in her footsteps over the last few years. I am doing everything possible to steer clear of that kind of relationship, that kind of life. Most importantly, I have avoided my hometown like the plague. It seems those kinds of relationships are like tornados there. If you stay, no matter what barricades you erect, you are destined to get caught up in one and will be chewed up, spit out, and forced to live with the consequences.

***

3

I finish up my shift with little fanfare. I really can't blame her for closing through the break because we have been dead these past few days. I exit into the dark, deserted street; and I realize we aren't the only ones closing for the holidays. It seems like everyone has pretty much left Oxford. Apparently, there aren't too many students dreading visits home. Most kids are probably thrilled about getting their clothes washed, meals cooked, and basically being waited on hand and foot for a couple of weeks.

I, however, have a whole other set of worries. Maybe…I think…maybe it will be different this year. I mentally feel a little jolt courtesy of my Psyche 101 class as Einstein's maxim pops unwilling into my head…"the very definition of insanity is doing exactly the same thing and expecting a different outcome…" *Well, one can still hope, Einstein.*

I take a deep breath and steel myself against all my negative thoughts and the biting wind. I step into the street and turn around to make sure I've turned off the sign. Of course, the sign glows back brightly at me. I'm not surprised, being so preoccupied. Then it hits me. Wow, Your Next Best Friend Bookstore. I've worked here almost my entire college career; and I've loved everything about it: the cheerful customers, the search for the elusive book, the challenge of matching a reluctant reader with just the right book and turning them into a lifelong reader.

Sometimes, I think I might be just as happy here as in law school. But I like everything that a law degree will give me—a shield, authority, protection. An image of my future self floats before my eyes. Future Lorraina is strong, successful, and impervious. I can't wait to be her.

I shake myself from my reverie, close my eyes, take a deep breath, and go back into the store to kill the lights. Daydreaming about my life, or lack thereof at present, isn't going to help me get this over with any sooner.

Chapter Two

There's No Place Like Home, Thank Goodness!

It just smells like home. Before I can even open my eyes, I know exactly what the day will hold from the smells wafting through the house—timber, red beans and rice, laundry detergent, bleach. My brothers will be splitting wood all day, my step-dad will be directing and drinking two beers for every tree felled, and my mom will be cooking and cleaning.

I begrudgingly open my eyes to survey my small, but tidy, room. Quite literally everything is brown. Brown paneled walls, brown furniture, brown clothes hamper, brown shelves, and brown bedding. At least that has the decency to have little white and yellow flowers.

I throw my covers off and think about getting up and seeing my family. I roll my eyes. I love them, but I'm really not in the mood to face the reality of them. It's sad but true.

I reach for my phone to call my friend Ginny and see about meeting up for a little Christmas shopping.

I close my eyes, willing her to be there and to say yes to my desperate shopping trip.

"Hello?" I hear her mom answer.

"Hi, Ms. Cuevas. This is Lorraina. May I speak to Ginny, please?"

"Sure, hun. You home from school?"

"Yes ma'am. I was hoping Ginny and I could go do a little Christmas shopping today."

"Oh great! I'll get her, hun. Take care."

"You too!"

"Hello?" Ginny asks in a sleepy voice a couple of beats later.

"Hey. It's Lorraina." I try for nonchalant. "I'm home. What are you up to?"

"The usual. Just working, taking classes, raising Aubrey," she answers, sounding exhausted. "How's school?" She punctuates the question with a yawn.

"Good. I can't believe I'm about to graduate. I guess it doesn't seem real because I'm going straight to law school—"

"Ya know," she perks up, "that's exactly what I need. A friend who's also an attorney...that will come in very handy."

"You're damn right it will you evil girl." Ginny had always lived life on the edge. She never did anything unforgivable—just slightly morally questionable. "How are you? How's Aubrey?"

"I'm good. Just tired. Aubrey's great. She is midway through kindergarten if you can believe that. She's a lot more levelheaded than I am. Believe it or not, she stays out of trouble."

"Well, it's only kindergarten. Give her time!"

"Bitch!" she laughs. "She's better than me," she replies thoughtfully. "You would think she was your kid as together as she is!"

My smile dies on my lips. "I can't wait to see her." I had bought her one of those cute little t-shirts that alerted everyone to the fact that her aunt went to Ole Miss. Southern tradition dictates that if we're far apart in age but close relationship-wise, I become your aunt. It's the respectful thing to do. "So, what are you up to today?"

She sees straight through me, "Hmm…just got home and trying to get out of the house already, huh?" I laugh. I don't know why I ever thought I would fool her. "Have you even had a cup of coffee?! Have you even said good morning to your mother?! You better go ahead and tell her that you're stuck with me, of course. Aubrey and I will come by and get you in an hour, OK?"

Ginny's idea of an hour and the reality of an hour existed in completely different realms. "Uh, Ginny," I stutter nervously, "when you say an hour, I really need you to use actual human time and rescue me in one hour. Got it?"

"Yeah, yeah. Got it."

"Thanks. See ya then." I hang up with a much more cheerful perspective on the day.

***

It was early afternoon and we had already finished up the last bit of our shopping. It doesn't take long when you've only got about fifty bucks to spend on a handful of people. I felt guilty for skipping out on my mom so quickly that morning, so I put extra care and dollars into her gift. It was an iridescent angel bookmark. The only thing she reads is her Bible, but I guess that counts as something. I bought Ginny a whimsical coffee cup that had no rhyme or reason to it, which is probably why she will love it. I put a great deal of thought into my guy gifts for my step-dad and brothers, but they were still my least favorite gifts. That was probably due to the fact that I had no idea what to get them but wanted in some small way to say, *Hey! I cared enough to do my very best!*

I was carrying Aubrey, who had fallen asleep on my shoulder, when we made our last stop. We always saved this shop for last because it had been our favorite place since high school, and we could quite easily spend the rest of the afternoon here.

As I open the door, a familiar jingle rings in my ear; however, the sight that greets me is anything but familiar. I stretch my neck back to double check that I am in the right place. Yep, Mona's Book Bag, but underneath that "& Café" now graces the entrance. "Huh," I murmur to myself. To Ginny, I hiss a little louder, "What the hell happened here?"

It had been painted all sorts of earthy, yet vibrant, colors. On the walls, what looks like local art is scattered throughout the store. Leather couches are askew in and around a few bookshelves that hold mostly magazines, newspapers, and greeting cards. The shop had been expanded on both sides to encompass the other stores that used to surround it. There are people sitting everywhere drinking coffee, reading, and conversing.

"Umm…You could've warned me?!" I snap. Finally drawing my eyes away from the scene and cutting them at her.

"Yeah! I know," she giggles, truly enjoying my torture. "I wanted you to be just as shocked as the rest of us were. Mona decided to upgrade us to one of those new-fangled coffee shops from Seattle. However, she also decided to outdo them in the process. It is truly a sight to behold, isn't it?"

She was right. It was incredible. I make my way to one of the tables while she orders us a couple of cups of coffee. I can't believe my eyes. It's a store to rival all other stores—a bookstore, a coffee shop, an art house, a library, a Hallmark store, and apparently, a popular local hangout. I was impressed. I was intrigued. I was robbed of my little used bookstore.

Ginny finally makes her way back over to me and Aubrey. I gingerly take a sip of my coffee, "Mmm...Wow! This sure is different from our little pot of Community Mona always had at the ready." It's delicious, but I long for simpler times.

We chat for a while, enjoying our coffee and grown-up time while Aubrey is passed out. She tells me of her latest drama with Aubrey's dad and her new boyfriend. I tell her I don't understand why she and Jimbo don't just get back together. It is obvious to everyone that they are destined to be together. She insists that, while that may be obvious to everyone else, it is obvious to her that Jimbo is, was, and always will be a piece of shit. I absolutely adore the fact that Ginny never minces words. She says what she means and means what she says; therefore, I now consider the case forever closed. She doesn't do fickle.

"So are you seeing anyone?" she asks.

"No, I wish I had time to date. Things are just crazy," I reply, giving her the standard acceptable answer.

"When's the last time you had a boyfriend or even a date for that matter?" She asks pointedly.

"Um…It's been…a while," I hedge. Thankfully, Ginny turns our conversation to less awkward topics, and I get caught up on the latest gossip surrounding people I haven't thought about in a long time.

We agree to take turns checking out the book selection since Aubrey is still asleep, so I make my way back to my rows and rows of used books. This is what I had come for. I plan to spend most of my break catching up on my "fluff" reading. As an English major, I never have time to read anything I want to read, which, of course, is the ultimate in irony. There is always a reading assignment lurking. I am a voracious reader, but I am really tired of being told what to read and forcing myself to analyze all the little details when all I really want to do is just devour something for the sheer joy that reading for escapism provides.

Surprisingly, I find myself toting around some books that I had already read a time or two mixed in with a couple of others that look they had been read quite a bit, which is a good indication that I won't be disappointed. Because my reading time is always so limited, I decide to reread a couple of my "sure things." Getting some good stories in before tackling my final semester is crucial to my mental health. I spend way too long deciding, so I hurry back to Ginny.

On my way back to our table, I spot it. On one of the greeting card shelves, sits a drawing I would know anytime, anyplace. *No way!* It's like the card has a tractor beam fixated on me because before I know it, I'm standing directly in front of it with my mouth hanging wide open. I snap it shut and glance around to see if anyone noticed my weirdness. I don't see anyone staring at me, so I continue my mission. I lay my books haphazardly on top of the shelf in my eagerness to confirm who has designed the cards. As I reach down to examine one more closely, all my finds tumble to the floor. I hear Ginny tsk from across the room. I roll my eyes at her and bend to pick them all up. By the time I have them gathered and stacked properly, she is standing next to me explaining how she's going to book shop another time because she really needs to get out of there and get some things done.

I nod, barely aware of what she is saying. I pick up one of the cards and study it. It is beautiful, and I know this rose. I imagine it falling out of my locker during freshman year. I wince as I remember crumpling it up with frustration. If it isn't his, I will be completely shocked. If it is his, I will still be completely shocked. The last I'd heard he had gone to jail for a DUI and had been written off by everyone as trash just like his daddy. I pray that it is his, though, and that he's sharing his talent. Finally, I turn it over and gasp. I am in awe. I am so impressed by this little card that I can't speak for a moment. Tears have pooled in my eyes.

I blink them away and look at Ginny to ask if she knows who had designed the card. She shakes her head. I whisper, "It's Michael's. How in the world?"

"Michael? Oh, Bang?! Oh, right. I heard he was drawing and designing stuff. I didn't know he was making cards too. That's cool."

"It's more than cool. It's amazing," I reply fervently. "Do you have any idea what this means? I mean, I know it may not seem like much; but it's actually a huge deal. It means he's taking steps to straighten out his life, or he has straightened it out." I can hear the awe and wonder in my voice, but it can't be helped. I am reeling from the implications of this. I had resigned myself to the fact that he would probably turn out like every other guy from my town and that had been that. Now look. Wow! Just wow. I feel tears spring to my eyes again. I know we aren't close anymore, but I can't help the immense amount of pride I feel for him. He deserves every bit of happiness he can wring out of life. He's the most deserving person I've ever known.

"I didn't even realize ya'll were friends."

"Yeah, we were," I mumble distractedly. "That was before you and I met. I was in eighth and ninth grade. He used to be my best friend, but we lost touch." I give her a very simplified version of our very complicated history.

There were ten cards on the shelf. There are now ten cards in my hand. I didn't even check to see how much they cost. I head to the register.

I hear Ginny laughing behind me and she says, "Hey, spaz, you left your books over here on the shelf."

"Oh yeah, let me go put some back. I want to get these cards too, but I don't have enough money for everything."

We make our way back to the register so that one of the new faces can ring me up. As she totals up my purchase, she volunteers, "Hey, you know he's playing here tomorrow night, right?"

"Who?" I ask. I give her what I'm sure is an annoyed look because I am lost in my memories at present. Just ring me up and be done with me already so that I can get back to my daydreaming.

"The guy who designed these cards. Mike Bang. I figured you'd be interested since you bought so many." She is looking at me like I am some kind of psycho or, worse, not from around here.

"What do you mean 'playing here'?" I ask. Now, I am truly intrigued. I haven't heard his name said out loud in years, and I wasn't quite sure what to make of the effect that the invocation of it just had on my body.

"Mona features singer/songwriters every weekend after hours. She calls it her 'Create Café' because she loves to give undiscovered artists a shot," she giggles at her coffee house pun.

I already know the answer to my next question but am curious to know what others think about him; so I ask, "Is he any good?"

She breaks a huge grin out. "Oh, yeah! He's super talented and," she leans in to whisper, fanning herself, "super cute!"

"So, you said he's playing here tomorrow night," I say with sudden interest in conversing with her. "What time?"

Chapter Three

The Joke's on Me

I remember leaving the store and getting in the car and saying goodbye to Ginny and Aubrey. But pretty much everything after that is a blur. I'm pretty sure I ate and hung out with my family a little. I remember a drab game of Clue in which I, very uncharacteristically, did not win. I'm lying in bed now, so I must've had a shower and readied myself for bed. I have been so preoccupied with thoughts of Michael that I have been on autopilot all evening.

I stare at each of the cards one at time, poring over and analyzing every little detail. Of the ten, there are four different designs. The rest are various copies of the four. In my haste, I didn't even notice that they weren't all unique. Each of the four roses is quite unique, though. I suddenly recall how Michael had never drawn me the same rose twice. His very mood decided the type of rose I would receive.

It had been so very long since I'd held one of his roses in my hand. It had been so very long since I'd even seen him. Our last conversation comes flooding back to me, and I push the memory away violently. It wasn't a favorable one.

Instead, I search for a different memory. A peculiar one springs to mind. One that I had never really reconciled. Sometimes, I marvel at the way my scheming mind used to work.

Even with all my scheming, though, things always had a way of backfiring on me.

Because Michael was on to me and so much wiser, he had loved every minute of my torture. I didn't think it was very funny at the time, but I can laugh about it now. I will never forget the look on Stacy's parents' faces when I set her and Michael up to go on a double date with me and Tony. It was so ridiculous that it was absolutely priceless.

Michael had actually backed off of his constant hounding of me to go out with him. We had become friends again—even best friends. This was how I loved us. He was my confidant, my rock, my everything. But every time he pushed, I fled. He hadn't pushed in forever. I was ecstatic, yet I was desolate. Was he finally over me? I decided to test him, so I offered to fix him up with Stacy. He accepted without blinking or seeming to think twice. I throw my head back on my pillow as I allow the memory to take me back.

Michael met me after biology and offered to carry my books for me. I shrugged him off and said, "You know it would be cool if we could hang out more without arousing Tony's suspicions. He doesn't get the whole 'best guy friend thing.' Why don't you go out on a double date with us? I could invite Stacy?"

"Sure, OK. Why not?" he said nonchalantly.

Something inside me protested and my stomach churned; but instead of giving a voice to all of that, I said, "Cool. I'll set it all up. Friday?"

"Yeah, OK."

That was easy, I thought. He really must be over me. He didn't even flinch or protest like he had when I had pressured him to date in the past. Stacy was going through her rebellious phase, so I knew a date with Michael would seem like the perfect ammunition to start a good fight with her parents, but she might also like Michael. He was unpredictable enough to challenge her, and she would like that.

Friday night rolled around. My mom would only let me go out on double dates since I was only in ninth grade, so I was not allowed in Tony's car alone with him. Tony picked Michael up first, and then they came to my house. I heard Tony blow his horn, so I started outside. As I put my hand to the door, the doorbell chimed. It was Michael. He looked adorable. He wore all white with a skinny, loosely knotted turquoise tie. His sleeves were rolled up. The first two buttons were undone so that his pewter cross was visible. The all white was in direct contrast to his dark skin. I'd never seen him dressed up before. I told him how cute I thought he looked. If his dark brown skin could've blushed, I know his cheeks would've been pink. "What?!" I said. "I can think my friend looks adorable, can't I?!"

He gave me the quintessential teenager reply, "Whatever."

I noticed that Tony was still sitting in the car as I was shutting the door. I said, "Don't say it. I know."

"Know what?" he asked.

"Know that Tony's a jerk." I laughed nervously because bashing my current boyfriend had gotten us dangerously close to

trouble one time before. "Anyway, I'm only dating him until Homecoming and then we're breaking up."

"'We're breaking up'? Sounds like you're breaking up," he replied with a cocked eyebrow.

I shrugged. "Yeah, I know. It's just inevitable. I know he's not the boy for me so why prolong it."

"That's exactly what I told you two weeks ago," he reminded me sardonically.

I just raised my eyebrow as a response since we were now within hearing range. Michael opened my door for me and hopped in the back.

When we got to Stacy's, Tony's chivalry had unexpectedly revived itself. He opened my door, and we all went in to get her. I entered first and called for Stacy. Her parents must've heard me because they quickly joined us in the living room. I watched their faces go from composed to shocked to horrified and back to composed in the space of about 3.5 seconds. I actually had to turn my head to keep from laughing aloud. As I did, I caught Michael's eye, and I actually got kind of pissed as I realized the reality of their disdain. Did Michael notice? If he did, did it bother him? I was beginning to regret my impulsiveness in setting up this experimental double date.

They had collected themselves enough to introduce themselves. By that time, Stacy had joined us. She looked positively pleased with herself. I pursed my lips and silently begged her with my eyes to get us out of there.

Her parents began asking the usual questions. Where are ya'll going? What time will the girls be home? Etcetera, etcetera. Then, out of nowhere, "Michael, what is your family background, son?"

I turned to look at Michael. Who very calmly stated, "American Indian—Choctaw, sir. And yours?"

When he said this, Stacy and I both lost it. I needn't have worried about Michael. He was perfectly capable of holding his own. Her parents shot us a dirty look. And Stacy's dad answered with all seriousness, "Irish."

As we're heading out of the house, I hear Stacy murmur, "Thanks. That's exactly the reaction I'd hoped for." They shared a laugh, and I fumed. I had no idea why it ticked me off so much that they had bonded over that moment; but from that moment on, I found myself stealing glances at them. Well. Didn't they seem to be hitting it right off? I couldn't fathom what she saw in him. I couldn't fathom what he saw in her. This was supposed to be a little experiment. I never really thought that it would actually go this far and that they might actually like each other. At this point, all I really wanted to do was punch both of them in the face, and I didn't even really know why!

I tried to pinpoint my irrational anger and a terrible thought occurred to me. Michael really was over me and falling for Stacy. But was she falling for him too? Crap. What if all she could see was his potential to piss off her parents? What if she breaks his heart? I didn't know the answers to any of my musings. All I knew was that I was a horrible person for having set him up to get hurt.

19

When the guys dropped us off at Stacy's, I followed Stacy in her house to have our sleepover; but all I really wanted was to go home. I thought about calling my mom and pretending to be sick, but any night away from my responsibilities waiting for me at my house was a good night. So I tried to get over it. Inevitably, Stacy and I started rehashing the night; she recounted how many times Tony's gaze lingered on me and how many times he "accidentally" touched me. I changed the subject and told her how much Michael's friendship meant to me and that I was glad that they had hit it off.

She looked at me like I was the village idiot and barked, "I couldn't possibly date Michael for real. You know that. I just did it to piss off my parents. Mission accomplished. They told me when I went to their room to check in that we're going car shopping tomorrow, which is exactly what I had hoped for. Can you imagine me driving my brother's hand-me-down?!"

I felt tears spring to my eyes. If that's really all it was, why did she seem to have such a good time with him? She hung on his every word, laughed at all his jokes, and shared food with him. It all seemed a little too personal to have been faked on either part. Now, I really did feel sick to my stomach. Calling my mom suddenly seemed like a great idea.

On the ride home, I let myself consider all of the implications of what Stacy's little rebellious standoff might have. What if Michael really did like her? What then? He would be crushed. He didn't deal well with rejection. I knew that all too well. I had set him up for this. I just had to have a little experiment to see if he really was over me. I felt like a naïve, meddling nitwit.

Once I was at home, I sneaked the phone to my room and called him, breaking my phone curfew. Customarily, I hung up on the first ring.

I called him right back. He answered on the first ring. "You know, you don't have to do that anymore. My brother doesn't care, and he won't tell a soul," he said sleepily.

"I know. It's just habit," I snapped back.

"Er…What's with all the hostility?"

"I'm sorry." I said aloud. To myself, I amended my apology to I'm sorry for existing.

"For what?"

"For setting you up with Stacy." To myself, for acting like I don't care about you when clearly I do. I just don't know what to do with that.

"Oh yeah? Why's that? I had fun."

"Yeah. You really liked her, and she's a spoiled little brat." And I'm the biggest brat of them all.

"Yeah. I know, but it was fun hanging out with her and helping her piss off her parents."

"What? You were in on it?" My voice rose incredulously.

"In on what exactly?"

"On Stacy getting her way and her new car."

"I don't know anything about that."

"You knew she was using you, though?"

"Of course, you'd have to be completely oblivious to not have known that that's why she agreed to go out with me in the first place."

It was the first time I'd ever hung up on him. Almost two years we'd been talking, and he'd pissed me off on countless occasions, but I picked that moment to hang up on him. The cool part was he wouldn't dare call me back for fear of getting me nice and grounded. Or so I thought. When my phone rang, I nearly jumped out of my skin. "Hello?" I breathed.

"Don't ever hang up on me again," he said through his teeth.

I'd never heard him get angry with me before. I cringed. Then, a part of me delighted. I didn't get that. "That's what you get for calling me oblivious," I shot back. "You know better than to call me. If my mom had picked up and realized the phone was for me at this hour…"

He ignored my protests. "I wasn't calling you oblivious. You're just too kindhearted to get that she was only using me for my good looks and rebellious appeal," he snickered, losing his anger quickly.

I contemplated this a moment and decided to level with him. "I'm not kindhearted. I set you up as a test, and I knew that was the only reason she would go out with you. It's just that you two seemed so—"

"Yeah. I knew that too."

"Really? Why, then, did you agree to go?" He was really starting to piss me off. Freaking know-it-all.

"Because you wanted to know whether or not I was over you, and I wanted to know what you were like when you were on a date." He hesitated for the briefest of moments before he proceeded to completely blow my mind. "When we finally have our time together, I want to know that it's different for you. That I'm different from the boys you date."

I heard my sharp intake of breath. There it was. He was back. Hadn't I known that he really hadn't gone anywhere, though? He didn't skip a beat.

"Lorraina, you had to have known that I was bluffing when I acted like I was over you. I have your initials tattooed on my arm. I have your face tattooed in my brain. I have your soul tattooed in my heart."

"Damn it, Michael! What the hell?!" I demanded as loudly as I could without being discovered. Why did my heart do that thing again? "You're the one who's oblivious. We. Will. Never. Be. Together. I'm sorry, but that's the way it is. If we can't just be fr—"

"You know. I really hate it when you cuss. It's very unbecoming. You're far too beautiful to be that foul. Besides, didn't you learn your lesson about profanity last school year?"

Of course that was the part he heard! How many times over the years had I begun that sentence only to be silenced with his acquiescence or deflection? "I've gotta go. I don't feel very well."

"K. Call me tomorrow, K?

"Yeah. OK."

As I was lowering the receiver, I heard him whisper, "I love you, Lorraina. Only you. Forever."

"Fuuuuuck!" I screamed inside my head. It reverberated throughout my body and I pushed the air of my lungs forcefully, throwing myself back on my bed. I promptly curled into a ball and cried myself to sleep. I kept asking myself why I was crying. But I had no idea, which brought a new round of tears.

I jolt awake, look at the clock, and blink; it's two in the morning. I run my hand over my chest. I must have dozed off thinking about him because he has just starred in the most unexpected, shockingly pleasant dream I've ever had. My heart is beating rapidly, and my throat aches for a drink of water. I grab the glass beside my bed and drain it of its contents in one gulp. I take a deep, steadying breath, trying to hold tight to the images from my dream. It wasn't the first time I'd dreamt of him over the years. It was, however, the first time I'd dreamt a dream like that. Huh, I thought only guys dreamt like that.

Chapter Four

Gotta Get It All out on Paper

Since I can't go back to sleep and can't get into one of the books I had purchased, I decide to do something I haven't done in years. I reach into the back of my nightstand to find my journal. I open it up and thumb through my memories from my senior year of high school. Just as I had hoped, there was plenty of blank paper because I had stopped journaling shortly before graduation. So many memories were fighting to get through that I felt the need to get them down on paper.

It was the craziest feeling. I was seeing Michael in a whole new light—one where doubt and fear didn't plague my every emotion where he was concerned. For years, I struggled with my need for him. I never was quite sure where I stood. I loved him being my best friend. At times, I wanted him to be more than that, though. Every time I thought about giving into that desire, he would do something that would make me doubt that it would be good for me. His intensity scared me, yet I couldn't walk away.

I had already made up my mind what I wanted out of tomorrow, well tonight. Now, I just had to bide my time and figure how to handle the impending situation. Writing out my memories might just help me do that. I quickly write down my memory from before I had fallen asleep. Then, I move on to the first time I'd ever heard his name.

*It was early in my eighth grade year, and my brothers and I
were waiting at the bus stop. I was reading some Nancy Drew, and
they were seeing how far they could throw their rocks across the
road. Suddenly, Jerome is standing beside me. I look up and
demand, "What?"*

*He says, "Don't be mad at me, but I forgot that I was
supposed to tell you something."*

*"OK. I promise I won't be mad. What is it?" If I get in trouble
for doing or not doing something, I was gonna wring his neck.*

*"Well, I was supposed to tell you that Mike Bang has decided
to marry you," he explains.*

*That was one thing I never expected Jerome to say to me, so I
didn't really have a response. I don't even know who Mike Bang is.
Nervous laughter bubbles out of me, "What are you talking about?
I don't even know anybody by that name."*

*"Yeah, you do. You just don't talk to him. He sits in the back
of the bus with all the older kids. He's in like 9th grade and…" my
brother starts to get distracted by the rock throwing competition
and tries to walk off mid-sentence.*

*"Hey! Wait a second. Are you talking about the boy with the
really black hair and dark skin? He lives by the Taylors?"*

*"Yeah, that's him. He told me that he hung out with Daddy at
the river this summer and knows all about you. He says he's going
to marry you one day." With that, Jerome rejoins the competition.*

*I vaguely know who he is but have no idea why he would tell
my brother that. I am flattered, of course, being the vain person*

that I am. However, since I am new at the school, pretty much every guy wants to date me. It isn't vanity for me to think that part, though. It is a reality of small town living.

That day on the bus I pay special attention when we near his stop. I want to see if he will make eye contact with me after telling my brother something so brazen. Unfortunately, my curious nature would be denied; he doesn't get on the bus. I don't dare ask anyone where he might be less I be accused of liking him. I may not know him very well, but I knew enough about his type. Bad boy. As if to prove my thoughts just, one of my friends offers up intelligence as to Michael's whereabouts. He had been suspended from school for fighting.

Later that day, while cleaning up at the barn, I hear my brother on the phone in the tack room. That's weird. Who would he be talking to? It better not be a customer. I open the tack room, and his guilty gaze meets mine. "Jerome, who are you on the phone with?" I snap.

He has the nerve to laugh and say, "It's for you."

"I didn't hear it ring," I state as I move toward the phone. "Hello?"

"Hey, Lorraina. Do you know who this is?" a velvety voice asks.

All I can think is that it's a boy and my parents will beat me senseless if they find out I am talking to a boy. "Um…no," I utter.

"It's Mike. Mike Bang from the bus."

"How did you get our number?" I demand. I look over my shoulder for my brother, but he is long gone. Little rat!

"You do realize that your grandparents' business phone is in the book, right?" Before I can offer a retort, he explains, "I had a friend ask your brother to call me actually. I thought it would be better if he just handed you the phone and I was on it rather than you having to decide if and when you would ever get around to calling me."

"Oh, really?" I laugh, "And why would I ever want to call you?"

"Well, how else are you going to get to know your future husband?"

I hear myself laugh a flirty little laugh, but it is bravado for sure. I don't know what game he was playing at, but I do know I don't want any part of it. "Well, it was nice talking to you, Michael; but I have to go and get my chores done."

"That has a nice ring to it—Michael," he rolls it around on his tongue as if savoring the thing.

"Well, that is your name, right?!" I bite out; his voice had taken on a new quality—a dangerous one.

"Yeah, but everyone usually calls me Mike."

"Oh, then. I guess I should call you Mike." I mentally shrug. I've just never been one for nicknames.

"No, Lorraina," he replies thoughtfully. "You should call me Michael."

Confused, I ask, "Why's that?"

"Because you're not everyone. See ya tomorrow, Lorraina."

That was the whole of our first conversation. Short, simple, to the point. Names, brief introductions, marriage proposal. I really was intrigued even though I knew I shouldn't be. I also very much liked the attention that he was giving me. That feeling would wear off quickly enough, though.

I look back over my journaling and realize that I'd written my memories in present tense. I puzzle over this for a moment, and then I recall the conversation that took place after I had spoken to Michael.

After that disturbing conversation, I had noticed my dad sitting on the front porch alone, so I decided to ask him about Michael and his family since they seemed to be friends. I made my way out and struck up conversation on an unrelated topic. Finally, I meandered enough to find out what I really wanted to know.

Surprisingly, it seemed Michael was off limits to me. I was told that in no uncertain terms the whole Bang family was trash and that I'd better steer clear. If I was caught so much as talking to Michael, I would get the whooping of my life. I knew he meant it too. Daddy never was one for empty threats.

What I didn't get, at that time, was that it was OK for my dad to be friends with them, but I couldn't be. He was guilty of the same sins as Michael's father, yet we were to hold those against him and his family but not my dad and his. What made me any better than Michael?

I throw my pen down as I realize that I get it now, though. Even though my dad acted like trash and lived in poverty, he had a respectable family name. We were able to cross that almost tangible line. My grandparents on both sides of my family were respected and that courtesy was extended to me, ensuring I never really fit in with anyone. I always felt like an impostor.

I had always felt like everyone knew exactly the kind of person my dad was even though I never understood why nobody seemed to hold it against me like it was held against Michael and others like us. That was just it, though. Because of our name, no matter what my dad did, he would never really be held accountable.

Chapter Five

If Only I Had Listened in the Silence

I look back over my journal entry and smile. It had been so long since I did any writing or journaling. It feels amazing as I put the pen to paper, get out of my head, and pour out my heart. As I pause from my writing, I'm surprised to feel this level of relief over this little purge and something else—longing. I've always known that I loved Michael, but I'd managed to convince myself that it was a friendly, or even brotherly, love. The feelings that are threatening to consume me now are anything but platonic. I am overtaken with the need to see him and see him soon. Aah…It's only three o'clock now. He won't be at Mona's until around seven this evening.

As I start to imagine seeing him, nagging doubts bombard me. What if he doesn't even recognize me? That would be humiliating. "And, you are?" What if I see him and this was nothing more than my romantic fancy taking over and I have to deal with the loss of something that never was meant to be? I may be completely romanticizing him and our past relationship. Even more likely, what if he has a girlfriend? If the girl at Mona's was any indication of the way girls were overtly responding to him nowadays, he probably does, indeed, have someone. What if I go there and lay my heart bare and he turns on me? Our last encounter was truly awful. He may still be holding a grudge.

I focus on my journal again and grimace as I remember how humiliated and angered I was about his own declaration of love.

Michael and I had been talking for many weeks now. We still didn't sit together on the bus or even acknowledge each other. I was petrified at the thought of my dad finding out that we were friends. Every night, I would sneak up to the barn and call him. I always let the phone ring once to signal him. He would run over to it, and I would call right back. If his parents answered the phone, they might wonder who I was and trouble would most definitely ensue. We felt very safe with our little ritual.

Our phone conversations lasted for what seemed like hours, but I'm sure that I never found that much time away from my parents. We would talk about everything. He would play me songs from the radio, read me poetry, strum me songs on his guitar. Most importantly, he would listen. I had never felt like anyone had ever listened to me. It was an amazing feeling, proven by his asking me probing questions and offering me the sagest advice.

He hadn't confessed his love to me or told me that he was going to marry me since our very first conversation. I began to believe that I'd imagined it or that he had gotten to know me and changed his mind. The latter was the most probable. One night, he played back Poison's "Every Rose Has Its Thorn." I liked the song. It was beautiful in its simplicity. I expressed that thought only to be subjected to a fifteen-minute lecture on the intricacies of the song and what Brett really meant when he was writing it.

I reveled in his insightful analysis of one of Billboard's Hot 100. He was too cute talking about getting what your heart desires only to realize that it doesn't come without a price. "Even the most beautiful flower, the rose," he argued, "has the thorn that makes it imperfect." I argued that the thorns were what made the rose so beautiful. Without the thorn, the rose wouldn't be as magnificent as it was. He agreed that I made a fair point. He pontificated upon several more points, and then he strummed his heart-wrenching acoustic version of the song. I was so impressed. The song had only been popular for a few weeks.

It was the loveliest thing I'd ever heard, I thought to myself. Better than the glam rocker's version even. Instead of admitting that, I say, "Cool. You learned to play that really fast."

"Yeah," he says, "the song means a lot to me. It expresses how I feel about a number of situations."

"Oh...well." I fidget, beginning to feel uncomfortable. "My parents are sure to be wondering about me by now. I'd better go."

"OK. Good night, Lorraina. Sleep well..."

"Yep. I'll see ya tomorrow."

As the bus bumps along the road the next morning, I have my nose buried in a book. I register some out of character early morning laughter but ignore it. It grows louder. I, then, began to hear my name being whispered. "What the hell?!" I think. There's no way they're talking about me. Why would they be? When we come to a stop in front of Michael's house, my friend hops up in the seat to see what all the commotion is about.

33

She flops back down on the seat and looks at me with a horrified expression. Her mouth forms a wide "O" but nothing comes out.

"Well, what?" I hiss.

By this time everyone is standing and staring and laughing at something or someone in front of the bus. I'm too scared to look. Unwillingly, I glance out and see my name spray painted on the road in front of the bus with hearts all around it. It takes up the entire two-lane road and is prominently displayed just beyond where the bus comes to a stop. OH! MY! GOD! I'M! GOING! TO! KILL! HIM!

Of course, he doesn't get on the bus. He's suspended again. The bus driver doesn't realize this, though, and sits and honks and waits for him and calls even more attention to the fact that my name is branded on the road by a boy who everyone considers a lost cause. A boy who my dad would kill if he thought I was interested in. A boy I want to kill for instituting my public ignominy.

On the way home that day, I notice my name is completely covered up with fresh black spray paint; nevertheless, it's too late. Everyone still gets a real big kick out of it at my expense, of course. I will probably never live this down, I think. I'll probably never have a decent boyfriend. I'm forever tainted.

The evening is one of my longest ever. My anger fuels my resolve to get my chores done at a breakneck pace. As soon as I am able, I slip off to the barn.

"Hello?" he asks all innocently.

"Don't hello me. What the hell were you thinking?!?!" I bark.

"Well, I know it wasn't my best work; but you weren't even a little impressed?" He asks disbelievingly.

"Um...Let's see...NO! Not even a little!" I am shouting at this point. I hear the horses whining at my outburst. I take a deep breath and release it. "What were you thinking, Michael?" I ask more calmly. "My dad takes that road to the store at least twice a day. What if he would have seen it? He would've killed us both." I wince as I recall my dad's last lecture on my treasured virginity. It's not something that I want to revisit. Ever.

He takes a steadying breath and replies as if he is speaking to a mental patient who is on the verge of cracking, "Lorraina, I've been so patient. I've been giving you time to adjust to the facts. The time for me to push the subject along was imminent."

"You didn't push. You gave it a violent shove!"

I hear him gearing up his well planned argument "That's purely semantics, I—"

"Just stop," I beg. I know I will get nowhere with him as I don't even know the definition of the word semantics. I'm pretty sure I couldn't even pronounce it properly if asked even though he's just said it. "Michael, I just...If we can't—"

"Don't start that again. You know that you and I will never be just anything. I've made my feelings on the subject very clear," he replies matter-of-factly.

"Well, let me make myself clear, MIKE," I wield his name like a weapon. I hear an angry rush of breath, and I can practically feel him glaring through the phone line at me. "I will never…You will never…We will NEVER be anything other than friends."

Instead of fighting with me, he replies flippantly, "You know what they say—Never say never, babe." Surprise, surprise. His cockiness rears its ugly head. He's not in the least bit deterred.

"I gotta go. Bye." I hang up without waiting for his response. There was no talking any sense to him. He would NEVER listen to reason. Well, he would have to cope with silence then.

I ran from the tack room, throwing open the door leading to the horses' stalls in my anger. The horses jump to attention and whinny. I feel immediately contrite. I force myself to calm down. I locate Shadow, go to her, and lay my head against hers. I feel tears burn the back of my eyelids. I just don't understand. I love Michael, as a friend; but that's never going to be good enough for him. Why does he keep pushing me?

Resolved to make him realize that he couldn't behave like that with his grand gestures, I didn't acknowledge him for two months. I hated it but felt like I didn't have any other choice. He tried passing me messages through my brothers. I wouldn't listen. He tried my friends. I wouldn't listen. He even conned our bus driver into talking to me, which was awkward at best. I wouldn't listen or respond. Radio silence. It was the longest two months of my life, and I almost gave in so many times. Then I would remind myself that I didn't have any other choice.

Finally, he seemed like he was forgetting about me. He no longer stared holes in the back of my head. He no longer sent messages. He no longer made any grand gestures. So how do I react?

I call him, of course. His mom actually answers. I freeze for a moment. "May I speak to Micha—Mike, please?" *I stutter over the name that only I call him.*

"Yeah," *she mutters.* "Michael!" *she bellows.*

Hmm…interesting. I guess I'm not the only who calls him that.

"Hello?"

"Hi."

"Umm…Hi?"

Uh oh! He sounds…indifferent. My heart protests violently. Anger, I can handle. Even obsession, yes. Indifference, big fat NO! "I'm sorry," *I hear myself saying. Well, I certainly didn't plan to say that. What am I sorry for exactly?!*

"I love you, Lorraina. You're gonna have to accept that because I'm not going away. As much as you think that's what you want, it's not going to happen."

I can't believe he is leading with that. What the hell?! "Michael, I—" *I, what? I don't even know. All I know is that I've been miserable without him. I can't tell him that so instead I ask,* "Have you learned any new songs?"

He laughs a strained, terse laugh. "Yeah. Have you heard Bon Jovi's 'Living on a Prayer'?"

"Yes. I love it. I'm sure you play it even better than they do." I hear the pride in my voice. He's so very talented. I know exactly what his response to my flattery will be.

"Whatever."

Yep, just like I thought. Until confronted with praise, he's extremely cocky. I roll my eyes. "Michael, I swear..." and I chuckle at his true humility lurking behind that arrogant exterior.

"What a lovely sound."

"Huh? What sound?"

"Your laughter. I didn't realize exactly how...starved for it I was. I'll try not to offend you any time soon so that I can have some more of that." His voice had taken on a husky tone, but what he'd said was incredibly sensitive.

Of course, I inadvertently oblige him with more laughter. I'm taking the proverbial giggling schoolgirl to a whole new level. I roll my eyes at myself now. How does he do this to me?!

"Right on cue," he taunts.

Before I can get irritated, he launches into his version of Bon Jovi's latest hit. Just as I predicted, it's beautiful. He has to stop and restart a couple of times, but it sounds perfect to me.

Chapter Six

The Best Laid Plans

I open one eye and check my clock. Ugh…it's already eight. I can't believe my mom let me sleep in. I stumble into the bathroom and wash my face. When I pop back up, I survey myself in the mirror. I look different than I looked last time I looked into this mirror. My hair is longer, almost to my waist. It's darker blonde too. Probably from a lack of sun. Yep, I look paler. My skin seems to be glowing though. I hadn't noticed that before. Oh, I need makeup. I honestly can't remember the last time I wore any. My mom would have a cow. I snicker. She wouldn't agree with many of my choices of late. I don't even know that I have any friends besides Ginny at the moment. I'd become a recluse, a pariah, a hermit.

I try to recall the last time I went out, relaxed, and enjoyed myself. It was disastrous. I wasn't ready. Hmm…I'm long overdue, and I feel ready. Suddenly, I'm very happy that I have several hours before I plan to be at Mona's. Nothing in my closet is good enough for our reunion. I wonder if Joe would let me borrow some money. Probably. Can't hurt to ask. I finish with my bathroom duties and make my way to the kitchen to find my mom.

She has her back to me, leaning over to wash the dishes. She looks really thin but beautiful. She hears me and turns. Her smile is brilliant. "Morning. Did I wake you up?"

"Oh, no. It was past time for me to get up. I couldn't sleep last night, though."

"Huh…Excited about Christmas?"

Yep, excited but not about Christmas. "Yeah, I guess."

"Well, I got your sheets and comforters washed. I had Weldon put them back in the car for you. I didn't touch your pillows, though."

"Oh, thank you. I was putting off doing that. That's why they were still in the car. I didn't even realize that I'd thrown my pillows in the car too."

"You're welcome. You deserve a break. Things are about to get tough. Don't you think?"

"Yeah, I guess. One more semester then law school. I think that's what I need to gear up for. I'm not really feeling it, though."

"What is that supposed to mean?" I can hear the disapproval in her voice.

"I don't know. I just…seven years of school straight through." I hesitate, wondering what exactly my problem with school is. "It seems superfluous at this point…"

"What are the other kids feeling? The same? Or excited?"

"I couldn't tell you."

"Are you seeing someone?" She asks pointedly. "Is that where this is coming from? You don't have the luxury of burnout, ya know?"

Really?!?!…Have I ever not persevered? Does she not know me at all? "Mom, I'm just tired is all. And, no, I haven't met anyone new." Will she catch my little qualifier? I smile a secret smile.

"Well, I just don't want you to get caught up in something that will keep you from your studies. You've worked too hard to quit now or get distracted."

Umm…OK. "Who said anything about quitting?" I can't keep the angry tone from entering my voice. "And, I'm not distracted." *Just because everyone you've ever known including yourself has quit doesn't mean that I will.*

"You know Jerome is looking at welding school, huh?" Right on cue. Change of subject. Extremely effective in avoiding any situation that rings of emotion.

"No, I had no idea. That's good." Where's she going with this? Just catching me up or what? "Oh, hey. I maintained my four-point-oh this semester," I say, hoping to cheer her up.

"Good job. Anyway, your brother could use your support. This is a big deal."

"Oh, yeah. Of course…"

"What are your plans for the break?"

"I don't know yet. I was thinking about looking for part time work. I wanted to see if Ms. Jeanine needed extra help at Santa's Sleigh this year. I have absolutely no money."

"You should just borrow a little from Joe to get you by. He would be happy to do that for you. You really need to relax before your final semester."

I consider this for a moment. It would be better to owe Joe a little money if it will give me more time to spend with Michael. *If he will have me, I mentally amend.* "Yeah, you're right. I'll ask him in a bit. Is he in a good mood this morning?"

"Pretty much. Better ask early though," she giggles nervously.

***

My step-dad is in a good mood. I get my advance with a promise to pay him back as soon as I clear my first paycheck back in Oxford. I head to town to pick up some much needed beauty supplies and something better to wear. It's been so long since I've shopped that I feel awkward. I contemplate seeing him after all these years. Should I dress up? Sexy or demure? I don't have a clue. I want to make a good impression, though. I wander around the store not really wanting to buy anything but knowing that I need to. My wardrobe consists of jeans and hoodies and Converses, and they just won't do.

I finally decide on something moderate as is where I always seem to land. As I'm approaching the register, I spot a familiar face. One I haven't seen in about ten years. *Oh, shit.* There is no way I can speak to her. Talk about awkward. My most prominent memory of her invades my previously mundane shopping thoughts. I laugh aloud. I swivel my head around as she does. I'm suddenly very interested in *People's* latest celebrity updates. I have to get to my journal.

I've never run so fast in my life. As soon as the bus came to a stop, I fled. I don't know how serious the girls' gang is, but I'm not taking any chances. I dodge unsuspecting students as I make my way to my second bus. Why, oh why, are they so pissed at me?! It's not like I've encouraged the attention from the boys at my new school. Well, maybe a little. I've never quite had that kind of attention before, so it felt pretty good. I may have flirted back a little. That's not exactly a crime that I deserve to get beaten and bloodied for, I think. I'm lost in this line of thought as I plow into the back of a skinny leather clad boy. I land square on my butt and am jolted back to the urgent matter at hand—saving my ass. He turns around and scoops me up off the ground in one quick movement. Oh!

"Hey, what's your hurry?" he asks in a heavy, almost familiar voice.

I brush my hair off my face and look up at him. So, this is THE Michael Bang, I think. I open my mouth to speak. All that I'm able to utter is, "Uh...I...They" It wasn't exactly rhetorical fireworks.

He saves me from further embarrassing myself. "I was plotting about how to go about having a face-to-face conversation with you today but couldn't quite figure out how to do it," he laughs. "I guess you've saved me the trouble. How fortuitous." A smile plays at his impossibly full lips. Why am I staring at his lips? I mentally shake myself a little.

"Some girls are trying to kill me," I blurt out. "They're chasing me from the junior high bus." I'm immediately embarrassed all over again. Why did I just say that to him?

His look suddenly turns serious. "Go get on the bus, Lorraina. Don't even look back." With that, he thrusts me forward into the throng of students waiting to load. I decide to skip ahead, eliciting all kinds of comments as I stumble around the other students.

I make it on the bus and head to the back. I make a, very uncharacteristically, gutsy move and decide I'm going to sit in his usual seat so that I can talk to him when he makes it back. After what seems like forever, I see him board the bus. He looks furious. Note to self—never piss Michael off.

He slides down in the seat beside me. All his anger seems to slide gently from him as he does. What a transformation. He casts me a glaring white crooked smile from his copper face. He really is quite cute. "Well, that was interesting," he grumbles.

"What?"

"It seems they wanted to kick your butt for flirting with Cory Austin."

"If speaking is flirting, then, I guess I'm guilty," I bristle. I don't like the way he sneered Cory's name at me. What's he got against him? He's a nice enough guy.

"Well, they won't be messing with you again."

"What did you say to them?"

"Let's just say that I told their 'fearless leader' if she and her flunkies even so much as look in your general direction or allow your name to cross their minds or lips, they will be sorry."

"Oh, and why should they listen to you?" I scoff. This is a good thing. What do I care if he's too cocky?

"I'm authoritative," he decrees as if that explains it all.

I let it go. He asks me how things are going for me at the junior high other than my lack of female admirers and what teachers I have. Before I know it, I'm divulging my entire schedule to him, whom I eat with, what lunch I have, what activities I participate in. I tell him I don't really have any real friends yet. I'm really a social person, so I hate this fact. I realize that he has told me nothing of himself.

I ask him about his schedule at the ninth grade. He mutters something about it not being of consequence and tells me that his favorite class is English. I giggle. Mine too, I tell him.

"What's your favorite book?" I ask.

"The Tragedy of Romeo and Juliet," *he responds with a sigh.*

"Well, you don't seem too happy about that."

"It's a tragedy," he says dryly.

I laugh. "Yeah, I get that; but you obviously love it. You shouldn't sound so agitated."

"It's not that," he releases a sigh. "It's just overwhelming, bittersweet. I mean to feel that kind of passion and fight for love like that. Going against everything you've ever known, ever loved…"

I'm lost in thought as I imagine that kind of love. I realize he's stopped talking and I blink fast, trying to focus on something semi-intelligent to say. "I haven't read it yet, but I know the premise. I get what you're saying."

"What's your favorite?" He perks back up. He slides one of my notebooks off of my lap and begins to doodle. I wonder for a second why he doesn't carry any books or notebooks.

I try to focus on the question at hand. "Um...hard to say. I guess Black Beauty *or* Julie of the Wolves *or* Charlotte's Web--" His laughter interrupts me. It pulls my gaze from his drawing on my notebook. I shoot him a frown. "I find it hard to decide favorites." I shrug. I don't think a boy has ever touched my belongings before. I'm mesmerized by his familiarity.

"All good, solid choices," he declares. "They all have bittersweet endings as well."

"Yeah, I guess they do," I muse.

"Oh, here's my stop," he says with what seems like regret. I glance up. Sure enough. That was certainly the fastest bus ride ever. Usually, it feels like I'll never get home. I look back at his half frown. I feel myself regretting the end of our conversation as well. He's interesting, smart, unexpected.

"Can I call you tonight?" I hear myself ask. I feel a thrilling spark shoot through me. Did I just say that? My mother would be appalled.

He gives me the most brilliant smile. "Yeah, of course." He writes his number on my folder underneath whatever he's doodled on it. "What time do you think?"

"Around seven..."

"Great! A thousand adieus, Lorraina."

My name sounds so beautiful coming from him, so when he says it, I feel this pull in me to try to keep him talking. To ask him to say my name over and over again. It's just weird. I'm so weird. Before I can further engage him in conversation, he places my folder on my lap and makes his way off the bus.

I watch as Michael climbs the hill to head toward his house. He throws his head back in laughter as he dodges his friend's jabs. In this moment, he seems so carefree and alive; but if his life is anything like mine, I know this moment will be fleeting.

I'm pulled from my reverie as I hear one of the older girls from the very back of the bus address me as she shuffles off behind him. "Whore."

I baulk and slide down in my seat, bringing my knees up on the seat in front of me. What in the world did I ever do to deserve this level of hostility?!?! I don't get it. I barely speak to anyone, yet everyone seems to hate me.

Once he's out of my line of vision, I glance down at my notebook. It isn't doodling. It's the most intricately drawn rose. His phone number is below it along with his signature in perfect cursive.

***

Later that night, I call Michael for the first time. We set up our trusty signal and commence to talk about everything under the sun. He wants to know everything about me. I insist that I'm boring, but he assures me otherwise. I try to pry information from him but don't get very far at all.

I confess to him that I am so lonely at my new school. In a moment of weakness, I ask him why he thinks all the girls hate me.

"You have no idea, do you?"

"Umm...No. That's why I asked," my smart mouth, which has a mind of its own, blasts.

"You're beautiful, you're smart, you're different, you're you," he states matter-of-factly.

Whoa, I think. "You have a way of wording things, don't you?"

"I just don't believe in wasting time. I see that all around me. People who live like they will be here forever. Using people, hating people, hating themselves, destroying the ones they love, destroying themselves. I believe in figuring out what you want and reaching out and grabbing it. Is that so bad?"

"No, I think it's pretty amazing for a ninth grader actually."

"Well, I did get held back a year," he jokes. I laugh because I know he wasn't held back because of his lack of intelligence. He's the wisest person I've ever spoken to. "That's not funny," he pouts.

"No, that's not why I'm laughing," I promise.

"Will you sit with me on the bus tomorrow?" he asks.

"Oh, no. I'm sorry. I don't think that's a good idea. What I did today was very risky. My dad, umm, doesn't allow me to talk to boys." I leave out the part about his particular threat about Michael and the fact that he's a paranoid lunatic.

"Yeah, I really can't blame him there. So what's the deal? Will we talk tomorrow?"

"Can I call you again? Same time."

"I'll be waiting."

"OK. Night."

"Night, Lorraina."

And so it began, our nightly ritual of what would become hours upon hours of phone conversations. We rarely acknowledged each other on the bus. Michael saw my dad many times but never let on that we were friends or that I sneaked away at night to call him. I quickly realized that I had never trusted anyone the way I trusted Michael.

I suddenly wanted to be the best possible version of myself for him. I read even more than before and memorized quotes and poems so that I could contribute to our conversation. I listened to the radio religiously so that I could discuss new songs in the same analytical fashion that he did.

After we started talking, I found my confidence increasing and found myself making friends, finally. The girls' gang left me alone. My admirers started to calm down and back off a little. Little did I know at the time that word was out—Michael had staked his claim, and I was off limits. The new friends I made were also because of him. Years later, they would tell me how Michael talked to them and asked them to be nice to me and watch out for me. His probing questions that day about my schedule were to ensure that I had a friend in each class, at lunch, and during my various activities. I'm sure I kept the friends once made, but he was responsible for delivering them to me. Unfortunately, that wouldn't be the only way he meddled.

Chapter Seven

No Guts, No Glory

I managed to kill another couple of hours shopping and journaling. As I start to get ready for my outing, I tell my mom that Ginny and I are going to have dinner and hang out so that I don't arouse suspicion. I would feel bad for lying, but I'm just too excited to care about that right now. I toss my journal and my emergency cell phone in my purse. At the last minute, I decide to take some extra clothes with me. Who knows what this night will hold?

I walk into the living room to say goodbye, and my step falters as I realize that everyone is staring at me. *Shit!* Do I look silly? I glance down. Nothing seems out of place. My confidence flies straight out the window. "What is it?" I ask, hearing the tremble in my voice.

Joe clears his throat and says, "You look different."

Oh, great, as opposed to what exactly? "Is that good or bad?"

"Oh, good, good," Joe rushes.

"Thanks," I mutter. "I'll probably end up staying the night with Ginny if that's OK."

"Yeah," my mom says, "just let me know for sure so I don't worry." Her dark brown eyes meet mine as she says sincerely, "You look beautiful."

I give her a genuine smile. She has no idea how much I had needed to hear that. "Thanks, Mamma. I'll let you know. Good night."

***

My plan is to arrive much earlier than he is scheduled to play. I want to sit somewhere where I can listen to him without being spotted. My conscious whispers, "Creep." I hear Radiohead's lyrics on repeat in my head. For so many years, it was Michael that was the Creep. My, oh my, how the tables have turned. I giggle. He would love this. It would do wonders for his ego.

I arrive at Mona's. I have an hour before he starts to play. At least there is plenty to read here and keep me from considering what I'm doing. I order a smoothie, best not to be too jittery. I ask if it will be Michael who plays and where he will set up and take a seat toward the back of the store. This is perfect. There's even a little half wall to block me. If he looks this way, all he will see is the back of a dirty blonde head. I make my way to the restroom, deciding to check my hair and makeup one more time. I can't believe I'm so nervous: it's just Michael! My feelings have morphed into something unrecognizable, and I fret that he will be able to pick up on that immediately.

I stare into the mirror, focusing on what I can control. Not half bad. At least I hadn't forgotten how to apply makeup. My eyes look fuller with eyeliner and the turquoise shirt brings out the green in my eyes. I try smoothing the frizz from my waves one more time and practicing smiling. I spin around and am, for once, grateful for what my mom calls my bubble butt because it quite nicely fills out my black mini-skirt. My legs even look halfway decent due to the sheer black hose and slightly high heels. I tried on a taller pair but got no more than a wobbling gait out of them and decided not to push it. Clumsiness wouldn't get Michael to see what I hoped looked like the grown up version of me.

Back at my table, I take out my journal and reread what I've written so far. It makes me giddy. I'll need to purchase a new one soon at the rate I'm going. I'm so excited to see him but full of mixed emotions. I only pray that I'm still everything he once loved. I know I don't measure up to the girl he idolized all those years ago. I hope I'm just being overly hard on myself; on the other hand, he always had impossibly high standards where I was concerned. Another memory bombards me, so I give in and put it to paper.

"I haven't heard from you in forever. What's been going on? Are we OK?" He plies me with questions before I can respond to the first.

"I'm fine. I just got 'ungrounded,'" I complain. I don't tell him that I also couldn't sit down for a week because of the lashing my dad had given me.

He busts out with a relieved laugh, "What did YOU do to get grounded?"

I grimace. "I'd really rather not say."

"Did you not clean your room? Forget to feed the horses? Bad grades? Leave the milk out? What?"

"Ugh...You're gonna drive me insane until I tell you, aren't you?"

He laughs. "How'd you guess?"

I release an answer on an impatient breath, "Fine. I wrote a profanity laced letter to Missy McIntyre."

"Really?! How interesting. I've never even heard you cuss. Well, not anything major anyway," he amends. "It must've been bad."

My behind stings with the memory of just how bad it was. "Yeah, I was feeling pretty good when I told her off in the letter for talking about me behind my back. She was spreading rumors about me making out with some boy I barely know, and it really pissed me off. I decided to, very authoritatively," I stress the word he taught me when he curtailed the girls' gang from killing me, "cuss her out in writing, but I signed my stupid name to it. She promptly handed it over to a teacher."

I have to sit there for a good couple of minutes listening to his laughter. Finally, I crack and am laughing too. What an idiot, I think.

"What an idiot," he says aloud and elicits another round of laughter from me. I proceed to tell him how I drafted the very angry, threatening letter filled with every curse word I'd ever heard. I tell him I even took pride in my excellent penmanship and elegant signature. He admonishes me for my lack of civility and tells me that kind of stuff will ruin my reputation not only with the *students but also with the teachers and administrators. Great, disappointment. As if I didn't feel bad enough.*

"Anyway, what's been going on with you?" I ask, changing the subject.

"You haven't been the only one in trouble. My dad and I got into a fistfight a few days back. I'm pretty sure he loosened a molar. My mom left for a couple of days and threatened to make it permanent if he ever hit me like that again. I feel so bad for her. She's had a miserable life being married to a drunk and raising a black sheep."

"You're not a black sheep!" I protest vehemently. "I know all about black sheep. Remember who my dad is. I can't even look people in the eye when I say my own last name for fear they will know which Dabney my dad is. There's no telling who all he's screwed or screwed over around here. You're NOTHING like that!"

There's a pause. I wonder if we got cut off for a minute. He finally replies tersely, "Thanks for that."

"You're welcome; but I mean it, Michael. I hate it when you put yourself down. You're a good person, Michael. The best actually. And, I…Anyway, what did you do or not do?" Did I really almost tell him I love him? That would have been a huge mistake. It's true. I love him, but I love him as a friend; and he wouldn't get the distinction.

"Well, it seems that I will reprise my role as a student at the illustrious Harrisonville Central Ninth Grade School next year." Stuck at that awful school another year, ugh!

"Oh no," I gasp. "Why? You're so smart." I offer the compliment unthinkingly.

"My intelligence is not in question here."

"So, what's the deal? Miss too many days?"

"I failed on purpose."

"Umm...Why exactly would you do that? I've heard it's not the best of environments." I don't believe him. No sane person would do that. Why doesn't he want me to know the real reason?

He releases a long pent up breath like he's about to make a confession. "It's pretty simple. You'll be at the ninth grade next year."

Oh, shit. My gut twists. Like I thought, no sane person. "Are you friggin' kidding me?!" I yell.

"Nope. It'll be fun don't you think?" He asks, warming to the subject.

"Michael, that's just crazy. You lost a whole year of school just to hang out with some girl?"

"Yes and no. Lost a whole year. Not just some girl," he replies glibly.

"I don't even know what to say to that."

"There's nothing to say. I am gonna drop out when I turn sixteen anyway and start working. I might as well spend my last year with you."

"Oh, well, now that you put it that way it just makes perfect sense," I spit scornfully.

I'd almost told him I loved him in that conversation, but I knew he would take it the wrong way and get his hopes up. Having him at the ninth grade was great, though. I'd had an awful summer. That was the summer my dad really lost it, and my parents divorced. We moved into town, but he was there for me like no one had ever been before or since. He managed to get three classes with me and secure the locker right next to mine. Almost on a daily basis I would find a note, a poem, a drawing, a song stuffed in my locker. I threw it all away. It made me crazy. Why couldn't he just accept our friendship? I treasured our friendship, and he was one of the most important people in my life. However, I could only take so much of his incessant pushing and shoving. Then again, sometimes his meddling was very much welcomed.

I'm at my new house that I love. My old house was a perpetual construction zone. Alcohol and partying came before lumber and nails. We have actual walls and floors throughout. It's even close to civilization. At times, I'm glad that my dad torched it all. I hear the doorbell, which also takes some getting used to. No one who would have been required to ring the doorbell, if we'd had one, ever came to my old house. I run to the door to prevent my little brothers from getting to it before me. I throw it open in my haste, not even checking the peephole, which I can never seem to remember exists.

"Hi," he says on a smile.

"What are you doing here?" I grab him and hug him, taking us both by surprise. "I missed you, Michael."

"I missed you too, Lorraina. I have good news." He hesitates a moment and squeezes me back and drops his face into my hair. I can feel him breathing me in. My eyes widen, and I suddenly feel as if his is a crushing weight. I pull back quickly.

I step out onto the porch, closing the door behind me. "Really? What's the good news?" My voice sounds scratchy to my ears. I try to clear it.

He pinches at something in my hair, and I watch as he flicks the almost invisible fuzz away. "I moved in with my brother."

"What brother? Where? Do you have to change schools?" Why would this be good news? I had no idea he even had a brother. In the whole year we've been friends, he has never mentioned a brother.

"No, I'm still going to the ninth grade. He lives two streets over. He's my half brother. We have the same mom."

"Two streets over from what?"

"From you," he pronounces carefully as if I'm the slowest person on the planet.

"Nuh uh!" This is very good news. I fling myself at him again and give him a quick hug, releasing him before he can wrap his arms around me.

"Yep. You're glad?" he asks incredulously.

"Absolutely. You're my best friend."

He groans at my proclamation, "Usually, when I manipulate situations to be closer to you, you get pissed. You're really not pissed?"

"No, this time I'm not pissed. I'm happy."

And I really was. Having him near was amazing. We rode bikes together. We walked the neighborhood. We rode the same bus again. My mom didn't know about my dad's feelings toward Michael, so he was even allowed over to hang out. He was so good to my brothers that my mother trusted him implicitly. It was like she knew that Michael would protect me from everything and everyone. He always had. He would never hurt me. Why couldn't I see that then? I was so blind. At least I know I was not completely impervious to him, though.

Chapter Eight

One and Only

"Do you really have to go? Can't you ask your mom for more time?" I'd been over at his house playing Mario Brothers for a couple of hours. He was pretty impressed with my video game prowess. I had two younger brothers. I couldn't let them beat me— ever. I had to be good at it, I told him.

"My mom's blown the horn twice. Yeah, I better go so that she doesn't come storming in here." I stand up to leave and reach down for my bag. When I straighten back up, he's standing in front of the now closed door with his arms spread, effectively blocking my exit. *"What are you doing?"* I laugh nervously.

"You can't leave until you give me a kiss," he demands.

I roll my eyes toward the ceiling. *"Michael, there is absolutely no way that I am going to kiss you,"* I respond scathingly.

"Lorraina, I don't ask you for much. I'm asking for one kiss so that you will prove to yourself, once and for all, that you have feelings for me. It's time for a shove."

I have tears in my eyes. I just don't get why our friendship is not enough for him. He always tries to mess everything up. If I kiss him, it will be awkward. He will see that, feel that. Then, we won't be able to be friends anymore. I tell him of my musings.

He offers me a challenge. *"It will be anything but awkward. You will feel. And we will act like nothing ever happened until you decide otherwise. I promise."*

Maybe if he sees that I don't have these allegedly hidden feelings, he will back off. I move toward him. Am I really going to do this? "Don't touch me," *I tell him. He barely nods. I recognize the look he gives me. It's the same look I give a skittish horse that I'm trying to coax.* "Don't open your mouth," *I insist. This elicits a little laugh from him. He quickly squelches it and takes a deep breath before closing his mouth.*

I'm standing directly in front of him now, looking into his deep brown eyes. They twinkle with what seems like anticipation. The whites around his eyes are a gray-blue. Interesting. He's interesting. I notice how long and thick his dark eyelashes are. Pretty. He's pretty.

I close my eyes and lay my hands on his chest. This little move feels very intimate. I lean in. I feel my lips touch his for the briefest of moments. His lips are so soft and full. I move my lips over his for a moment, relishing the feeling of—I pull back quickly. His eyes are closed. His arms have dropped to his side. He looks so serene that it freaks me out. I grab the door handle and swing the door open, ducking under his now extended arm. He deftly avoids getting hit by the door.

I move quickly toward the front of the house, looking back over my shoulder to see if he pursues me. He's still standing in the bedroom. His back is toward me. I stop and watch as he runs his hands through his hair. He wavers on his feet. He turns slightly, leaning on the door. His back slides down the door until he is on his knees. His head falls forward as he expels his breath.

I take a shaky breath and continue to my mom's car. I buckle up, feeling like the most powerful woman on earth. A secret smile escapes me. I brought him to his knees with my kiss? How? What will this mean for our friendship? Do I want more with him? I'd kissed other boys before, but that kiss felt different from any other. I liked it. I touch my lips with my fingertips. They felt tender and overly warm. If he asked me to be his girlfriend now, I don't think there is any way I could deny him. He would be able to see right through me. I feel as though our kiss has branded me.

As always, Michael was true to his word. Weeks went by, and he never mentioned our kiss, acted like it never happened. What was I supposed to do with that? Did he not feel what I felt? Did he finally realize that I wasn't all he'd made me up to be? I couldn't bring it up. I was too embarrassed.

As I journal about our one and only very chaste kiss, I reread the entry. My eyes linger on his words. *"And we will act like nothing ever happened until you decide otherwise. I promise."*

"Oh," I say aloud and feel like a veil had finally been lifted to reveal the true nature of what had transpired between us. True to his word, he had been waiting for me to make a move. He promised me that he would never bring it up. I had to be the one, and I was too much of a coward. I was always such a coward when it came to him. His intensity scared me. I was also afraid that I would never be able to live up to the ideal person he had built me up to be.

All of those fears caused me to lose seven years with him. After that kiss, we only hung out a handful of times before he dropped out of school; and he would only reappear in my life sporadically over those next few years. I think about my one failed relationship since then and all of the heartache that one person had brought me. I think about how often I felt so lonely and desolate and how I'd actually always had true, unconditional love staring me in the face. I had been more loved and cherished than probably any other person had ever been. Instead of wrapping myself in all of this and reveling in those feelings, I had taken his love and acceptance and affection, balled them up with both hands, and tossed them aside as I had all of his declarations. I'd been such a fool. Resolute, I vow I will remedy that.

Chapter Nine
When Push Comes to Shove

I glance at my watch. He would be here soon. I'm giddy with anticipation yet fraught with nerves. I pick up my book, flip to my bookmark, and dive into the story. It's like a pool without any water. I land smack dab on the concrete. It is dry and without feeling. I throw my head back on the little love seat and smile. I can only think of him and our past and what may lie ahead. Our far too brief time together seems so very precious at this moment. I allow myself to indulge in another memory and reach for my journal.

"Did you hear what he was suspended for this time?" Sheryl asks me.

"Er...No." I answer hesitantly. Do I want to know?

"Smoking in the boys room," she singsongs.

I chuckle. "I'm not surprised. I think he wants to get thrown out of school. He hates it. It kills me, though, because he is so freakin' smart. He could do well if he wanted to, and I have to work my butt off for my A's." My frustration with him shines through.

"Yeah, it's not fair. He has that bad boy thing down to a fine art, doesn't he? He's troubled and untouchable but gorgeous and talented."

"You think he's gorgeous?" I ask incredulously.

"Um...Yeah, all the girls do! They just won't admit it because of his reputation. Pretty much everyone adores him."

"I thought they were fascinated with him because of his reckless nature and behavior."

"Well, that too." She waves her hand around in the air. "It's all a part of his bad boy persona."

Oh, am I the only one oblivious to his looks then? I never really paid that much attention to them. I mean, I didn't think he was hideous or anything. He was just Michael. Flawed but good. Off limits to me but the most grounding force in my life. I was pretty sure that he had once again forgotten his obsession with me as we are currently in a good, friendly place—emphasis on the friendly.

"He is pretty cute," I admit. "But he is more than just that. I wish everyone could see that. I mean, he's kind and thoughtful and sincere." I look over at her with a startled look on my face. Did I just say all that aloud?

I flush, embarrassed by my admission. She gives me a strange look. She is used to me shutting down on the subject of Michael. I'm usually too irritated by his antics to discuss him.

***

That night, I went to the baseball field for practice. I was pitching for our mock scrimmage—first string vs. second string. I, of course, was second string. I saw Michael climbing into the bleachers. He sat down and started talking to one of the other girl's boyfriend. I had pitched a no-hitter up until this point, trying desperately to be noticed by our coach and be declared a starter. I was sick of warming the bench for the first few innings. Michael and I make eye contact. I grin and try to refocus on the situation at hand. I pull it in with a deep breath, bring my arm back, and release. It's a pretty pitch, I think. Straight down the middle, but is it too fast to be hit? My answer is the crack of the bat as it slams into the ball. Shit! I watch in horror as it soars over the entire field, dropping flawlessly behind the fence. Home run. Shit! Shit! Shit! I glance over at coach and he's nodding his head as if to say, "Yep, I knew it. You're not ready." I guess those four perfect innings were effectively wiped from his memory with my one screw up.

I refocus and finish the inning without another incident. After our end-of-game pep talk/gripe session, the girls and I meet Michael and the other boys in the bleachers to watch the next game. He has a handful of bubble gum and a Coke for me. That was the least he could do since he'd ruined my perfect game! I tell him so. He laughs at me.

"I can't help it if you find me distracting," he mocks. He suddenly finds his fingernails very interesting. I notice he is chewing on his bottom lip.

"You're acting funny. What is it?" I ask as I blow a bubble. Sudden fear cripples my movements. Did Sheryl tell him about our conversation on the bus that afternoon? Oh, crap. Yes, I'm willing to admit to myself that I think he's great and has potential. No, I'm not willing for him to know that anytime soon. I'm just not ready for the all-consuming force that is Michael, and I know this.

He puts his finger through my bubble, popping it, takes a steadying breath, and grabs my hand. Oh, this is not good. "I have something to show you actually."

"What?" I demand.

"Well, I don't want to show you here. Can we go over to the playground? There's hardly anyone over there."

We make our way to the playground. I'm sweating bullets by this point. What is it that he wants to show me? Is he going to try to kiss me? I'm covered in red clay from sliding. I know I probably smell bad since I've been sweating for the last two hours. I have a huge wad of gum in my mouth. Oh, and I have my baseball cap on. Can't take that off—hat hair. Please, please, please don't try to kiss me, I will him. These are not ideal conditions for my first kiss.

He leads me to the rear of the playground and hops on a swing. He proceeds to show me how high he can go. The metal starts to click loudly as it protests the unknown height it is being forced to endure. I tell him he's going too high and making me nervous. That is not why I'm nervous.

"You care for my safety?" he asks. I give him a bland look. "Watch this." He propels himself from the swing at the highest possible point. He lands skillfully on his feet with his hands out to the side for balance. "Ta da!"

"Aren't you amazing?" I tease coolly. "My mom's gonna be here soon to pick me up. Are you gonna show me or not?"

"Well, I don't want you to get mad, but I know you're gonna. I'm just hoping you won't be mad for too long. I can't take another two months of silence."

This worries me. It must be bad. He's usually not hesitant about his antics. He plunges headfirst and the consequences be damned. "Well, are you going to keep me in suspense much longer?"

He grabs my hand with one of his and with the other begins to roll up his shirtsleeve. Oh my gosh! He's gotten a tattoo. What an idiot. He's only fifteen. How'd he get a tattoo? Isn't there some kinda law against that?

"Really, Michael, a tattoo? That's what you occupied your time with while you were suspended? What were you thinking?" I ask dryly.

Not answering me, he finally completes the rolling up of his sleeve so that I can see it. I move closer so that I can see what he's gotten. It's small. It looks like writing. Not at all what I had expected. He turns toward the light a little so that I can see it better.

I am finally able to make it out. I hear my sharp intake of breath. I jerk my hand from his and am jogging away. I hear him call out to me to stop. Oh, hell no. I'm not stopping. I'm crying and he will not see me cry!

From out of nowhere, his arm snakes around my middle, pulling me to him. "Shh, shh...It's not that big of a deal." He lays his forehead on my shoulder, and his free hand strokes my ponytail. He soothes me for a few moments.

I'm crying harder than I thought. I wipe my arm across my face and choke back another sob. "How could you? How could you go and put my initials on your arm? It's forever! Don't you get it?!"

"I'm very aware of how long it will be there. That's the appeal."

"Nice," I sneer. I spin out of his arms, and I look at it. It's hideous. It looks fresh. It's definitely homemade. My initials stare back at me, taunting me— **LD**. I absolutely hate my initials. I rear my fist back and land a punch on the offending letters. "Hey, dumbass! Do you know what LD stands for?" I shout over his groaning.

"What?!" He grits his teeth and looks up at me inquiringly, holding his arm. "Lorraina Dabney," he answers matter-of-factly.

"How about Local Dummy or Learning Disability?" I raise my eyebrow at him, waiting for this realization to kick in.

"I don't care. No one's going to give me shit about it."

"Well, I've gotten shit about it my whole life. What makes you so special?"

"No one messes with me. And everyone will know exactly who it stands for."

"Yeah, even my dad?" I sneer.

"Oh…" His head drops.

"Yeah, oh! I guess you didn't consider that, did you? He's gonna freak and probably try to kill you." I'm ranting I know, but I can't seem to stop myself. "You're so over-the-top! Why can't you be like a normal boyfriend and draw my name all over your notebook or your room or something a lot less permanent and obvious?"

His head shoots back up, and there's a look of wonder on his face. "You want me to be your boyfriend?" I roll my eyes heavenward. Of course, that was the part he heard!

"No, not now! You've just further proven that I can't trust you to behave in a normal manner. This is NOT normal!" I screech.

I leave him standing there, wondering about my strange behavior. He's probably thinking does she or doesn't she. "She" doesn't even know.

When I get home, I get cleaned up quickly and sneak out to call him. I really don't want to speak to him at the moment, but I have to know what he will tell people.

"I'm sorry I hit you," I tell him. "You just scare the shit out of me."

"I know. I knew you would be angry, but I needed your initials on my arm. That's just how I felt. Feel," he amends.

I ignore all that. The deed is done. I figure I must focus on damage control. "I need to know what you're gonna tell people. What are you going to say they stand for?"

He's quiet for a moment. "Long Dong!" he exclaims. "Yeah, I'll tell people they stand for Long Dong!" He seems very proud of his quick wit and laughs at his joke.

I'm pretty shocked by his perverted reply. I've never heard him say anything even slightly inappropriate. Then, I laugh too. That is actually pretty funny. Pretty stupid? Yes. But pretty funny too. Crisis averted, I hope.

Chapter Ten

How Does He Know?

I'm shaken from my memory as I hear that familiar jingle of the door, and I glance at my watch. It's time for him to be here. I steal a glance over my shoulder. It's him. My breath quickens as does my heart. It feels as if it will burst out of my chest any moment now. I watch him walk over to the coffee bar and joke around with the server. He looks so good. He's wearing his leather, of course. It looks thoroughly worn and soft. I imagine myself running my hands up over his arms and the feel of his soft, supple leather. I don't stop there, though. My hands run up his coppery neck, and I'm holding his face to plant a kiss on his velvety lips. *Holy shit!* I remember exactly how soft they felt. I run my hands through his now longer hair where it falls in disarray just above his collar. It is as black as midnight sin.

I try to stop daydreaming about him in this manner. Nah, that's not what I want. Where this came from, I don't know; but I'm enjoying it. *Just keep talking so I can keep checking you out, I will him.* His jeans are well worn, too. They are faded and frayed perfectly around the back pockets and seams. They fit him like a second skin, allowing me an unfettered view of his tight behind. My eyes are drawn to the shape his wallet has made, and I follow the chain around his hip. He's still pretty slim but broader. He wears scuffed up black biker boots. He is not anything like anyone I've ever been attracted to. I'm usually drawn to the clean cut, athletic type. Of course, I haven't been attracted to anyone in a very long time. I guess our tastes do change as we get older.

I see him start to turn toward the little platform where he will perform. I jerk around and scrunch down on the loveseat. I hear him readying his instrument and doing his sound check. I hear the canned music click off and Michael say, "Hey ya'll. Thanks for coming out to Create Café tonight. I'm Mike Bang from the Big Bang Theory." His voice forces me to swallow hard. It's smooth yet raspy. Although he's still full of contradictions, his voice has changed and is deeper, more mature. "If you have any requests, I'd love to hear them. If I know it, I'll play it. If I don't, well, I'll try to play something similar," he ends on a laugh and launches into a recent hit that has received lots of airtime lately.

I just sit and take it all in, closing my eyes to imagine his fingers skimming the chords. Are his eyes closed to revel in the music too? I remember how lost in the music he would get the couple of times I saw him pick on his guitar. His whole countenance would meld with the guitar, making him look like he was born with one in his arms, born to play that way. This song is so…darkly passionate.

I'd only ever felt that passionate about one thing in my whole life, yet I let it slip through my fingers. How did I do that? Oh, yeah. I didn't allow myself to feel anymore. It's hard to create when you're numb.

I steal a glance at the patrons sitting across from me. They seem to be enjoying him play. The woman is really staring hard at

Michael. She keeps trying to focus on what the man is talking to her about. *Distracting, isn't he?* I think. I chuckle to myself. *Eyes off, lady! He's mine.* Well, I hope he will be anyway.

He wraps up that song and starts a slow build up to one of my favorite John Lennon songs. Oh, how does he know just what to play? John is seemingly apologizing for being overzealous. He's saying it's the only way he knows how to be, and she just needs to deal with it. Ha! Sounds very familiar.

I take out my journal and jot down the names of the songs in his first set. I love every song that he plays, and I never want to forget which ones I hear him play this first night. Some I remember from my youth, some are current hits, and one love song I don't recognize at all. On his seventh song, I decide to let him know I'm here despite the overwhelming urge to curl up on the couch and let the butterflies, currently residing in my stomach, take over completely.

I draw my knees up on the seat and turn to the side, working my way up to turn completely around. My stomach suddenly pitches violently. I turn and sink back down on the couch. Tears spring to my eyes. All of those "what ifs" are back and taunting me. It suddenly feels like the first day of class in a new school, and I'm naked in front of everyone. I can't just sit here all night and not acknowledge him. I feel like I've wasted enough precious time living without him in my life. It's now or never. I bolster my resolve and turn a little more quickly this time so as not to change my mind.

I look across the room to make eye contact with him. He's staring right at me—hard. He gives me a grin and a knowing look like he's known all along I would be sitting right here on this very couch at this very moment in time. The look at once causes something in me to tense, but that is immediately replaced by a strange sense of calm. I smile back and fold my hands on top of the couch, resting my head on them and maintaining eye contact with him. After a couple of minutes, he seems to signal something to the server.

Suddenly, the server is standing in front of me, wanting to know if I would like anything.

"Oh, um…I already had a smoothie. I'm not sure. What else do you have?" I ask shakily.

He rattles off a list of drinks I've never heard of. I shoot an unsure glance toward Michael and ask, "Uh…What's Michael drinking?"

He tells me the name of a very intense sounding concoction. That sounds exactly like Michael. I have a sudden query for the server, "Does he send drinks to a lot of females?"

He seems to consider my question for a moment, purses his lips, and says, "No, actually, you're the first; and we've been working together for a while." He makes a tsking sound and appears thoughtful.

"I'll just have what he's having," I stammer.

Once I have my drink, I lean back on the arm of the sofa and enjoy the rest of Michael's set. He seems to have a pulse on the place because everyone is enjoying his music as they are doing a lot of clapping, singing along, and swaying back and forth. I'm immensely proud of him for pursuing his talent and his dreams.

I suddenly hear him launch into our Poison song. Oh my! I wasn't expecting that. I bite my lip and look at him. We keep eye contact throughout the entire song. Again, intense would be the proper adjective for the feelings passing between us. Does this mean I'm forgiven?

He wraps up his song, finally closing his eyes on the last note. I close mine too and turn back around on my couch. I sink into its comfortable embrace. I hear the canned music start back up. I feel him heading my way. I take a deep breath and say a little prayer that our first conversation in almost five years goes well.

Chapter Eleven

Off Kilter

He saunters over to stand in front of me. I open my eyes and look up at him. He really is gorgeous. I suddenly don't know what to say. Small talk seems so pointless between us; however, I can't lead with everything that has been flowing through my brain. My brow furrows. I can't believe I didn't plan that far ahead. That is highly unusual for me.

He interrupts my thought process, "You looked happy to see me a few minutes ago, Lorraina. Now I'm not so sure."

Any thought about how to approach this conversation flies right out of my head. I shake my head a little and grin around my confession, "No, it's not that. I suddenly recalled something odd."

"Hmm…Mind if I sit down?"

"Oh, yeah. Of course." I move to one corner of the loveseat. I close my journal and slide it into my purse. I wish I'd thought of a more seductive opening. "How are you?"

He sits in his corner and throws his arm up on the back of the couch. He looks completely at ease while I feel like all my nerve endings are exposed. "Good, good. How are you, Lorraina?" Oh, my name on his lips. My heart skips a couple of beats. It has just the same effect as I remembered.

"I'm pretty good. Home for a visit. You sounded good up there."

"Yeah, not too shabby, I hope. I've been playing professionally for a few years now. We even started a band. It keeps me out of trouble."

I haven't stopped smiling since we started talking. My smile spreads on that note, though. "I'm glad to hear that, Michael."

"So, what's up with you and college? Aren't you graduating soon?"

"I am but I'm going straight to law school, so I'm not really focusing on graduation like everyone else."

"Really, law school?" His face wrinkles up like he's smelled something foul. "I didn't figure you for law school." He seems embarrassed to have admitted that.

"Why not?" I'm wounded. Does he think I'm not smart enough or is it that my family is a walking contradiction to the law?

"I don't know," he shrugs and smiles a little. "I guess I just always imagined you writing or teaching or both."

I relax, knowing he's not insulting my intelligence. I feel silly thinking that's what he meant; I should've known better. "I'd considered it, but there's absolutely no money in it. I had to be more sensible than that, I guess."

"Hmm…Well, what do you think of Mona's transformation?" He holds his hands up to encompass the shop.

"I love it. I miss the old place, but this is really neat."

"Yeah, I like it too. I've been playing here for quite a while. She's been very good to me."

"I'm so happy for you. You seem to be doing well." Of late I've been a succubus. Would I mess this up for him by bringing to the surface old feelings?

"I am, I think. I have like four jobs and go to school full-time, but it's good. Like I said, keeps me out of trouble," he nudges my knee and winks at me. My knee tingles where he's touched me, and my heart beats a vigorous tattoo.

I clear my throat and decide to address my pink elephant. "The last time we saw each other wasn't very pleasant. Am I forgiven?"

"Are you still dating the child molester?" He asks bitterly.

"Oh, no. Definitely not." I hesitate. "I'm not seeing anyone actually."

"Focusing on your studies?"

"Yeah, something like that. How about you?"

"Yep, focusing on my studies." He gives me a slanted grin.

I giggle. That's not the question I wanted answered, and I can't imagine him putting school before anything else. He always hated it so much. I voice these musings.

"That's because I was sick of other people telling me what to think and what classes to take. I take whatever classes strike me as interesting and allow myself to think whatever I want now."

"What classes have you taken?"

"Lots, but some of my favorites have been Creative Writing, Greek Mythology, painting, World Literature, oh yeah, and Women's Lit."

That all sounds well and good, but how will he earn a degree taking only what he's interested in? "What will your degree be in?"

"I'm undecided. I'm not in a real hurry to get a degree, honestly. I just want to learn. I've been thinking, eventually, I might go the creative writing path."

"Oh, I could totally see you doing that." I picture him running his hands through his hair at a mahogany desk, trying desperately to pen the perfect sonnet. Then, I picture me, his self-appointed muse, sitting in front of him on his desk to give him some inspiration. I feel myself blush and grin at my thoughts.

"You seem happy," he interrupts.

"I'm happier than I've been in a long time, Michael," I admit. The look in his eyes allows me to go further. "I feel very fortunate to be enjoying your company." I give him a look that I hope communicates all that I'm feeling, all that I want to say but can't just yet.

He studies me for a moment. I wait patiently for him to say something. He doesn't say a word. I begin to fidget, realizing I've revealed a great deal, yet somehow he's revealed nothing. He finally grabs and holds my hand and runs the fingers of his free hand over mine, making some unknown pattern. My fingertips grasp his. This feels so right. He lifts my hand and plants a small kiss on my knuckles. Slowly, he arranges my hand back on the couch and gets up to make his way back to the platform.

I melt into the couch as I revel in what I can only deem is an encouraging first encounter. Does he fully understand why it is that I am here? And what kind of change has occurred in me? I'm far more mature than the thirteen-year-old girl he fell for all those years ago. I'm even more mature than the seventeen-year-old young woman he tried to reason with a few years back. I allow our confrontation and last conversation to run through my head and flow onto my page.

"What are you thinking?! You know, I left you alone for these last couple years for one reason. I wanted you to have a normal teenage experience and meet a guy with some kind of future who could give you everything you desire, everything you deserve. And you choose him?" His tone is admonishing. It pisses me off even more. Who is he to reprimand me? I've heard what he's been up to lately.

"Look," I try, "you don't have to agree with my choices, but it really is none of your business. We've gone our separate ways, you and me. You've made choices as have I. I'm not too happy with the ones you've made either, but I don't want to waste our time fighting about it. I haven't seen you in forever." That all sounded very reasonable to me.

He doesn't agree, "That's just bullshit," he says in a calm, clear voice. I don't remember him ever cursing in my presence before, especially not in anger. It catches me off guard. I open my mouth with a comeback, but he continues unhindered, "You need to call it off with that fucking child molester now!" He is pointing at the ground and looking up to the heavens for divine inspiration, I guess.

His words hit their mark. I feel as though he's just punched me in the stomach; his summation of my relationship has taken my breath away. I open my mouth to defend him or myself or our relationship, but I realize that he's dangerously close to the source of my own unease about my relationship. "You know," I try again through gritted teeth, "he cares about me like no one else ever has. He doesn't drop out on me. He doesn't run around with other girls, getting drunk, getting high, fighting, getting arrested. He holds down a job and cares about me. Is that so bad?"

"Yeah, it's disgusting. He's twenty-fucking-six years old, Lorraina!" I back up with each of his hatred-spiked words, fighting the urge to cower. He keeps advancing, but his voice gets soft. "You're a baby compared to him. A very sheltered one, I might add."

"Oh, really. You think my growing up with my dad was sheltering, huh? You don't know the half of it!" I turn to walk away, but he grips my shoulder and spins me back around.

"I mean sheltered when it comes to human nature, Lorraina. You are far too good a person to believe that he means you any harm, but I'm here to tell you that any MAN who would date a young GIRL has anything but good intentions."

"He loves me. He wants to marry me one day," I protest, and it sounds weak even to my own ears. He hones in on this in an instant.

"What does your mom say?"

Oh! He's got me there. I see in his eyes that he knows it, too. "She doesn't know," I whisper. More forcefully, I add, "And don't be the one to tell her, OK?"

"I can't stand by and watch him use and discard you," he says resignedly while shoving his hands into his hair

I fold my arms across my chest and cock my hip. "Well, you're in luck!" I snap. "You don't have to. We aren't even a part of each other's lives anymore. I don't know anything about the man you're turning out to be other than you are reminding me a lot of my dad, and you don't know anything about me. We just need to wish each other well and forget about each other."

My comment hits home. He knows that I value my dad about as much as I value pond scum. I regret it immediately. He nods his head and looks me up and down for a minute as though searching for something or committing me to memory. He jerks his head once in a final nod. "All right, I'll see ya around then."

My voice turns apologetic as I watch him back away from me. I never wanted to hurt him. I try to move toward him. "Michael, I—"

He throws his hands up, warding me off. "No, it's all good. Take care, Lorraina. See ya around."

I watch him hop into his friend's waiting car; and they speed off, leaving me standing in front of my work. I wipe angry tears from my face. Fine, if that's the way he wants to play it. Then, fine.

Yeah, he tries to warn you and tell you that he left you alone for all the right reasons and you blow him off and talk to him like he's garbage. You compared him to the absolute worst possible specimen of humankind that you've had the displeasure of knowing. You chose a complete loser over one of your oldest and dearest friends. Smart. Real smart.

I close my eyes and shake my head, trying to dislodge all these thoughts. I'd paid dearly for that choice, too. Would Michael forgive me for those choices that I made so long ago? How could he if I still hadn't forgiven myself?

Chapter Twelve

Don't Look, Just Leap

I gather my belongings and move over to the stools at the counter so that I can be closer to Michael. He's playing an infectious melody that I find myself humming. He raises his brow at me and smiles into the microphone, closing his eyes and reveling in his song. How did I ever resist him? Was he always this confident and self-assured? I think there were bits of him that were but not quite like this.

I take out my journal and jot down the names of the songs he's played during his second set, making myself a soundtrack for our first night together. It reminds me of the few gifts he gave me back when we were friends. He's only ever given me three presents. Two of which were mixed tapes that he'd made while I was in eighth grade. They'd burned along with the rest of my things, however. The other was a tiny little pewter cross hanging on a strip of leather that he used to wear. I knew where that was even though I hadn't looked at it in forever. Maybe I could make some kind of gift for him from this soundtrack.

He opens his eyes and sees me sitting at the bar. He looks relieved. I wonder if he thought I was leaving. I'm not going anywhere. Realization dawns on me, I don't ever want this night to end. I don't want for another day that he's not a part of. I ignore a nagging little thought that chants something about me being the obsessed one.

"Can I get you anything else?" The server asks, pulling me from my musings.

"Oh, no," I say, "I'm good."

"Well, just let me know."

I try to pull him into a conversation. "So are you and Michael friends, then?"

"Yeah, we hang out." He offers me a huge grin and his hand. "I'm Jason."

I shake it and grin. "I'm Lorraina."

"How do you know Mike?" He asks.

"We went to school together. We were good friends before I went away to college." I have to bite my lip quickly to keep from shouting that he is the love of my life, but I was too stupid to do anything about that before and am here to rectify that tonight!

"Oh, yeah. Well, he must really like you. I've never seen him act so...not tortured. Sorry, that's the best way I can describe it," he finishes with a shrug and continues wiping the counter down.

I feel so "not tortured" myself. "I really like him," I admit with a sigh.

"Good, I get good vibes from you. And Mike is good people. He deserves someone good." He gives me a smile.

I smile back at him. "He really is a good person," I agree.

I turn my attention back to Michael and enjoy the rest of his playing. He wraps up his second set, thanks everyone for coming out, and starts to pack up his guitar. I'm nervous. I wonder what we will do. Does he already have plans? I hope not. I don't want to share him.

He comes over and leans on the bar. He picks up a coaster and spins it quickly like a top. "They're closing. Do you have any plans tonight?"

Oh, yes. I certainly do. "Um…No, what about you?"

"I do, unfortunately." He's looking down so he doesn't notice my crestfallen expression. I quickly rearrange my face, hoping for a neutral look. "I have another gig in about thirty minutes. My band is playing at Grey tonight; it's the new club at Starlight Casino. I'll probably be there until around one or two." He looks up and his face holds a look of disappointment.

This makes me smile a little. He doesn't want to leave me either. I've never been to a casino, though. "I could wait for you, but that's really late for me to be out," I say hesitantly. Obviously, I'm old enough; but I just feel intimidated for some reason.

"I know. It's not a bad scene, though, if you'd like to go with me."

"I don't know," I hedge. "What are you doing tomorrow?"

"I'm off tomorrow until my gig here at seven," he replies quickly.

I don't want to wait until tomorrow to see him; I suppress the urge to stamp my foot like a petulant child. "Well, could we do something tomorrow then?" *Please say yes, please say yes.*

"I would love that. I'll give you my number so you can call me when you wake up."

"OK." He grabs a napkin and writes his number down for me. I tuck it inside my journal.

"I'll walk you out," he tells me. He settles his business with Jason while I pack up and ready myself. Jason waves goodbye to us. *This sucks,* I think.

He walks me to my car, mentioning a few different things we could do tomorrow. I'm not really hearing him because I am nervous about how to say goodbye to him. I came here hoping for…for what? I don't know. I just know it wasn't a goodbye, even a temporary one.

I must've responded in a positive way because he seems not to notice my distractedness. He grabs my hand again as we reach my car. I latch on to his hold. "Lorraina, I can't tell you how good it was to see you again."

I smile up at him, "I know. I feel the same." *That was eloquent, I chide myself.* I'm just reeling.

"I'll be waiting for your call in the morning."

"Is eight too early?" I ask.

"Nope, sounds perfect."

"K. Until then." We hold hands for another moment. He picks up my hand again and brushes it with a soft kiss. He turns to go and I want to say something clever and memorable, but I can't muster anything. When he looks back at me, I manage a little wave.

With a sigh, I get in my car and fire up the engine. I watch him as he jumps into his Jeep, gives me a final wave, and heads out. I watch his Jeep pull out, thinking even his mode of transportation is sexy. I don't know too much about cars, but I know it's an older model Jeep with big tires, dark navy, and chromed out. It fits him even though it's not what I would expect for him to drive, but Michael is nothing if not unexpected.

I lay my head on my steering wheel. My eyes puddle up. They are tears of joy. He seems very open to me. I hope I'm reading him right, though; there wasn't much time for talking.

I look at the clock on my dash. It's only nine. That's too early to go home. I guess I could go to Ginny's and hang out. Then, at least I wouldn't be telling a complete lie to my mom. I put my car in gear and make it out on the highway.

I replay the entire night again. I smile. I think it was a success despite having ended earlier than I'd hoped. I can't believe how unsure of myself I am around him. The stakes are just so high, though; and I don't want to loose him again. I don't think I could bear it.

I put my turn signal on and merge with the traffic flow. I'm glad I know these roads so well as I am completely consumed with thoughts of him. I guess I need to decide where it is I am actually going: home or Ginny's?

He has four jobs and school? He seems consumed much like me. Why is he working so hard? Is the temptation of his former life that strong that he needs to work like a dog? Is he trying to bury himself in work like I've buried myself in school? What or who is he running from?

I park my car and look up at the flashing lights before me. I laugh at myself. How did I know I would end up here? I never had any intention of going home or going to Ginny's, did I? I bite my lip. Should I go in? I've never been in a casino before. *Ugh!* If I don't go in, I'm afraid I will lose whatever momentum we've established this night. I think, too, that he would see this as a sign of my pursuit. Will he be flattered or repelled? Only one way to find out.

Chapter Thirteen

Rolling the Dice

The noise and the smoke are the first things I notice about the casino. There are flashing lights everywhere. Some people look ecstatic. Others look downtrodden. It's a stark dichotomy. I make my way to the marquee, looking for directions to the club that Michael's playing in. I think I can find my way there after studying the map for a few minutes. I walk toward the escalator, flashing my ID as I pass the security guard. I hope I look acceptable to enter the club. I went to a couple of clubs while I was in high school with *him*, but that was so long ago.

I find the club. It sounds like there are lots of people and the music is very loud. Quite different from Mona's.

Michael's band is playing a Southern Rock classic. It's one of my favorites. Maybe, I think, all the songs he's playing are becoming my favorites because I love to hear him play so much. I giggle at myself.

I stand back for a few moments and take in the crowd. Not surprisingly, they are really enjoying the band. The dance floor is pretty packed, but I'm able to gain an unobstructed view of the stage where I can watch Michael for a few unbeknownst minutes. His stage presence is completely different from his unplugged performance at Mona's. His dark hair is damp with sweat, which makes me realize he's really been working the crowd. As if to provide me with evidence of my guess, I watch him stride to the edge of the stage and lean into the crowd punctuating each beat with a shake of his head. He pulls back up, stretching his powerful neck and holding a long note. I notice the female fans' collective disappointment at having lost the moment to pull him down further to them.

I head toward the bar to order a drink and find a seat. It's pretty crowded. I have to shuffle my way through the throng. When I break through to the bar and turn to face the stage, we make eye contact. Again, he raises his eyebrows at me and gives me a brilliant smile. I've surprised him. *Good,* I think.

I get the bartender's attention. Uh, now what? I haven't ordered a drink in forever. Honestly, I can't even think of any names of any drinks. "Um…Cherry Coke, please?" I suppress a grin.

"ID, please?"

"For a Cherry Coke," I gasp.

"Kidding. I'll be right back," he laughs and winks at me.

He's definitely laughing at me, not with me. I spin around on my stool to watch the show. The guitarist is starting up the insanely long guitar solo as the song demands. I see Michael making his way to me. Darn! I thought I would have a minute to acclimate before trying to speak coherently. Vaguely, I take note of all the women clamoring to get his attention. He is so gorgeous I can't lend it serious thought, though.

He reaches me and leans over to speak in my ear, "Hi! What are doing here?"

"I couldn't resist," I say. I pull back so he can see my meaning in my eyes.

"You have completely made my night, my week, my year!" He laughs.

"You've made mine as well. I just…just couldn't say goodbye to you yet."

The bartender interrupts with my drink, "Hey, Mike, can I get you something?"

"I'll have what she's having," he shouts.

He chuckles. "Are you sure you're man enough?!"

Michael turns a surprised look on me. "What are you drinking?"

"You'll have to wait and see," I respond coyly.

"You're just full of surprises tonight, aren't you?"

"I hope so," I say breathlessly.

He grabs his drink and takes a deep pull. I laugh as he squishes his face up in surprise. "Cherry Coke, really? Just livin' on the edge, huh?"

I giggle and confess, "I don't really drink that often, so I didn't know what to order."

He gives me a wink and leans over to shout something at the bartender. He takes another pull from his drink and rubs my knee. Before I can visibly react to the chain reaction his touch sets off with just that little graze, he's off to sing again.

I appreciate the view as he makes his way back to the stage. He's taken his jacket off since Mona's, and his black t-shirt pulls quite nicely across his shoulders and arms. I notice he has a tribal band drawing attention to his nicely toned right bicep. Again, it doesn't escape my attention that I'm not the only one noticing his exceptional good looks either. He leaps and spins onto the stage, grabbing his microphone and singing into it right in time with the music. *Oh, he really has this whole rock star thing down pat,* I muse.

I watch in awe as he works the stage, works the crowd. His movement is so fluid, so focused. I watch him focus that gaze on those around the stage. As he moves from girl to girl, each one turns and either screams or offers a dreamy sigh. I snicker at how ridiculous their behavior is until he turns his heated gaze on me. He takes me in from toe to head. When he eyes reach mine, I almost gasp aloud as I see all the passion, all the emotion emanating from his almost black eyes. I'm practically melting on my bar stool by the time he releases me. *My apologies, groupies.*

The bartender interrupts my infernal suffering and offers me another drink, "Mike ordered you a Mai Tai. Enjoy!" It looks beautiful. It reminds me of a sunset and has a wedge of pineapple, my favorite fruit, and wedge of lime. It even has a tiny umbrella. Cute, I think. I take a cautious sip. Mmm…It's good too. I can't even taste the alcohol.

I spot a table that looks inconspicuous and a little away from the crowd and head that way. I sip my drink and watch as Michael and his band interact with the audience and play a variety of songs.

They sound good. It sounds like they even play a couple of original songs. Impressive.

I'm enjoying Michael play, but I'm anxious to have him to myself. The night seems to stretch on forever. Finally, I hear Michael make the last call announcement. I straighten in my seat and mentally clap my hands together.

After their last number, he makes his way to me. Several people, mainly underdressed women, stop him and try to chat him up. He gives them a few words and a polite smile and moves on quickly. He finally makes his way over to me and puts my thoughts into words, "Finally, I thought the night would never end."

"My sentiments exactly. Do you have to stick around or can you go?"

"My band is gonna take care of everything tonight. Speaking of which, they're headed this way to meet you."

"Oh, OK," I rush out, trying not to be nervous and failing miserably.

"This is Josh, Nolan, T.J., and Taylor," he announces pointing quickly at the various members. "Guys, this is Lorraina." We make small talk for a couple of minutes during which they give him a hard time about being a diva since they have to take up his slack tonight.

"Yeah, thanks ya'll," Michael mumbles.

One of them gives me a pointed look and informs everyone that it's not Michael's thanks he's looking for.

My face drops and Michael cuts in, "Dude, what the hell?! I'm standing right here."

Josh, I think, smacks the other one on the back of the head, causing him to wince. "Yeah, T.J., shut the hell up! This is THE Lorraina." Four sets of eyes swivel around toward me, and I force myself not to shift to stand behind Michael.

"Well, if ya'll are done giving me shit, I think we'll cut outta here." They mumble their goodbyes. The rest of them all smacking T. J. around now. I giggle.

"Sorry, about that." Michael shakes his head at them as they walk away.

"They're fine. I'm just happy they finally went away. I've been dying to get you alone."

Michael turns and gives me a hungry look. "Let's get outta here," he breathes.

"OK," I manage to grab my stuff as he seizes my hand.

"You want to drive us?" He asks over his shoulder. "My Jeep has a bunch of equipment in it."

"No problem," I answer. And we're off.

Chapter Fourteen
Partial Confessions

I find myself sitting at the restaurant I worked at as a teen and the last place I saw him almost five years ago. I would've preferred to go somewhere else, but I realize that our options are limited at one o'clock in the morning. I vaguely recognize a couple faces, which means I shouldn't have to deal with any awkward "catching up" conversations as they probably aren't sure if they know me either.

I'm jolted from my thoughts as Michael rejoins me and slides into the booth across from me. "Whatcha thinking about?" he asks.

"We had our last conversation here," I reply. Better that he not know how uncomfortable this place makes me.

He fiddles with his straw wrapper, using water to make it worm. I focus on his long, full eyelashes. They jut out and curl up, making me want to run my fingertip over them. "I was thinking about that as well. I never got the chance to apologize for the way I spoke to you." He makes eye contact with me. He has the deepest, darkest brown eyes, making them almost black. Beautiful. He's always been so beautiful.

I start to speak but instead squeak. I clear my throat and try again, "There's nothing to apologize for. You were painfully accurate on every count."

"I'm sorry that I was right then," he gives me a slanted smile.

"Me too. But I learned some crucial lessons. I wouldn't be who I am without them today, so it's hard to be bitter."

He takes my palm and makes a little pattern with his fingers. "I'm sorry that you had to learn that way."

"I always was obstinate," I joke.

"Aah…very true," he finally laughs. "Here's the thing. I've been torn up over that conversation more than anything else over the years. Regretted it because I hurt you; but at the same time, grateful because it helped me so much. It was a wake up call, Lorraina. That conversation changed almost everything about me and for the better. It made me take a long look at who I was and what I was doing to myself. I was hurting my mother in all the ways that my father had hurt her. I was drinking. I was lashing out. Indians and hard liquor do not mix, ya know? The result is not pretty. More than that, I realized that I could never ever deserve you while I was on that path."

I flip my hand over to grasp his in mine. "I wish more than anything that I had listened to you back then. I was too proud and too stubborn to hear the wisdom of your words." I hesitate. The time for me to be honest about it all is upon me, but I can't bear to see love replaced by hatred in his eyes. Not now. Not yet. I know I will tell him the full truth eventually. I've always struggled with being honest, and that's a character flaw I will conquer for him as much as for myself. I settle with a partial truth, "Michael, I have to tell you something."

He looks worried. I ache to massage away the lines created by his frown. I look away quickly, afraid that he will read my thoughts. "Yeah?" he prompts.

"It was no coincidence that I was at Mona's tonight," I blurt out.

"Really?" he cocks his eyebrow and looks immediately relieved. Maybe he won't be put off by my obsession then. I glance down and focus on our hands again.

"Ginny and I were at Mona's yesterday. I bought your cards, and the cashier told me that you would be playing there. I couldn't resist." I look up and smile tentatively.

"So let's see if I got this right," he leans in and whispers. "You're the one stalking me now?"

I feel my cheeks warm. "Yes," I admit on a sigh.

"Interesting."

Our food comes and we enjoy the reprieve, switching the talk over to less serious topics.

I learn that he has his own place, a studio apartment by the ocean. He assures me that it is slightly larger than a walk in closet but that he is comfortable. He thought about getting a bigger place and a roommate; however, he likes his privacy too much.

I tell him about life at school. It's pretty boring, though. I assure him that Ole Miss and Oxford both have a lot to offer; but I don't partake, working and studying with any spare time that I have.

As the server clears our plates, he asks, "Do you have to go home now?"

"That depends."

"On what?"

"On what you have in mind."

"I want to show you something beautiful," he hesitates and pins me with his hot gaze, "and I'm reluctant to let you out of my sight."

I feel the exact same way as if he might disappear on me once again. "I'd love to see something beautiful," I tell him.

Chapter Fifteen

Through My Father's Eyes

I find myself sitting on the beach with a monstrous cup of coffee. This is turning out to be quite the night. I can track its progression by the rollercoaster of beverages I've consumed—smoothie to relax me, espresso to pep me up, Cherry Coke to keep up the pep, Mai Tai to make me look cool, and coffee to get that energy up again. They mirror my emotional rollercoaster ride as well. We sit on a large stretch of grass under one of the small oak trees that exists on what locals call The Point. I've been here a few times over the years, but I've never been a beach person. This little area is neat though—no sand.

Michael tells me that he comes here often after his gigs to decompress. He says that he falls asleep for a couple of hours and wakes to the most magnificent sunrise on God's green earth. Sometimes he writes or strums his guitar or draws. It sounds lovely to me. Very bohemian.

We sit in comfortable silence for a while. I'm loath to break it but there's something I need to know, have always wanted to know. I'm not quite sure how to ask, so I decide that being direct is probably best. "Michael, I have to ask you something. Something I've always wondered about."

"Yes," he breathes heavily, "I've always been this irresistible." I stare at him and raise my eyebrow. Cocky as ever.

"Anyway," I roll my eyes, "I never really understood why you were interested in me or how you even knew about me."

"That's not a question, English major," he replies sardonically.

"OK. How did you know about me? Why were you even interested in me?" I continue undaunted.

"That's two questions," he laughs as I playfully smack his arm. "Well," he begins, "I first found out about you from your dad. He and my dad were river rats. Always drinking and hanging out. I ran beers for them, ya know? I would run them theirs, and I would grab one for me and my friends to share on the down low. Your dad was a talker, though, when he would drink; and he talked about you all the time."

"Me?" I interrupt, shocked. "What would he say?"

He squeezes his eyes closed for a second, "He told stories. I don't know that he ever intended to tell me about you specifically, but he would always wind up telling Lorraina stories about how amazing you were with the horses, how beautifully you sang, and how well you did in school. How you were kind and gentle. Oh yeah, and how mature you were in dealing with people. He said you never met anyone you didn't like."

I feel tears well in my eyes. *It's too bad he hates me now,* I think. "Is that all?"

He shifts uneasily and looks at me. "No, not all of it; but I don't think you want to know the other things he said."

He's probably right, and I know where this is leading. Nevertheless, I ask him to continue.

"Are you sure?" I nod my head. "He talked about how he hoped you never turned out to be a whore or ended up with trash. He was quite vivid in his descriptions about that. It was odd the way he talked, though. Like he owned you."

Yep, I think to myself, it was exactly like he owned me. He used to tell me that if I ever kissed a boy or had sex with a boy that it was the same thing as breaking the adultery commandment and that I would go to hell. That God had given me to him and I was his until he gave me away on my wedding day. I do not share these thoughts with Michael, though. He doesn't need to know exactly how twisted my dad is if he hasn't yet figured it out for himself.

"You OK?" he asks.

"Oh, yeah. The possessive thoughts aren't what I find baffling or disturbing. I'm more surprised he said anything flattering about me. He never was very nice to me."

"He spoke of you almost reverently. The way he described you made me want to find you and make you mine forever. I remember thinking that one day. Just out of the blue after weeks of talking to him about you. I thought: 'I have to make her mine,'" he admits and laughs as something occurs to him. "I had to be kinda sneaky getting him to talk about you, though. He offered information at first. Then, after a while, he quit talking about you, so I had to invent all kinds of segues that would get him to talk about you without letting on that that's what I was doing."

I imagine him sitting around dreaming up ways to get my father to talk about me without provoking his wrath. It makes me laugh. "You always were so smart. I always wondered why your feelings were so intense for me, though. I barely knew who you were, but you seemed to know all about me."

"Well, after school started, I watched to see if I saw those qualities in you. I saw the way you looked out for others, especially your brothers. You always were so thoughtful. Do you remember Clark getting his fingers smashed in the door?"

I raise an eyebrow at him. Of course I remember; it was the scariest thing I'd ever seen. Clark lost the ends of two of his fingertips. "Yes, I was scared out of my mind, but you weren't there."

"Oh, I was there. You just weren't aware that I was there. When he smashed his fingers, everyone jumped back like they were scared to help him. You didn't though. You rushed forward and freed his hand in nanoseconds. I couldn't even react. I had the thought to help ya'll, but you had him freed and were carting him off to the nurse before I made it to you."

"Wow, I can't believe you were there. I missed the bus home that day. My grandmother had to come and get me, and she was not happy. I tried to explain, but nothing would come out quite right. I was pretty freaked out by the time she got there. I ended up just taking my punishment."

"I tried to get the bus driver to wait for you, ya know? She wouldn't hear of it. I finally convinced her to at least let me run your book bag and purse to you. I knew someone would come and get you. I, however, would've ended up walking home had I missed the bus; or I would have waited with you. Besides, you didn't know I existed yet."

A laugh escapes me, "Ya know. I never could remember how my stuff got to the nurse's office. When I walked out of the back, I thought I needed to track down my stuff and there it sat on the front counter. I had no idea that it was you. I just figured I was so freaked out that I'd only imagined tossing my things in my desperate attempt to help Clark."

"Yep, doing my good deeds where I can." He pauses for a beat and then blurts out, "*Where the Red Fern Grows*." I give him a questioning look. "That's the book you were reading." A satisfied sensation pervades my entire being, making me feel warm all over. He remembers the book I was reading almost ten years ago. Unbelievable.

He shifts again, looking uncomfortable. I suddenly realize that I'm not very comfortable either. We've been out here for a while now, but I don't want him to call it a night. Suddenly, I have a solution, "Hey, I have a blanket in my car!" I practically run to my car and grab all my sheets and pillows. We spread them out and get comfortable, lying side by side.

We get quiet again. I love that he seems as comfortable with silence as I am. So many people feel that they must fill silence when there really isn't anything of value to say. As if we can't live without inane and incessant chatter. Why doesn't everyone realize that we need silence to process and feel and exist? That has always baffled me.

I must've dozed off. I feel so warm all of the sudden and realize that my head is cradled next to Michael's chest. I smile slowly and close my eyes again. I'm not sure how I got over here; but if he's OK with it, I'm not budging.

The next time I rouse, it's to Michael's voice and the magnificent sunrise he promised me. "When the child of morning, rosy-fingered Dawn, appeared, we admired God's wondrous gift to us."

I'm impressed as he paraphrases some lines from one of my favorite epic poems. "Homer, huh? It's so beautiful. You're incredibly insightful to have remembered that phrase." I laugh at myself and confess, "I've always thought that the dawning sun resembled the end of an orange sherbet push up pop. How creative is that?"

"Very, actually. Mine is from memory. Yours is original."

I run my hand up his chest and turn my head to look up at him. "I'll never forget this moment here with you, ya know?" I'm finally starting to realize that I've memorized every one of my moments with him. I will add this one to my stash.

His words are an echo of my thoughts. "I've never forgotten any moment I've spent with you. A couple of them I tried to forget because of my stupidity but couldn't quite manage it because, however stupid I was, you had starred in that memory."

I stretch myself along his body and place a light kiss on his mouth. I quickly turn my head to look back at the morning sun as embarrassment warms my cheeks. I feel like a new person lying here with him. Better than new actually. I feel revived. Almost like the old me.

Chapter Sixteen

Brings Me to My Knees

I wake up again to find the sun a few hours further in the sky. Michael's breath is even under me. I gingerly scoot over and stretch. I sit up and stare at him for a few unencumbered minutes. He looks so peaceful. I can still make out the faint scar on his eyebrow from one of our dirt bike riding accidents.

I flip through my purse without taking my eyes off of him and try to locate my journal.

My mom had found two small beat up dirt bikes for sale around Christmas the year she finally left my dad and had hocked her class ring and engagement ring in order to buy them for my brothers along with a beautiful gold wishbone ring with a tiny little pearl for me. Of course, she told my brothers they had to let me teach them how to ride because they were still pretty young. That meant I got to enjoy the dirt bikes as well. It was a couple of days after Christmas, and Michael showed up at my house asking about going for a ride since I'd been bragging about my skills on the hills.

When we tried to start them, he insisted that his wouldn't start and that he could just ride on the back of mine. I suppress a giggle as the reality of that dawns on me. I was too naïve to see his motivation for lying then, but it had to have been a lie because later that morning it had cranked right up.

"I can just ride on the back of yours for a while," he says.

"Um…OK." I was nervous about our weight on it but not too nervous to deny him a ride. He throws his leg over the side. Before he has his hands around my waist, I gun it.

"Shiiiit!" He shouts and then laughs as his hands grasp my waist.

I laugh and maneuver our way out of the developed part of the neighborhood. My hair is flying back in the wind that stings my eyes. I feel him rest his head on my shoulder. It has been two weeks since our kiss. I wonder if he will ever bring it up. We ride for a while, jumping puddles and mounds of dirt. I hop off for a little while and let him show me up with all of his wheelies and jumps. He's far more daring than I am.

I yell at him that I'm starting to get cold. We decide to head back for a while and warm up and go out again later. He pats the seat behind him and winks at me. Of course, I'm hardheaded and just quirk my brow at him. There's no way I'm getting on the back of my own bike, I think.

"Fine, have it your way," he pouts and scoots back.

"I will. Thanks for your permission, O' Great One!" I mock.

We're almost to my house and I, in my infinite wisdom, decide to shake some warmth in my hands as I slow down to turn on my street. I don't understand the fact that my hands have shrunken with the cold and are now smaller, so my new ring goes flying off in the tall grass that borders our street. I almost wreck as I try to get stopped as quickly as possible. Michael yells at me to inquire about my sanity. Before it fully dies out, I'm off the dirt bike and running toward the grass.

"Lorraina, what's wrong?" he shouts the question at me.

"My ring! My ring! It flew off my hand when I was shaking it out! Oh my God, Michael! My mom bought it for me just two days ago!"

"OK. OK. It's gonna be OK. We'll find it," he assures me.

We searched for at least an hour before being overcome with the unusually cold weather. My face was chapped from my tears. My throat ached with the unshed ones. Michael didn't want to give up, but it felt hopeless. He assured me that after we went home and warmed up some we would search again. And we did to no avail, of course.

Later we sat on the porch holding hot chocolate. My mom was still at work, and I was scared to tell her what had happened when she did arrive. We were silent as we had been since my complete screw up.

Finally, Michael breaks the silence. "Lorraina, your mom will understand. It was an accident. You would have never been purposefully careless with her gift. She'll know that."

I start crying again. When I finally stop, I mumble, "Michael, my mom hocked her class ring and her wedding rings to buy us our Christmas presents. She's working two jobs, going to school, and providing for us while my piece of shit dad blames the world for his drinking and arson problems and what do I do? I lose her precious gift to me." I choke on another sob and can't speak anymore.

He waits until I quiet down again. "I'm so sorry," he offers.

And he is. I can hear it in his voice. Most people utter these words unthinkingly, not considering what they really mean. He would take this pain from me if he could. He understands that it was more than just a piece of jewelry that I am mourning for. My mom was killing herself, and I was a klutz.

I prayed that my mom would know how much her sacrifice meant to me even if I did lose the token of that sacrifice. I wasn't ungrateful. I was just stupid. Moms understood that, right?!

He sat there with me for a long time. Not talking. He was just there. A strong presence in my infinite sadness. I gathered strength from him as I prepared to face my mom.

Over the next few weeks, to make up for my foolishness, I did all kinds of things around the house to show my mom how much I appreciated her. She wasn't mad at me, which I had feared. Worse, she was disappointed. I hated disappointing people. Still do.

***

A couple of weeks later, Michael meets me as I get off the bus. "Walk with me," he says.

I give my brother my book bag and catch up to Michael, who has already started walking away. His hands are in his pockets, his head down, his shoulders pulled taut. He looks as if he is in pain. I feel something akin to panic steal over me, freezing me in place for a moment.

111

"Hey! Wait up!" I yell.

He spins around. "You know how much I love you, right?"

I skid to a stop. The look he gives me scares me. It looks like resignation. I've never seen Michael give up before. What is he giving up on? Or is it who is he giving up on? "Michael, you're scaring me. Are you OK?"

"Do you want the bad news, the crappy news, or what?"

"Just tell me!" I hate the unknown. "Whatever it is; we can deal with it."

"There is no 'we,'" he thrusts the pronoun back in my face.

I take a deep breath to defend myself. His look stops me. I don't know how to handle this Michael. I'm sorry just won't cut it. I'm at a loss for what would be appropriate. But, he's right—there is no we.

He runs his hand through his hair and sighs, "Look, I didn't mean it like that. I'm just... I..."

This is crazy. I've never seen him at a loss for words or unsure of himself. "Michael, whatever it is, please tell me." I want to reach out and comfort him, but he wouldn't appreciate it right this moment.

"Well, for starters, I tried to find the pawn shop where your mom hocked her ring; but it was impossible. Either I didn't find the right one, or it's already sold. Either way, I can't help you get her class ring back."

I relax a little. This is not the end of the world as his demeanor was suggesting. This wasn't what I was expecting. I had no idea *that he had even been searching for it. My heart warms. "Michael, I can't believe you—"*

"I'm dropping out," he deadpans. His eyes don't meet mine. My gratefulness flips like a switch to emptiness. He can't leave me.

"Michael, please don't do this," I beg. "You're better than this. I know school sucks, but you can stick it out for a few more years."

"That's not the issue."

"Then what is?" I scream. "There's nothing worth quitting for. Is it me? Are you that pissed at me?!"

"No, no! I have to be able to support myself. I can't make enough money at Cricket's to help my brother with the rent, and I...I can't go back home. I got a decent job offer, but it's full-time work."

What can I say to that? I know exactly the situation he would face with his dad, and I know all about the struggle to make ends meet on your own. My mom's living proof of that battle. I bite my lip and try desperately to think up an alternative. I know nothing about his options, though. I have no wisdom to offer him. I do the only thing I know to do: I grab him and give him a hug. I don't know how long we stand there. I hear him sniff a few times and feel him run his cheek over my shoulder.

After we say our goodbyes, I walk home and know that nothing will ever be the same. I run my hands through my hair and feel his tears there. I hate this! I freaking hate this! What can I do though? We're both powerless to stop this. This is what being poor means—powerless, weak, defenseless. Two deadbeat, drunk, violent fathers result in our two crappy, meaningless lives.

"Whatcha doing over there? Whatever it is, I don't like it. It makes you unhappy." I look over to see that serene look on his face still. Is it possible that, despite all the crap we've been through, we might actually make something of ourselves? Might actually be happy?

"Good mornin', Michael," I say on a smile.

"Mornin', Lorraina."

I sigh. So simple, so lovely. "I was journaling. Something I haven't been able to do in a long time." *It's because of you,* I think. *I'm able to journal again and confront my feelings because of you. It's always been you.* "Anyway, I was writing about some unpleasant memories, but it's therapeutic to get them out, ya know?"

"I get it." Of course he does; he's the most intuitive person I've ever known.

"I'm sure you channel your pain and unpleasantness into your music, right?"

"Among other things," he agrees.

I glance at my watch. "Oh! It's almost eight. I should get home. My mom will be worried."

"Yeah," he agrees, "you've totally screwed up my routine."

"Oh, gee. Sorry about that," I sneer. Curiosity trumps my irritation. "You have a routine?" I ask disbelievingly.

114

"Rote breeds predictability. Predictability breeds favorable conditions for my sobriety."

That's a non-answer if I'd ever heard one. "Aah…I'd like to see what you do to keep yourself occupied," I hint.

"And so you shall," he stretches. As he does, I see his tobacco-colored abs pulled taut. I see a bit of ink of another tattoo. How do I make him realize that he's the sexiest thing I've ever seen? I can't wait for that. I quickly busy myself with putting my journal away. He stands to help me up. "But not today," he continues, "like you said your mom will be worried."

We pack up, and Michael drives us back to his Jeep. He insists on following me to my road, at least, even though it's way out of his way. He worries that I may fall asleep at the wheel. If I'm wondering about him driving behind me and analyzing me and our night together, I'm sure that will keep me awake; so I agree.

I pull off to the side of the main road before we approach my road. He whips his Jeep around my car and pulls over as well.

I'm so exhausted, but I don't want to say goodbye. *Absence makes the heart grow fonder,* I think. *Can't have him get too used to you yet. If there's no challenge, he may get bored with you,* I chide myself.

Michael hops out of his still running Jeep, and I can hear "Desperado" pouring out of his speakers. He makes his way back to my car, and I get out and lean on my door. He puts his hands in his pockets, pushing them down into fists and looks at me shyly.

We just spent the entire night together and he's shy! Typical Michael and his contradictory nature.

"When can I see you again?" I ask. I'm done being coy and shy and nonchalant. I know what I want and I'm going to get it. Afraid he may see all that in my eyes, I look away a little.

"When do you want to see me again?" *Oh, who's playing coy now, Mr. Bang?*

"Well, I'll be home for spring break," I tease and glance at him.

The look on his face says he's done with coy. Good! Got his attention! "This afternoon?"

"I can't wait," I declare. "So, what is this?" I gesture between the two of us. "Is it safe to say that we are dating or that we are boyfriend/girlfriend?" I bite my lip. I couldn't resist asking; but now that I have, I fear his response.

He shakes his head and grins at me. I fight the sudden urge to run my hands through that silky midnight hair of his. "Always so quick to label and categorize. I guess that's what will make you an excellent attorney. Assess. Label. Categorize. Add up the W's. " He leans in a little and whispers, "How about we just go with the flow? See where it leads us. Label later?" He raises his brows, offering my type-A dominant personality a direct challenge.

Caution to the wind, very atypical for me, I reply, "OK. I'm up for it." Challenge accepted. "You?" Challenge returned.

"You bet, Lorraina," he rasps softly.

He leans into my door and places his hands on top of mine. I'm suddenly quite anxious and ever so grateful for the door between us. My hands get clammy and my heart races. Blood races and pounds in my ears, making me feel very much awake now. One hand moves up to brush my hair from my forehead and moves down feather light until his knuckles brush across my cheekbone and lips. He pulls his thumb slowly across my lips. It's excruciating. It's exquisite.

Both of his hands come forward to frame my face gently, and he pulls me in for a kiss. A too quick kiss. It's over before I realize it's even begun. He gives me a half smile and turns and walks away.

"Michael!" My voice barely sounds human. More animal in nature. It's raw with ache.

He turns and takes two long strides back to me. This time when he grasps my head it's anything but gentle. He pulls my lip in and nudges my lips open with his. All rational thought escapes me. I mirror his grasp and enjoy the fullness I feel with him in my mouth. I give as good as I get. This kiss is nothing like our two before. I savor it.

When he turns to walk away, I release a long pent up breath. If he would've looked back, he would've seen that I was the one on my knees now.

Chapter Seventeen

Forbidden Fruit

"So what made you decide to go to law school?" he probes. We had met at a local grill to have a late lunch. We'd been here for a couple of hours now. The wait staff was starting to give us dirty looks, but neither of us made a move to leave.

"A lot of things. Mainly, I think, to make sure that women and children don't get screwed over at the hands of an inept, male-dominated system."

"That's very specific. I don't think I'm too far off base to presume that this is in direct relation to what happened with your father."

"Nope. You would be extremely safe in deducing that."

"You know, of all the reasons for you to choose law school I think that is the most noble. You will be able to help so many people. I just know it."

"Thank you for that. I want to work for the D.A. and specialize in family law for a while and see where that leads me."

"Those will be some lucky women and children to have you on their side. Your passion is already shining though. You can't ever let it become just a job, though, ya know?"

"Exactly," I agreed. I'd never told anyone why I wanted to be an attorney. It felt good to have someone know the truth. Most everyone assumed that it was for the prestige or the money, and I'd never corrected that assumption less I'd have to explain myself.

The beauty of it was that Michael already knew most everything there was to know about me. He completely understood, without my having to go into all of the gory details as to why I would feel so connected to my chosen line of work.

"Well, how about we head out? Wanna head to my favorite spot until my gig?"

"That sounds great."

***

I spread my blanket on the ground beneath the oak as he takes his guitar out of his Jeep. I watch him from the corner of my eye. I love the way he moves. So fluid, so sure of himself. His transformation from a cocky boy to a self-assured man has been majestic. I feel tears in my eyes and my throat aches. I love him so much. I want to tell him right now, but I fear running him off. Would he doubt my sincerity since I'd held back on him for so long? *Take it slow, I caution myself.*

"So, I'm off tomorrow," he breaks my reverie.

"Really? That's great. Me too," I joke. I turn toward the water to dry my eyes. The breathtaking beauty of the setting sun moving over the Gulf shocks me. I'm thinking that he makes everything more beautiful just by being present.

I feel his hands on my shoulders. I shift my head to brush my cheek across his knuckles. When I've exposed most of my neck, I feel his calloused fingertips brush my hair from it. Everything in me clenches in anticipation. I feel his warm breath before I feel his lips place a long, lingering kiss there. I hear a groan. When I realize it came from me, my eyes fly open. I'm so transparent. I need to get a handle on that. As soon as the thought enters, it dissipates as his kisses turn hungry and demanding. My knees weaken, and I lean back against him for support and realize that I'm not the only one affected.

I lick my lips, which are suddenly very dry, "Michael?"

"Aah...Lorraina. I've dreamt of this. Lying in this very spot. I've dreamt of nothing but you and having you and making you mine." He pauses and clears his throat a little. "Umm...We should do something else for a moment."

I laugh, and it sounds foreign to my ears. He has no idea what his words have done to me. They've warmed me to my very core. Not too long ago, I thought I was destined to never feel this for anyone. I don't know why I'm suddenly so blessed. I fear questioning it.

He takes my hand and pulls me down beside him. He places a gentle kiss on my knuckles, quickly releasing my hand to pick up his guitar.

I make myself comfortable on my pillow, staring up at him and waiting for my private show.

He strums another favorite of mine. I watch his fingertips move across the strings. So intricate. His nails are perfectly shaped so as not to interfere with his playing, but his fingertips are calloused from years of playing. I love that someone so gentle has these telling, rough parts. His voice sounds shaky at first as if warming up. I wonder—did I do this to him? He was so polished last night.

I close my eyes and enjoy his playing. Suddenly, he launches into a song I vaguely recognize. I open my eyes to question him. When the lyric permeates my brain, I gasp. He continues his song and, in his unique way, tells me all that he can't put into his own words. He wonders what I've been up to while he has been waiting for me to come and make him mine and who I've been loving.

On the last note, I pull myself up to my knees and take his guitar from him to lay it beside us. I pull his face to mine and lay my forehead against his.

He transforms the other Michael's words into his own, "My plan has always been to find my way back to you. I never gave up on you, ya know? I guess the old adage is true…'If you love someone, set her free. If she returns, it was meant to be.' I just knew that I had to be better for you, though."

"Michael, no one could ever be better than you. You were never bad to me, by the way. I just knew I wasn't ready for what all you were offering me. However, I've come to some realizations myself lately. I've realized that I *have* to be with you and only you. I've been wondering how you would feel about that, though."

"Amazing is the word that springs to mind. But you need to know some things about me first."

I lean back a little, taking his hands in mine. "You can tell me anything, ya know?" I prompt.

"Well, I was worried about being too overzealous. I don't want to scare you off again. But you seem…different. More open."

I smile up at him. "I am. I've realized how much time and effort I've wasted, and I don't want to waste another moment."

"Me either. Me either," he reiterates and shakes his head with what seems like disbelief. I can't believe it either. "Lorraina, when I said that I've made myself better for you, I meant it. I've completely changed my life, and I need you to be a part of it. More now than ever before…I think it will require you to make some changes as well, though."

OK. Anything, I think. "Like what?" I wonder aloud.

"I'd rather show than tell if that's OK with you."

"You're kinda worrying me. You're not in a cult or something are you?" I joke.

He laughs, "No, nothing like that. It would just be easier to show you."

"OK. I'm in." I trust him implicitly.

"There is one thing we can and should discuss. It'll probably be awkward but…I'm celibate."

Whoa, this catches me by surprise. He practically oozes sex! I squeeze my thighs together on that thought. Not helpful at all. "Really? That's…interesting."

"Yeah. I figured out a couple of years back that it really wasn't fair to others, or myself for that matter, to have relationships or 'arrangements' with other girls since I was…spoken for." He grins sheepishly at me. "Then it morphed into more than just abstaining. It became a way of life, and it helped me with a multitude of things."

"Hmm...Now, who's being noble?"

"I guess what I really need you to know, especially since the uh," he clears his throat, "kiss we shared earlier, is that I don't plan on having sex again until I marry."

"Really?" It's all I've got.

He laughs a self-deprecating laugh. "I'm not trying to sound like a prude or sanctimonious, but it really just fits with my chosen lifestyle."

I wrinkle my brow at him. "Which you're going to show me rather than tell me, right?"

"Right. So are you OK so far?"

Yes and no. "Yeah, I mean. I think that's wise actually. Sex complicates everything, and we're just getting to know each other again. It's just...just that I really..."

"Yeah, I know. Me too, but I can promise that it'll be worth the wait." He leans over and gives me a kiss that leaves no room for doubt.

His promise and his kiss make me want him even more. Ah...the forbidden fruit. "There's no doubt about that. I guess this would be a good time to tell you that I'm not a virgin."

He doesn't break eye contact; instead, his eyes seem to pierce my very soul. "I kinda figured that. You couldn't have been with the Child Molester as long as you were if you hadn't been willing to sleep with him." There's a bitterness to his tone. It stings.

"Yeah, well, he's the only person I've been with. I had a couple of dates at school," I hesitate, "but neither went well." I avoid telling him how screwed up I've been over the last few years. I'm not ready for that conversation.

"I have to admit," he says as he grabs his guitar again, "I'm very happy to hear that."

Chapter Eighteen

Branded

I sit at the counter where I can keep an eye on Michael as he plays at Mona's. I've been journaling. It's transformed into more than just memories of him at this point although I can't help writing the old ones down as well as the new ones we're making. One thread that seems to keep reappearing is that of my father. Like Michael, I haven't spoken to him in about four years. I've picked up the phone to call him several times. Once, when I was home visiting, I actually drove by his house. I don't know what I want out of a reunion: forgiveness, acceptance, an apology? I do feel as though I've made peace with my Michael demons and that I need this peace as well.

Whether my dad knows it or not, he is partially responsible for Michael and me being together. Maybe he would be happy for me if he could see how Michael has turned out. How I've turned out.

"What the hell are you doing here?" a voice snarls.

I look up and try to focus on the person looming over my shoulder. Great. Missy McIntyre. I knew things were going too smoothly for me. "What does it look like I'm doing?" I deadpan.

"It looks like you're here, fucking with Mike's head again."

Well, look who turned out to be a freaking detective, I want to sneer. Can't get anything past you! "Don't even pretend to have his best interests in mind, Missy. I know exactly who you are and who you care about."

"You don't know shit. Who do you think Mike came to every time you screwed him over for the boy of the week?" The look on my face must give her great satisfaction. "Oh, you didn't know, did you?"

"It doesn't matter, Missy. We've all grown up now and moved on, right? I'm here visiting Michael and—"

Her look turns from disdain to pure hatred and she cuts me off with a snarl, "Do you have any idea what a condescending little bitch you are?!"

My efforts at diplomacy are fading quickly. She has no idea the temper I have. I shoot a glance over at Michael who looks concerned. I give him a smile, and he seems to relax a little. I turn a frosty smile back to Missy. "Yes, as a matter of fact, I'm very aware of my status as a bitch. I've come to terms with it over the last few years. Thanks for inquiring. Now, if you'll excuse me." I get up and put my journal in my bag. I don't know where I'm going. I just know that I have to get away from her before I end up knocking that smug look off of her face.

I hear the canned music click on. Thank God. I turn to make my way over to Michael, but she grabs my elbow and twists it to the side. I gasp as unexpected pain shoots through my arm. "Do you even hear yourself? You always thought you were better than everyone else! But if you hurt him again you're going to have to deal with me," she snarls.

"Got it," I grunt through my teeth. She releases my arm and proceeds to order a drink as though nothing has transpired.

I walk toward the door with Michael close on my heels. I spin around when we get outside and bark, "Really? Missy? You know how she tortured me in junior high. You're the one who put a stop to it!"

"What are you talking about?"

"She took great pleasure in letting me know that you had been together. I just don't get how you could be with someone like that." I fold my arms as my anger subsides. I really have no right questioning his choice in women. "I know I have no right to wonder about that, but I do."

"Well, your disbelief is on target. I was never with her. She grew up two roads over from me, and we became friends a few years back. That's all there was to it."

"She said she was always there for you when I hurt you. Like you ran to her behind my back."

"Really? Because we didn't even really start hanging out till you were far away in college. And even then it was insignificant."

"She was lying?" I surmise.

"She was lying," he affirms.

"Oh. Why would she do that?"

"To get a rise out of you. To bully you. Some people never change."

I shouldn't be surprised. I grew up with some extremely manipulative, backbiting, backwoods people. "Well, she certainly feels territorial where you're concerned. She threatened me with bodily harm if I hurt you."

"Really? I don't think that was necessary, do you?" His arms find their way around me. He pulls me tight. I needed this. I run my hands up his leather as I imagined myself doing before. *Was that just yesterday?*

"No, I will never hurt you like that again. I already know that."

We stand outside holding each other until we see her and her friends leave and deem it safe to go back in.

***

I'm nervous as we pull into Michael's apartment complex. I sneaked a call to my mom to let her know I was staying at Ginny's again. I don't know how many more times I'll be able to use that excuse. Telling her I'm spending the night with a boy, even sans sex, is not acceptable.

We walk up the stairs hand in hand. He opens the door and pushes it open. "Welcome to my humble abode. And, by humble, I mean miniscule and completely unassuming," he jokes and flips the light switch as I cross the threshold into his studio.

When my eyes adjust, I'm immediately impressed. It may be tiny, but he's made it into a lovely home. It looks way more inviting than my dorm room. It's decorated in tons of bandanas and Indian decor and his own art. He has a few posters of his favorite musicians spread throughout.

I laugh as I recognize the same Jim Morrison poster I have hanging on my wall. I run my fingertips over it and tell him he has great taste.

I make my way over to his bookshelf. It's always the first item I check out when I enter someone's office or home for the first time. It's automatic. I scan the authors — Whitman, Welty, Grisham, Gibran, Rice, Plato, a few I don't recognize. "You have quite the eclectic vibe going on over here, Michael." I turn to look up at him. The look in his eyes can only be described as hungry, and I'm distracted from my investigating. "What?" I ask, feeling a little self-conscious.

"I just can't believe you're here," he murmurs and shakes his head. "I keep waiting for the universe to demand payment or for you to say 'Never mind, this is too much.'"

I make my way over to him and wrap my arms around his waist. "I'm not going anywhere. You have no idea how fortunate I consider myself. I'm the lucky one, not you, Michael."

"Right now, I'm the smelly one," he jokes and plants a small kiss on my forehead. "Let me grab a shower real quick, OK? Make yourself at home."

While he's in the shower, I take out my journal and start to work through all I have to tell him. I try to put it into words since I've never uttered them before. It's not quite as hard as I thought it would be. Now if only I can gather the courage to engage in this conversation with him.

I glance up as I hear the door open and put my journal back in my bag. When I look back up, he's standing outside the bathroom and steam from his shower is pouring in the room. I feel my mouth drop open and hear my breath escape in a whoosh. It turns into a throaty little laugh.

"Sorry. The bane of studio apartment living. One room fits all."

"I'm not sorry. You're beautiful," I say without thinking.

His eyes widen as I make my way over to him. His damp hair hangs slightly longer than usual, and he is ensconced only in my favorite worn out blue jeans. His tattoo-covered chest and torso are damp. I see his bare feet peeking out from under his jeans. Placing my hands on his chest, I lean in to plant a quick kiss on his lips before I pull him over to the bed. I throw him down and lie beside him, propping myself up on my elbow. "What is all this?" I ask, curious about his tattoos.

"Too much?"

"No, they're sexy," I admit. I never have been one for tattoos, but on him they look delicious.

I trace the familiar profile on his right breastbone that reads Mary. It's the image I don't recognize, though. Mary's profile looks toward his heart, but the usual Marion features aren't there. Her features look more like Michael's if truth be told. I look up at him questioningly.

"It's a traditional Mary profile that I designed with my mother's face. I feared that it was kinda sacrilegious, but then I figured it was a fitting tribute to two of the most sacrificing women in my life."

I love how he talks about Mary as if she is a living, breathing person in his life. His love knows no bounds. He was always reverent like that when he spoke of his mother as well. "Isn't your mom's name Mary too?" I ask.

He nods his head, and I lean in to sneak a kiss. Drawing back, I focus on the area that covers his heart. An intricately designed heart is inked here. Its shape is outlined with a ribbon of thorns. Inside the heart, is my name in Michael's perfect cursive. I gasp. What a turn on! "You were that sure we'd end up together, huh? When did you get it?" I ask as my fingernail traces over it.

"Umm…on your birthday, two years ago." He grabs my hand to still it and brings it up to his lips.

Still pining for me after all these years. What did I ever do to deserve this kind of devotion? "Happy birthday to me!" I lean in and continue the pattern I had begun with my tongue.

He squirms out from underneath my ministrations and flips me over on my back, stretching out his length on top of me. His hands grasp mine above my head. "You're driving me crazy," he grunts.

I throw my head back and laugh. He attacks my throat with tiny little kisses and makes a path to my mouth.

Suddenly, I'm on my feet and spinning around the room. He's caught me in a little dance. "There's no music," I protest.

He dances me over to the complicated-looking stereo and pushes a series of buttons until I hear Dave Matthews serenading us with a sexy song of his. "Is that better?" he inquires.

"Well, for our entertainment, yes. For our libidos, probably not."

"Touché," he says on a laugh, rendering him more beautiful than ever.

***

I make my way out of the bathroom after having brushed my teeth and scrubbed my face. I have on my favorite pajamas, which means they're kind of ratty. I didn't have the time to shop for new ones, though. I don't want to lose another moment with him. He's changed from his jeans to dark gray pajama bottoms. I delight in the fact that he's still shirtless. I walk over to him and spot his first tattoo. The one that freaked me out all those years ago. If I were telling the truth, I'd admit the freaking out wasn't just about what other people would think.

"You've added to it. I'm surprised you didn't have this covered up or redone," I say. "It seems somewhat lacking in light of your other distinctive ones." My eyes trace over the rose that now adorns my initials. If roses had feelings, I would say it was the loneliest, saddest rose on earth.

"I added the rose shortly after you left for college. I actually thought about having it redone at the same time, but it is too precious to me the way it is." He suddenly laughs out loud, "Gah, you were so pissed," he grins.

"You want to hear something really funny?" I venture. "I wasn't angry about what you thought I was angry about."

His brow furrows, "What do you mean?"

"Well, I was angry about what other people would think, especially my dad; but that wasn't the entire reason I was so angry."

"Do tell, Miss Dabney."

I cover my face with both of my hands. There's no turning back now. I swore honesty both with him and myself. I run my hands up and over my hair, pulling it into a side ponytail and letting it drop again. Finally, "I was upset with myself," I hedge.

"How so?"

I can't seem to keep my hands still. "Well, when I first realized what it was, I was shocked; but then it…appealed to me."

"What do you mean 'it appealed to you'?"

I stop fidgeting and look at him, considering the impact my words will have on both him and me as I've only just admitted the truth of it to myself a few moments ago. Before I can talk myself out of it, I allow the words to tumble from me. "I…It made me feel powerful. Like, even though it was you who made the decision to get it and it wasn't my idea, it made me feel like I had a hold on you. That no matter what, you had this permanent reminder of me. That you could never deny me or forget me. Is that completely twisted?"

"Hmm," he appears thoughtful and runs his hand through his hair as if bewildered. "I don't know that it's twisted, but it completely changes how that certain memory has been playing in my head over the last several years."

I still don't feel as if I was as clear as I could've been. I don't want to leave any room for interpretation so I continue more succinctly, "I was angry with myself because I loved the fact that you had branded me on your body." My gaze flies to the floor. There, I've said it. *Chips, fall where you may.*

"That's incredibly possessive of you and, might I add, passive-aggressive."

I frown and stare holes in the floor. "I know, right?"

"And very hot," he murmurs.

My gaze flies up to his face to find a flirty little smile waiting there. He grabs me by my hips, pulls my hips to rest on his, and rubs his nose to mine. "Really?"

"Really."

***

I feel his calloused fingertips making their way up and down my arm. I've never stayed the night with a guy before, and I'm glad that he was my first. I grin as I remember how incredibly tender he was, talking to me about mundane details as if they were the most important things he'd ever discussed. Then, finally singing me to sleep in his beautiful baritone.

"Mmm...good morning."

"Good morning," he replies. "Did you sleep well?"

"I did. How 'bout you?" I peek at him over my folded elbow.

"I slept well. Are you ready to see my routine?"

"Already? What time is it?"

"It's about six," he puts a finger under my chin and tilts my head up for kiss. "It's passed time for you to get up." He takes my hand and pulls me into a sitting position. "Come on sleepy head."

He told me to bring comfortable clothes and tennis shoes, so I make my way to the bathroom to get changed. I glance in the mirror at my reflection and have to look again at myself. I look…happy. It takes my breath away for a moment. That's pathetic to be that shocked over my own happiness. I try to remember the last time I looked in a mirror and anything other than determination, denial, and defiance in my expression looking back at me. I shake my head and thank God for the way I'm feeling. That's a sentiment I haven't had in a while either.

When I return, I find him spinning his keys on his finger. "Ready?" He's wearing a tight black muscle shirt, black running pants, and well-worn black Nike's. As usual, he looks incredibly sexy.

I take a deep breath. "Yep, ready."

Chapter Nineteen

Ten Years in the Making

As we ride through town, I glance around at all of the changes my hometown has gone through. It's funny how, even though I'm all grown up, being here makes me feel almost childlike. Being with him makes me feel like I'm a teenager again. It's a euphoric feeling really.

"So where are we going anyway?" I inquire. I steal a glance at him. He's wearing his Top Gun shades and looking completely at ease with himself. I envy him.

"Oh, here and there," he teases and shoots me a lopsided smile.

"Ah…you know you're torturing me and my control-freak self, right?"

He laughs and raises his brow at me, "Oh, yes. I'm very much aware of what the unknown does to you."

We ride in silence for a few minutes before coming to a stop at St. Michael Catholic Church. I raise my eyebrows at him, "A church? What are we doing here?" I ask suspiciously.

"Funny thing about churches. They have services where anyone can go in and worship, etcetera, etcetera," he jokes.

There's no way I'm stepping foot inside. I try to hide my panic, "Michael, I'm not Catholic, and I'm not dressed for church." I grasp at my most inoffensive excuses.

"Oh, well, you don't have to be Catholic, and it's not a formal service. It's daily Mass, so you're fine. More than fine actually. Beautiful."

"Flattery will get you nowhere, sir. I'll just wait for you here," I offer.

"Come on," he cajoles me. I think you'll enjoy it, and it will offer insight into my lifestyle, which is what you wanted to know about, right? It helps me build my faith, stay strong, stay sober," he shrugs and looks over at me. "It's only thirty minutes or so."

"No, Michael. I'd really rather not." I turn a beseeching look on him.

"Ya know I'll help you with the rituals and all if that's what it is," he counters.

"No, that's not it. I don't want to get in the way of your time here, though; so please just let me wait here."

He sighs and I can tell I've disappointed him. "OK," he relents and kisses my hand, "I won't be long."

I watch his retreating back as he shrugs on his hoodie. I wish I could join him. It seems very important to him, but I haven't been in a church since I graduated high school. Too much judgment. Partially self-induced.

I journal while I wait for him. I frown as I realize it's mostly about my dad. This relationship has plagued me most of my life. When I was really young, we were very close. We share a lot of the same personality traits: creative, analytical, vocal. He was amazing with our horses, and he passed that love on to me. The similarities are abundant; however, he's an addict. Unfortunately, that dulls everything positive about him and amplifies everything evil about him.

I look toward the church as I see movement. I see Michael speaking to the priest. They talk for a couple of minutes and Michael turns to make his way over to the Jeep. Much to my surprise so does the priest.

Oh, no you don't, Michael. Don't bring him over here, I will *him.* Too late. They're practically upon me. I panic but try to maintain a cool exterior.

"Lorraina," he avoids meeting my eyes. Like he knows I'm staring daggers at him, "this is Father Patty. Father Patty, this is Lorraina Dabney."

"Hello, Lorraina," he says with an Irish lilt. "It's nice to make your acquaintance. Michael has told me much about you."

"Hello...Father." I'm pretty sure that's what I am supposed to call him. I watch Michael move off to the side of the Jeep, and I lose sight of him. *Now who's the coward?*

"So, Michael tells me you were reluctant to come inside for Mass," he doesn't mince words.

I'm going to kill him. This is so embarrassing. "Yes, sir. I...I'm not Catholic. I just didn't feel comfortable."

"Let me assure you that you are most welcome. I've known Michael for quite a while now, ya know? He's quite adamant about you being comfortable here, so I've offered my help in that area. Whatever is holding you back I can try to help you with, my dear."

I hesitate for a moment, "I haven't been in a church in many years. I'm...I'm a terrible sinner in so many ways."

"Aren't we all, dear?" He says on a wink. "I'll tell you what, though. How about we go into my office for a few moments so that we can speak privately?"

"Um...OK." I get out of the Jeep to follow Father Patty and see Michael sitting on the back bumper. I give him a tentative smile, and he returns it with a grand one. My entire attitude changes. If this is all it takes to make him happy, I'm all for it.

Once I'm in Father Patty's office, he makes me feel quite at home. He makes small talk, asking about my family, my religion, my schooling. He explains different artifacts and paintings that adorn his office.

As he wraps up a description of his miniature desktop edition of *La Pieta*, I realize it's now or never. "Father Patty, I have greatly sinned," I assert. I know how this part goes. I've seen *The Godfather* many times.

"No sin is too great for God to bear, and God's forgiveness knows no bounds, my child. The real question is have you forgiven yourself?"

He's hit the nail on the head. Wow. He's good. "No, no," I shake my head and clear my throat, "I...could never do that. What I've done is unforgiveable. I'm irresponsible, selfish, traitorous. In a word—evil."

"Dear, the very fact that you believe you are evil proves that you're not. You need to be reconciled to God. I can help you. It doesn't matter that you're not Catholic."

"Really?" he nods his head in assurance. "Thank you, Father Patty. I'll consider it."

***

The next part of his routine has me reeling even more than the first. I find myself jogging along a three point five mile bridge that runs over the gulf. I'm proud of myself because I haven't collapsed, and I don't quite sound like a bronchitis patient just yet either. "Promise you're not too mad at me," Michael implores me.

"I promise I'm not mad," I assure him for the third time in between shallow breaths.

"I knew you were ready for a shove."

"Oh, really?" My caustic comment has teeth. I try to temper myself. "You know this is what you've been doing our whole lives? Pushing me. Shoving me. Making me better."

"So, it sounds like a thank you is in order," he replies sweetly.

"I'm not thanking you yet, especially not for showing me this little part of your routine," I kid.

"Ah…it's good for you."

"Let me show you what I think is good for you," I turn and tackle him against the side of the bridge walkway. He grunts as I back him against the concrete. I bring his face down to mine and pull him in for a long, searing kiss. I pull back slightly and giggle.

"Oh, what are you doing to me? I abhor public displays of affection. Sorry about that. I just couldn't seem to help myself."

He runs his hands over my head and pulls my ponytail back to tilt my head back. He takes the lead this time, leaving me even more breathless than when I was jogging. "The feeling is mutual," he breathes.

We finish our jog in silence. He's right. It does feel amazing even though my shins are burning, and I'm pretty sure I'm going into cardiac arrest.

"So what now?" I ask as I drop my hands on my knees and peer up at him.

"I think we'll head to the store so that I can get some groceries for our dinner tonight." He stretches his muscles in a practical and precise manner. I imitate him.

"Oh, you're cooking?" I can't hide my surprise.

"It's one of my many skills," he brags.

"Oh, really? Is there anything that you're not good at, Mr. Humble?"

"Um…nothing comes to mind. I'll let you know if I think of anything, though."

"Please do." I laugh.

At the grocery store, he methodically goes through selecting his vegetables and his pasta and his bread. It looks like it will be a veritable feast. As we make our way to the checkout, I hear someone call out for Michael. I turn and it's a guy I recognize from high school with a cart full of beer and chips.

"Hey bro! What's going on?" he asks, giving me the once over. Michael releases my hand as they pull each other into a typical guy embrace.

"Hey brother! Nothing much." He introduces us, and they spend a couple of minutes catching up while I ogle Michael. I'm jerked from fantasizing when I hear Michael declining an invitation to a party later on that night.

"Don't let me hold you back," I offer.

"No, no. That's not it," he says to me. To his friend, "We'll try to make it over," he replies noncommittally.

I thrill at his use of that little pronoun.

***

"I can't believe you don't have a Harley yet," I call out as I glimpse yet some more Harley paraphernalia scattered throughout his studio.

"I know. Me either. I've been saving, of course. But crap always seems to come up. I'm getting pretty close, though."

"You're gonna look so good on a bike," I utter as the image of Michael riding his future Harley consumes me. I'm so entranced by it that I don't hear him come up behind me until I feel his hot breath and warm lips on my neck.

"You're gonna look so good on the back of my bike, babe," he murmurs against my skin.

I actually groan out loud. I feel him chuckle against me, and then he is gone back behind the divider to the kitchen. *What a tease!* The smells wafting from his kitchen are making my stomach rumble.

I've been exploring his studio while he has been cooking. My Michael is a genuine renaissance man. His art is inspiring, detailed, intense. The colors are subdued, lending them an otherworldly essence. His brushstrokes are heavy and rounded, reminding me somewhat of Van Gogh. He has several Choctaw rituals painted to perfection. After I analyze his art, I begin leafing through his sketchbooks. His sketchbooks contain many different art forms: landscapes, still life, music, poetry. *Wow!* I think. *He's so amazing.*

I saunter up behind him and wrap my arms around him, squeezing him to me. This feels so right. I release a shaky breath and take a deep, reassuring one. "I love you, Michael."

He stills and I hear his throat catch. I loosen my arms as he turns slowly to pierce me with his look. Is my confession too much? I worry and drop my eyes to his chest. "Ah…Lorraina, you have no idea what those words do to me. I've been waiting my whole life to hear them." He takes my chin between his thumb and finger and forces me to meet his gaze. "I loved you yesterday. I love you today. I'll love you tomorrow…forever," he seals his declaration with a kiss. "I've been dying to tell you that I love you since the moment I saw you sitting at Mona's. I had to put the ball in your court, though. I was afraid to push you too much."

My eyes puddle and I laugh, "Do you know that I've been holding back those words since our first night together? I was afraid of scaring you off, though. I also worried that I didn't deserve your love; but I've decided that, deserved or not, I'd be a fool to deny us again."

His brow furrows. "Why would you think you don't deserve my love? That's ridiculous. You're the most deserving person I know."

Hadn't I just thought this same sentiment about him? Instead of answering him, I lean in and give him another kiss. *Baby steps,* I think.

Over his delicious dinner, we talk about his friend from the store and the party that's planned for the night. He tells me that it's a going away party for his cousin, and I insist that we should go.

"I don't know that that would be a wise thing for me to do. I try to avoid hanging out with my old crowd, ya know? Wagon. Temptation. All that."

"I'll be there to protect you," I promise. "You should be there to see your cousin off. "

He takes a deep breath and releases it. "Aah…I can't resist you. OK. We'll go."

"Speaking of old relationships," I start but pause to take a sip of my water, "I'm thinking it's time I paid my dad a visit." I know my next admission is bound to bring on a round of uncomfortable questions, but he has to know. "I haven't seen him since I graduated high school."

"Really? I take it your last visit didn't end well."

That's the understatement of the year. "No, it sure didn't. We have some hard feelings that I think I should try to assuage."

He sees right through me. "That sounds terribly impassionate, which is not the Lorraina I know."

I drop my fork on my plate, making it clatter. "Well, Michael, he's hurt me so many times, over and over; so I guess it is a form of self-preservation. Honestly, I wish I could forget about him all together, but every time I try…I just feel myself being pulled back toward him. Guilt, I guess."

He seems to consider this for a moment. "You have absolutely nothing to feel guilty about." He seems to consider his next words carefully. "Ya know, I went to see him right after he burned your house down."

"You what?!"

"Yep, I had it in my head that I was going to beat him down until he begged for mercy. I've never wanted to hurt someone so badly. Well…he's one of two someones I wanted to beat down that badly, but that's another story. Anyway, when I got to ya'll's property and saw your home was in ashes and that tree that you always took pictures by was scorched, and your grandparents were so torn up, all I wanted to do was be with you. Nothing else mattered. Not even my vengeance. He was long gone by then anyway."

I smile as I remember my favorite tree that I made my mom take all my pictures by. It was a mimosa tree with silky soft pink flowers. How is it possible to miss a tree? "I never knew you went to see him. Why didn't you ever tell me?"

"I don't know. I guess I figured it wouldn't make any difference. I wasn't able to exact my revenge in your honor," he grins the young boy smile I remember from long ago.

"As contradictory as it may seem, I think it's sweet that you wanted to inflict bodily harm on my father. I dreamt of it for years myself."

"*You* dreamt of revenge?" he gives me a doubtful look.

"I did. I always thought, had I been there, I would have grabbed his shotgun, loaded it, and made it explode within him as soon as he spread those first drops of kerosene. I wanted to save my mother and brothers from all the pain they had to endure at his malicious hands."

I didn't realize tears were streaming down my cheeks until Michael was kneeling beside me and kissing them away. "You know? He hurt you too. Maybe it's not a good idea that you go and see him. It still seems too…fresh for you. Raw."

"How do you get over something like that? I don't think about it on a daily basis, so it doesn't control who I am every single day; but when I do stop to consider it, it overwhelms me. We didn't just lose our home that day. We lost everything: our family, our way of life, our horses, our community."

I don't know how long we held each other. It was long enough that the loss I was feeling was replaced with the fullness of Michael. I don't know if he has any idea how good for me he is; my mind whirls, trying to find a way to express how truly significant he is to me.

I try with my words, "Michael, I'm sorry that I wasted all those years. I will spend the rest of my life showing you and telling you and proving to you how very much I love you."

I hesitate and meld Gibran's words with my own, "The gates of my heart were flung open, and my joy flew far across the years, the miles, the room when I saw you that first night." I seal my promise to us with a searing kiss.

Chapter Twenty
Wanted

The party is much like I remember high school parties—a lot
of people drinking and bumping into each other constantly.
Michael and I both abstain from drinking. As soon as the crowd
starts to die down, more people filter in and revive it. It's on one of
these legs of newcomers that some girls I remember from high
school show. Michael and I visit with them for a little while,
catching up on the area's latest happenings. After a few minutes, a
guy who Michael introduced me to earlier appears at his side and
tells him that his cousin is asking for him in the back. Michael
gives me a questioning look, so I assure him that I'll be fine.

I visit with the girls for a while, learning all about who is
dating who, who is pregnant, who's gone to jail recently, who's
hooked on which drug. It doesn't take long for me to remember, in
all its vivid detail, why I've gotten out of here and, up until a few
days ago, sworn that I'd never be back.

"So, you and Michael?" one of them hedges.

"We're just hanging out," I struggle for detached when I really
want to shout, *Yes, Yes, can you believe it? We finally made our
way back to one another!!!!* Her next question snaps me out of my
internal diatribe.

"Would your parents approve? Weren't they really weird
about who you dated?"

"Um...well...I...I am almost twenty-two."

"True, I was just curious."

"My mom always loved Michael." I recall our conversation from a few days ago. I mentally amend she just wouldn't appreciate him right now.

"Well, I for one am thrilled for you guys. He's loved you as long as I can remember," another of the girls chimes in.

I look at her for a trace of sarcasm or disbelief. I smile and reply, "Thank you," when I find no evidence of either. Someone sincere. Who would've thought?

I decide that Michael's had long enough with his cousin, so I say my goodbyes and make my way to the back of the house. As I round the corner, I run smack dab into *him*. "Oh," my breath escapes me. I didn't expect this. What is he even doing here? My eyes dart around him to search for Michael. I need to get away from *him* now.

"Lorraina," he breathes my name heavily. It doesn't take long for the smell of alcohol to reach my nose. Not much has changed with him I see.

"Um…hi. Excuse me?" My calm words are in direct contrast to the tugging I feel in my gut. I try to move around him. Catching me by surprise, he puts his arms up on either side of me and backs me into the wall, effectively caging me in with his upper body.

"Where ya going? Don't you have a minute to catch up with me?" He leans in and I have to turn my head to hide my gagging.

"No, not really. Someone is waiting on me."

"Oh, yeah. Mike Bang. I saw you two talking earlier. Are you with him?"

I tilt my head up and meet his gaze dead on. "Yes."

"Really? Even after he beat the shit out of me?"

"What?!"

"Oh, yeah, I guess he had it in his head he was defending your honor. That's really not possible since you have no honor, right? He didn't really give me the chance to explain that to him, unfortunately. Maybe I should find him and explain that now." He turns to go, and I grab his arm to spin him toward me. Before I can beg him not to seek Michael out, he seethes, "Did you have a miscarriage or an abortion, Lorraina?"

I gasp, "What are you talking about?"

"Don't mess around with me! I know you were pregnant. That day when you gave me all those hypotheticals. You were pregnant, weren't you?"

I clench my teeth and spew my disgust at him with my one word reply, "NO."

"You know I've thought about you over the years and wondered what ever happened to you. It's like you dropped off the planet." He leans in further and runs his fingers up my jaw. It's all I can do not to slap him. "You know, you were a good piece of ass. A little rigid but definite slut potential. Don't you ever think about me?"

"You know you were the only person I was ever with, and I didn't drop off the planet. I just moved on, which I suggest you do.

And to answer your question, yes, I've thought about you over the years and each time and every time I do I have to fight the urge to throw up," I hiss each word at him so that he's backed off of me a little, and I'm able to drop under and escape his outstretched arm.

I need some fresh air before I can see Michael. I make it out onto the front porch. Thank God no one I know is out here. I find myself a little corner and slide down onto my haunches, breathing deeply to try to catch my breath. I think I handled that encounter as well as I could have. I don't think he would dare tell anyone of all that transpired between us for fear of making himself look bad, but I still can't take that chance. I have to talk to Michael about it before he hears it from someone else.

I don't know how long I sit on the porch. I know it's a while, though, because I look around and realize that I'm alone out here. I stand and stretch. My legs are screaming at me. I can't believe Michael has not come looking for me. The only reason I could stand to be away from him this long is because I just got mindfucked by the pervert. I wish I could've stood up to him before he spewed his venom at me. What's wrong with me?

I go back inside the house and try to make my way toward the back again. I give the room a cursory glance for Michael, but he's not in here. Unfortunately, I see *him* talking to another girl in much the same way he was talking to me in the hallway. Is that the only way he can get a girl now? Cornering her and intimidating her. What's a thirty year old doing at a twenty something's party anyway? *Oh yeah, mentally he's about fourteen, so I guess he fits right in.*

I speed down the hallway and see Michael's cousin standing in the middle of it speaking to another guy in hushed tones. He jerks his head quickly when he spots me. "Hey, Lorraina. I was about to come and find you. Mike told me to find you and give the keys to his Jeep. He told me to tell you to go ahead and grab your car from his apartment and that he'd call you tomorrow. You can leave his keys under his mat." He thrusts the Jeep keys toward me with a barely contained look of disgust.

I stare at them in confusion. What?! Just like that. Relegated to nothing more than a few obligatory details. "Um...OK. Is he OK?" I venture.

"Yeah, he's good. I'll bring him home in a little while."

"Did something happen?"

"Other than seeing you talking to your ex?" His snarky comment catches me off guard.

Oh no. "No, it wasn't like that," I try to tell him.

"Well, that's not the way Mike saw it."

"Can I see him please?"

"He doesn't want to see you right now. He said he'd call you tomorrow, OK?"

"OK." I turn to go but turn back to plead one more time, "Will you tell him that I was caught by surprise and it really wasn't like that?" I have to get out of here before I start crying. He nods his head. "Thanks." I turn to get to the Jeep as quickly as possible. I don't want anyone to see me cry. I feel crushed. I start the Jeep and figure how to make it go, which isn't easy through my tear-laden haze. Beginning to fume, I wonder if he thought of that when he made his little plan to avoid me. He should trust me more than that. Outrage replaces despair: how dare he not give me a chance to explain or confront me at the very least?

I pull up outside his apartment and lay my head on the steering wheel in an effort to get my mind to stop spinning. I'm not going home. He will not send me away like I'm inconsequential or a mere inconvenience.

I shuffle up his steps and lean back on his door. I don't want to go in without him; it'll be too depressing. I slump down and bring my knees up to my chest and rest my head on them. I replay all the events of the last few days. We've had an amazing reunion. How could it have gone sour so quickly? And not even from the thing that I feared but from something completely unexpected.

He wasn't harboring any long lost love feelings for me. I wasn't that naïve. I was always a conquest to him. The good girl— gone bad just for him. It was never really about me. Look at the way he spoke to me. I finally have a shot at happiness and with someone I've known and loved since I was thirteen years old. I will NOT let either of them ruin this. I will explain everything to him. We will be OK.

I briefly consider journaling while I wait. The next thing I am aware of is someone coming my way. I rouse myself. I must've dozed off. I jump to my feet as I see Michael leaning on his cousin for support as they make their way to the top of the stairs. I rush over and grab Michael's other arm.

Michael slurs, "I see you don't listen very well."

Oh, he's drunk. Shit! I did this. He didn't want to go to the party that I made him go to, and he saw me talking to my ex. I'm such an idiot. "I didn't listen because you wouldn't listen. So, why don't you just be quiet now?"

"Bossy little thing, isn't she?" Michael asks his cousin.

"I sure am," I reply without waiting for anyone's response. I unlock Michael's door, and we get him to his bed. Michael's asleep before we fold his legs onto the bed. "I can take it from here," I tell his cousin.

"You sure?"

"Yep."

"OK. For what's it worth, I did tell him what you said. He seemed better, but the damage was already done, ya know?"

"Well, thanks for trying." I try to hide my annoyance. I don't take my gaze from Michael's now sleeping form as his cousin leaves. He looks so vulnerable and so uncomfortable.

I sit down on the side of the bed and run my fingertips lightly over his brow bone, his nose, his cheekbones. I savor my stolen touches. What if he wakes up and wants nothing more to do with me? I try to make this stolen moment count. My path continues through his hair. It's so soft and silky and pitch black. The contrast between my pale hand and his hair is striking. My lips trace over the path I made with my fingers. *Oh, Michael, what a pair we are.*

With some difficulty, I remove his jacket and begin unbuttoning his shirt. Mmm...I've always loved these snap buttons. Very sexy. I climb atop him and sit astride him as I push his shirt aside and run my hands down his chest. I grasp his hips and lean in to plant small kisses along his chest and torso. I scoot my body backwards as my head drops to his abdomen where he has a complexly designed crucifix tattooed. I kiss it reverentially. My tongue darts out to swirl around his belly button.

I hear him moan, and I sit up guiltily. Oops! *What are you doing? I chastise myself.* I feel myself burning—with desire, embarrassment, longing? All the above.

I shake my head and try to focus on the task at hand, making him more comfortable. I push his shirt over his shoulder and under his back to tug it off and let it drop on the floor. I run my hands up his arms and lightly massage his muscles. Even in his sleep, they are taut.

My hands move to his jeans. My fingers hover. Should I remove them? It may send me over the edge and beyond any modicum of control where my longing for him is concerned. Before I can decide, his hand grasps mine. "No, leave them," he answers my unvoiced question. "You're not ready for that," he jokes, mirth dancing in his half-opened eyes.

I grab a pillow and playfully smack him with it. "I wasn't planning on taking advantage of you in your inebriated state." There was no plan but definitely the musings of an out-of-control control freak. He's joking with me. Am I forgiven?

"As evidenced by all your touching and kissing. Just take my boots off, will ya? The rest is fine."

I remove his boots and go into the bathroom to change my own clothes. When I return, he's under the blanket and with his arm spread out to the side. I sidle myself next to him and promptly fall asleep.

Chapter Twenty-one

Unconditionally

I hear him shifting slightly. He's across the room on the couch. "I'm sorry," I say before I even open my eyes or even become fully aware.

He scoffs, "*You're* sorry?"

He's upset. I pull myself up and pull my knees to my chest. I pat the bed for him to come and sit beside me. He shakes his head at me. This is going to be harder than I imagined. I clear my throat. "Michael, I screwed up last night. I forced you to go to a party you didn't want to go to. I allowed you to wander off when you told me not to let you. I had a confrontation with my ex. I almost compromised your virtue while you slept," I throw the joke in on impulse, hoping it will lighten his mood.

No such luck. He looks even more furious. He takes a deep breath and releases my name on an exhale, "Lorraina—"

"No, Michael, NO," I'm begging. *What?!* I scramble to the end of the bed. "I'm truly sorry. We can work this out."

His eyes are glossy. He just stares at me. I'm finally awake enough to take him in. He sits with one leg on the couch; his arm is draped over it and holding a glass of water. His other arm is folded on the couch arm; it's holding his head up. He looks tortured. Like he hasn't slept in a week. He didn't look anything like this last night. Yet, somehow, he still pulls off that gorgeous look of his.

My belly clenches and spirals out of control. How is it possible to want someone this badly? And to fear losing someone this much?

"Are you done?" he mutters.

"What?" *Done talking? Staring at you? Trying to figure this out?*

"You have nothing to apologize for. I am a grown man. I make my own decisions. I chose to go to the party. I chose to walk into that room, knowing what would be going on in there. I chose to have that first shot." He runs his hand through his hair and rotates and stretches his neck around until he is staring at me again.

"Michael, we all make bad choices."

"Yeah, but…"

"You're not perfect. Get over it," I half joke.

"I don't drink because it changes me, Lorraina. I become someone else. Someone…awful. I'm…no *you're* very fortunate that didn't happen last night. When Shane came back in and told me what you said about your ex, I, at least, still had the presence of mind to stop. If I had kept going…"

My gaze has drifted to the floor. When he says that drinking changes him, fear's icy fingertips wrap themselves around the heat I am feeling for him. That's what happens to my dad. Does he know this? Is it the same for him? I wouldn't ever want to see him that way. My dad scared the shit out of me when he was like that, and a little piece of him died every single time in my eyes. "You're scaring me," I admit.

"You should be scared," he warns me.

"I didn't know it was that bad," I lock eyes with him, "or I wouldn't have insisted on the party." *I can't give up, though, can I?* "This is something you will struggle with for the rest of your life, ya know?"

"Yes, I know. And now you know."

"Michael, I swore I'd never be with an alcoholic. After watching my dad and then my stepdad…"

"I know," his voice cracks, "I could never ask you to put up with this." His hands gesture to encompass himself.

I feel a fissure run through my icy-hot heart. "Oh, Michael. No!" I approach him slowly. I take the glass of water from his hand and slide down gently beside him on the couch. I take his arms and wrap them around me, placing mine around his neck. I lay my forehead on his. "We can beat this. You and I. Now that I know. Your willpower is a force to be reckoned with. So, you slipped. Everyone slips. They'll happen. They'll be rare, though. You didn't have my full support because I didn't really know what we were dealing with, OK? Now that I know, nothing can get in our way."

He just sits there. Taking in everything I said, I hope. Finally, he moves. He nuzzles my neck with his soft lips. "What did I do? Who did I please to get this lucky?" He pulls his lips from my neck and stares at me with wonder. "Are you for real?"

I giggle, "Yes, I'm for real. You scared me. I thought you were gonna make me go away."

"I should. If I wasn't a selfish bastard, I would send you away. It would be the best thing for you, but I have to be with you. I've always had to be with you."

"I'm glad you don't know what's actually best for me, then. You'd have to be really awful to make me want to disappear. My dads, they never fought it; they never cared that it was poison to them or whether or not anyone else was hurt by their actions or addictions. That's not who you are. I love you, Michael."

"And I you, Lorraina."

***

It's Christmas Eve morning, and I feel time turning its back on us. Michael and I take a brisk walk around the park. We hold hands and admire the sprawling oaks and squirrels and little kids running around. He seems much better than he did earlier this morning. We talk of nothing serious.

He wants to know my favorite movies and TV shows. I tell him I don't watch TV, but I love movies. I go into great detail on some of my favorites. I probably list about twenty; they are varied in seriousness and scope.

"So, you're on a deserted island," he challenges me. "One film has been left behind and you must watch it over and over and over....What do you hope it is?"

"*Forrest Gump.*" I hesitate for about two seconds. "*Steel Magnolias.*"

He laughs at me. "I said one, cheater."

"I know. I'm awful at the favorites game."

"And ever the one with the bittersweet endings. What's with that anyway?"

I consider this a moment. After all the books that I've read and stories that I've loved, I always gravitate toward the tragedies. "I think it's that I can identify with tragedies more. Life is tragic. A lot of people interpret that to mean all doom and gloom; but, to me, within tragedy there lies a chance for a new beginning, a new life. The optimist, the romantic in me looks for those little wormholes and that chance to find happiness. Some people don't search for that chance and let tragedy shape them, ruin them." I snap out of my diatribe and look at him, waiting for him to give me a where-did-you-go-weirdo-look.

He clenches my hand tighter and simply says, "That's beautiful. So, many people don't see the sweet within the bittersweet. Or that you have to have one to have the other."

I smile a little thank-you-for-not-judging-me smile. "Exactly." He gets me. "What about you? One movie, deserted island?"

"*Lonesome Dove.*"

"Oh, really? I love that movie! Another favorite. We could be on a deserted island together. OK. Real test for you. You can bring the entire discography of one musical act. Who do you bring?"

"Yeah, that's hard to say." He squints his eyes and tilts his head back as if this is the most important thing anyone has ever asked him. "Led Zeppelin."

"Interesting," I reply. "If I hit repeat on a song, which one should it be?"

"'All My Love'," he whispers.

"Mmm...Yes."

***

I have to go home for the night and at least most of the day tomorrow. This sucks. I try not to mope around too much and ruin our little bit of time together. It's hard, though.

He goes into the kitchen to make our lunch, so I grab my bag and dig through it for my book. I grab a blanket and pillow and make myself a little place in his window seat so that I can be closer to him while he cooks. He's using the leftovers from last night to make something that will be delicious I'm sure.

He frowns at me and says, "Look. It's killing me. I have to know what was going on with you and the Child Molester."

I was hoping we could avoid talking about that for a little while longer. "He...he caught me by surprise. What was he doing there anyway?"

"He and Shane worked together a while back. I guess they became friends at some point."

"Aah...So he says you kicked his butt?"

"Sure did," he answers emphatically.

"Care to elaborate," I prompt him.

"Not much to say. I ran into him at a party a few years back. I was drinking. I saw his face and saw red. I didn't even think about it. I just punched him square in the jaw and didn't stop until someone pulled me off of him. His face was a bloody mess, and I couldn't play my guitar for about two weeks. I spent the weekend in jail and paid a huge fine. That was that."

"Well, that was a mouthful for not much to say," I joke. Inside I delight, I'm really not big on violence, but if anyone ever deserved to get the shit knocked out of him, it was *him*. "I wish you wouldn't fight, but thank you for kicking his ass. Anyway, I don't know what his point was in cornering me in the hallway. He basically verbally assaulted me and threatened me where you are concerned. I'm surprised you didn't realize what he was up to."

"I invite him to follow through with his threats." His menacing tone makes me shiver. "I'm sorry that I jumped to conclusions," he says with disgust. "When I started down the hallway, I saw you grab his arm and you looked...intent. I thought you were trying to get him back, I guess. I turned right around and went back to doing shots."

I mull this over a moment, "I actually could've used your help. He was being a real jerk. He was drunk and talking trash. All I wanted to do was find you and get out of there once that happened."

He walks over to my spot in the window and caresses my cheek. I look up at him and his eyes are full of trepidation as he promises, "I will never let you down like that again. I will never doubt you like that again. I was a fool. Forgive me?"

"It's already been granted," I assure him. "This is new for both of us. It's natural to have doubts...questions. Don't you think?"

"Yeah, I'm just sorry I didn't handle it more maturely."

"Me too, but we're learning."

He leans and gives me a quick peck before heading back over to his cooking.

I curl up and start reading, surreptitiously stealing as many peeks of his profile as I can. He catches me several times and finally laughs at me. He's laughing, thank goodness! "What?" I pout. "I enjoy looking at you."

"Oh, yeah?"

"Yeah. Were you always this beautiful?"

"Um...I don't know about that, but you were impervious to all my charms back then," he complains.

I tsk, "I was somewhat. I had my moments of weakness, though."

He turns to focus on me, "Really?" he asks disbelievingly.

"Yep, do you remember the night I stayed over at Corrine's?"

"Yes."

"Do you remember what was supposed to happen that night?"

"Yes." He pins me with a look.

I narrow my eyes at him. "So why didn't you show up?"

He runs his hands through his hair, crosses his arms in front of him, and leans his hip into the counter. "Well, that's hard to say."

"Why don't you give it a shot? I was there, waiting for you. I felt like such an idiot. I planned to...to take our relationship to a new level, and you left me standing there. All the other girls' boyfriends showed up. But not Michael." I cringe at the memory.

His face registers his shock. "You were upset?" he asks incredulously.

"Yes, I had decided that, if you showed up, I would kiss you. You were supposed to be my first kiss. Instead, I ended up kissing Brian Gates on the merry-go-round at the ballpark a few weeks later."

"Thanks for waiting for me," he replies mockingly.

"Yeah, no problem." I admit, "Yours was the first kiss I really enjoyed, though."

"Yeah?"

"Yeah, and I think we're making up for lost time now. No pun intended," I laugh.

"I think so too," he agrees with a smile.

"OK. Deflection averted. Why didn't you show?"

He turns back around and busies himself with his cooking, "I knew if I showed that's exactly what would happen, and I worried about the consequences."

I let this sink in a minute. "You were saving me from myself?"

"Well, I didn't see it that way. I just knew I would put you in a compromising position. I'm just happy my fifteen-year-old horny self was able to see through the haze of my hormone clouded brain."

My face reddens. "You were horny?! For me?!" I can't believe he's talking to me like this.

"Are you kidding me? So horny. All the time. And I wanted you so badly," his breath hitches. He glances over at me, finally.

165

His gaze is heated, predatory. "Not much has changed on that front." He finally releases me from his stare.

This line of conversation might offend other girls, but I'm so turned on right now. I grab my book and try to grasp the words on the page. I can't respond because I know I will be truthful, which will alert him to the fact that I'm, all of the sudden, a pervert where he is concerned.

It doesn't help distract me, so I decide to read him a little *Wuthering Heights* aloud.

"Are you a Brontë fan?" I ask him.

"Charlotte, Emily, or Anne?"

Of course, he knows all the Sisters Brontë. "Emily, in this instance."

"She's my favorite Brontë."

"I have a hard time deciding between her and Charlotte. I love them both so much."

"Really?" he asks sarcastically.

"Yeah, yeah, I know," I laugh him off and begin reading, "'May she wake in torment!" he cried, with frightful vehemence, stamping his foot, and groaning in a sudden paroxysm of ungovernable passion. 'Why, she's a liar to the end' Where is she? Not there—not in heaven—not perished—where? Oh! you said you cared nothing for my sufferings! And I pray one prayer—I repeat it till my tongue stiffens—Catherine Earnshaw, may you not rest as long as I am living; you said I killed you—haunt me, then! The murdered do haunt their murderers, I believe. I know that ghosts have wandered on earth. Be with me always—take any form—drive me mad! only do not leave me in this abyss, where I cannot find you! Oh, God! it is unutterable!—'"

Michael cuts me off and finishes for me, "'I cannot live without my life! I cannot live without my soul!'"

I've read this passage so many times that I could repeat it from memory too. It's one of the most painful, most truthful moments of the book. It never fails to bring tears to my eyes. I look at him and his tears mirror mine. "What a pair we are," I mumble, aloud this time, and grin a secret smile.

Chapter Twenty-two

I Must Have Been a Very Good Girl

My time spent with Michael has made me more agreeable because I end up spending a pleasant evening with my family. It's a quiet one. Just my mom, step-dad, and brothers. We had a nice dinner that my mom prepared and then watched *A Christmas Story*, which is my mom's favorite Christmas movie. After that, we argued about when we should exchange gifts. I opted for tonight. Why wait? We're all adults. I prevailed, and we ended up exchanging presents. Everyone seemed happy with their gifts that I bought them with my very limited budget. My mom bought me a new camera in hopes that I would take more pictures. I even got some new pajamas from my "brothers". Ha! I would love to see them set foot inside a store and buy their sister something to sleep in!

I end up in the kitchen doing the dishes. My mom has a dishwasher but refuses to use it or even buy soap for it. So, here I am, volunteering my services. Michael and I did dishes together while I was at his house, I muse. I didn't mind so much then. I think about how playful he was. It took twice as long as it should've to wash the few dishes we dirtied.

My brother surprises me by nudging my shoulder and mumbling, "Move over."

"Um...OK. Thanks!" I reply, stealing a sideways glance at Jerome. He's looking good these days. I marvel at how dark his hair and skin are. Everyone in my family is dark like this with the exception of an aunt and a cousin or two. They love to give me a hard time about my questionable parentage. My mom gets angry and says I'm what our ancestors call a throwback, one of a litter who doesn't seem to fit in with the others and carries the genes of a bygone generation. I smirk as I realize that term could be applied to me in so many areas of my life.

We wash dishes in silence for a couple of minutes. I'm the first to break the silence. "Mamma told me that you're going to try welding school. Are you excited?"

"Yeah, I guess. Good way to make a little money. I want to get my own place. I think Weldon and I will move in together."

"Hmm…Do you think it's a good idea for Weldon to move in with you while he's still in school? It's only his junior year."

He looks over his shoulder and surveys the room quickly. He looks back at me and states, "He's droppin' out. Mamma doesn't know yet."

"Oh, no! Why?" Jerome hated school, wasn't cut out for it. It was disappointing when he dropped out, but Weldon—Weldon always did so well. I didn't see this coming.

"You know he's pretty serious with Mariah Johnson, right?"

"No, I didn't know that," I mumble. I'm ashamed to admit that I don't know much of anything about what my brothers do or don't do.

"Yeah, well, he and her started skipping school a lot, hangin' out at her house during the day while her parents were at work. Bing. Bang. Boom. She's pregnant."

I feel as though I was just punched squarely in the gut. "No," I whisper.

"Yep. So, he needs to work full-time, and Mamma and Joe are probably gonna kick him out when they find out." I knew exactly how disappointed Mamma would be.

"Does he have any idea how hard things are going to be on him? I mean, does he even know her well enough to have a child with her?"

"There's evidence suggestin' he knows her real well," he kids.

I splash dishwater at him and tell him that's not funny.

He looks over his shoulder again, conspiratorially. I wonder what other shocking news he has to impart. "Is it true about you and Mike Bang?"

My eyes widen with alarm. I'm not ready for my family to know about this yet. I narrow my eyes and feign innocence. "What do you mean? What about us?"

"Some of the guys told me that you were at that going away party for his cousin. They asked if ya'll were together. Ya know, some of them are still hoping for a shot with you."

"What? Nobody hopes for anything with me," I deny.

"Yeah, yeah, whatever. Anyway, how 'bout you and Mike?" he persists.

"I just happened to run into him at that party. So there's no me and Mike; we're just old friends. He's always hoped for more, as you know; but I just don't see it happening. We're hanging out but only as friends. I think he's finally accepted that."

"Well, that's probably better. He's a good guy and all, but he can't seem to stay outta trouble."

"You just described about every male I know," I reply cynically.

"True," he concedes.

***

As much as I didn't want to leave Michael, I'm glad to have some time alone to work on his Christmas present. I purchased a leather journal, which was all the money I could spare to spend. I decided that I would make him a present. He'll understand that whole starving student thing better than anyone. Besides, I know that Michael will appreciate the sentiment. He's incredibly sentimental like I used to be, am trying to be again.

I bought myself a fancy fountain pen to accomplish my little project. In the journal, I plan to write down all of our teenage memories and the memories we've made recently, making a copy of my own journal. I hope that he will add to the journal as our relationship develops. It would be very interesting to see his thoughts on the subject.

I start with inscribing our full names on the title page. I laugh as I remember how revelatory he thought our initials were. I'll have to add that memory in as well. As I glance through and prepare to copy them down, I notice again that I've written, all but the first memory, in present tense. I take a moment to ponder this. The inadvertent use of present tense has allowed me to relive each of these moments as though they are currently happening. Each time I've reread them, they've been so fresh, so powerful, so overwhelming. Who knew that tense choice could be such a powerful thing? Now, I get why. I decide that all of his should be in present tense as well so as to have that same unpredictable, therefore provocative, side effect.

I work long into the night, copying each memory in my best handwriting. I write my memory on one side of the page, leaving room for his on the other to create a mirror of sorts. I have a moment of doubt about this being a wise present, but my instincts tell me that he will love it. I wrap the journal with the leather tie and immediately fall asleep.

That night I dream of a young boy with shaggy black hair and copper skin. I can't remember much of it when I wake, but I do remember him assuring me that all of my dreams were about to come true.

***

I spend almost the entire Christmas Day with family I haven't seen in years. It's nice, but I'm dying to get back to Michael. The only thing that keeps me from flying out of here and to him is the fact that I know he's with his family too. I hope that is going well. He and his dad still don't get along, but Michael tries very hard to keep his cool around him for his mother's sake. He has older

172

siblings whom I've never met, but he speaks fondly of them. I pray he had a good day.

When I get back to my house, I quickly go into my room to grab my already packed bag. I double-check that Michael's present is there. I stick my head in my mom's room and tell her that I'm headed to Ginny's and I'll see her tomorrow.

Before I can make my exit, she stops me with what I can tell might develop into an argument. "Do you think that's a good idea? You've been staying over there a good bit. You don't have long to visit with us, ya know?"

Crap! Busted. I turn around and purse my lips. "Well, I really don't have any friends in Oxford. So I guess I'm just getting my friend fix," I venture. That might do it. My mom is a huge proponent of friendships.

"Is that all it is? You're not avoiding something?"

"What would I be avoiding?" Ironic that she question me about my avoidance tendencies. I learned from the best.

She shrugs her shoulders. "I don't know."

"Well, it's nothing like that. I'm just enjoying being with a good friend who I've missed incredibly. You understand, don't you?"

"Yes, I'm glad that you have a good friend like that."

I walk back to her and give her a hug. "Me too, Mamma. I love you."

"Love you too."

That was close. Lying comes very naturally to me, always has. But I do hate lying to her. She just wouldn't understand right now, so that's the way it has to be because I have to be with him.

***

Christmas evening with Michael is nothing short of amazing. He brought leftovers from his mom's so that we don't have to worry about being distracted by mundane matters such as sustenance. I wanted to give him my gift as soon as I arrived, but I suddenly feel very shy. My memories are making me feel very exposed and vulnerable. I know that I can trust him and, of course, he experienced them. It just seems strange to have them there in black and white for him to ponder over. Besides that, the memories are weaved in with my internal dialogue, which he has never been privy to.

Instead of exchanging gifts right away, he puts in the first of several discs containing *Lonesome Dove*. I know the action and adventure appeals to the guys, but does he have any idea how romantic I find this series? He's a romantic, so I'm sure that he does. He probably identifies with Gus since Gus never got over his first love, never stopped loving her or trying to win her back. Gus was always my favorite character. I loved his persistence and his own sense of romanticism even though he still fulfilled his own needs with an almost constant demand for a "poke." For the last several years though, I've held a more "Callean" view on life, trying to avoid any real feelings or get too involved with others, which is ironic because I always wanted to slap the shit out of Call when I was younger. I didn't understand how he could be so obdurate.

I'm shaken from these thoughts as Michael puts his arm around me on the couch and pulls me in closer. I take a deep breath and inhale the scent of him. He always smells of musk and an exotic spice that I can't identify. I just know that I love the way he smells—woodsy, natural, and sexy. I nudge even closer as I can't seem to be close enough to him. He smiles down at me and adjusts himself so that we are both comfortable.

I think about the first time I ever saw this series. It invokes feelings of belonging and commiseration. I grew up on a farm, so I knew the harsh day-to-day realities of making one run. However, I was also familiar with all the joys that came from that hard work and sacrifice.

I try to refocus on the movie but get caught up in thinking about how astounded I am that Michael and I are together. I can't believe my good fortune, but I wonder if we will make it. I pray that we do. He's so good for me, and I love him so much.

I absentmindedly trace a pattern on his shirt as my thoughts drift. Will I be able to accept and deal with his lifelong demon? I think so. I've learned a great deal about dealing with this kind of thing. It's not going to be easy, but I think I can handle it. I want to help him overcome it. Furthermore, he wants to conquer it, making him different, more stable.

Will he be able to handle my own transgressions? I'm just barely able to come to terms with them myself. Maybe he can help me with that. He could turn his back on me completely, though. I don't think I could bear that. I cringe at the thought. I relax my hand as I realize that it's bunched up, grasping his shirt tightly.

"You OK?" He probes.

I bite my lip and nod my head. "Yeah, I'm sorry. I was just thinking about the first time I watched this movie." I give him a half-truth. "It was really funny. All of the families on our property got together at my grandparents' house to watch it. Like it was the landing of the first space shuttle or something extraordinary like that. Every night that week we went up after dinner. It was an amazing experience because it brought our family together for a brief moment."

"That doesn't seem anything to be anxious over," he surmises.

"No, but it's one of the last moments I remember feeling that unity before my father ruined it all. Therefore, one thought always leads to the other."

"Yeah, I get that," he says and rubs my arm up and down, comforting me.

We relax and enjoy the first part of the miniseries in silence except for the few kisses we sneak from each other. As the credits roll, Michael plucks something from the floor and places it in my lap. Ah…gift time. I rub my hands together excitedly. I'm giddy with anticipation.

"Can I open it now?"

"Yep, go for it," he laughs. "I hope you like it. It's nothing extravagant."

"Why don't you let me be the judge of that? Extravagance is relative." He just snorts at me. I pull the package closer to inspect it. It in itself is a gift. He's taken what seems to be a brown grocery bag and drawn neat little patches of different gardens. It's all pen and ink, but the flowers are exquisite. I wish I were artsy like he is. I threw my present in a bag. I can't even wrap a present competently let alone design my own wrapping paper. "Well, that decides that."

"What's that?"

I tilt my head and smile up at him. "I know who will be wrapping all future gifts from us."

"Oh yeah?" He sweeps a lock of hair from my forehead. "I like the way future and us sound together in that sentence," he muses.

"Me too," I admit. I lean in and steal another kiss. OK, I'm ready. I gently open my gift, taking care not to ruin his artwork. Oh, it's beautiful. I gingerly take the dream catcher out of the box. I run my fingers over it. It looks very familiar. "Your tattoo?" I question.

"Yeah, I made it after the one I designed for my back with the exception of the paw print, of course. Do you like it?"

"I love it. I can't believe you made this," I whisper, astonished. The yarn of the web is a deep blood red and is intricately woven. Two feathers drop from the circle.

"Do you know about the dream catcher?" he asks.

"A little. I know that it's supposed to protect you from bad dreams when you hang it over your bed and, of course, that it's Native American."

"It begins with the webbing as it works like that of a spider and catches all dreams—good or bad."

"Neat," I finger the design. "So how does it work exactly?"

"Well, the Choctaw didn't invent it, but we adopted it so to speak. Legend says that the dreams are filtered by the web. Bad dreams are caught in the webbing, and the good dreams trickle down through the feathers to the dreamer." He runs his fingers through the feathers and up my thigh as he explains. It's almost too much. I take a deep, steadying breath. He continues undaunted. How does he do that? "That means that all you get are the pleasant dreams," he finishes softly.

I flush, thinking of all the "pleasant" dreams I've had of late. Maybe I can tell him about those one day, but definitely not today. "That's really beautiful."

"I'm glad you like it. There's something else in there too." He removes his hand and my thigh aches with the absence. He takes out a leather journal much like the one I bought him. I giggle. "What?"

"Nothing. You'll see in a minute."

He furrows his brow. "I thought since you write so much in yours that you would need a new one soon. There's a little bonus feature, though."

"It's much nicer than the one I have now," I observe. I flip it open and thumb through the pages. "Oh," I gasp. I glance up at him and see a little secret smile waiting there.

"I don't want you to look at it all now. I hope that you'll enjoy it when we aren't together. You know as a reminder of me." He shrugs on this last thought.

"I don't need any physical reminders of you," I choke out. "You're my first thought in the morning and my last thought at night. And, yet somehow, you manage to consume almost every single thought in between as well." My eyes are brimming with unshed tears. He helps me by running the pad of his thumb across my bottom lashes. I'm such a crybaby. "I'm sorry."

"For what?" He asks.

"I'm very emotional lately." I shrug. How do I put everything that I'm feeling into words that don't make me seem like a freak?

"I like emotional," he declares. "Emotion is underrated."

I laugh and get up to retrieve my present for him. "Don't mind the hideous bag," I tell him. "We're not all talented artists like you."

"Yeah, yeah," he mumbles.

He takes out his first gift. "It's a blank piece of paper. Um…you shouldn't have," he jokes.

Be brave, be brave. I chant. "I want you to design a tattoo for me."

He raises an eyebrow at me. "Really?"

"Yep, I want you to sketch a happy rose and a sad rose for me. The bitter with the sweet." I run my fingertips over his sad rose. "I want to have those tattooed on me," I hesitate for the briefest of moments, "along with your name."

He stares at me for so long that I start to get really nervous. *Is this too much too soon? I wonder.* We really haven't even discussed where this is going. "Michael?" I finally prompt him.

"Lorraina, I…" He pulls his eyes from mine, finally. "I don't even know what to say to that."

"You could say, 'Sure, Lorraina, I will design your first and only tattoo for you,'" I suggest.

"It's forever," he reminds me and meets my eyes again.

"This is forever," I correct.

His lips crush down on mine so unexpectedly that I cry out with a mixture of pleasure and pain. His tongue charges against my mouth, demanding entrance. I thread my fingers through his hair as I allow him to overtake me with his scorching kiss. I marvel for a moment about how intense my feelings are for him. Then, I lose all thoughts as he changes gears yet again and demolishes them all with a sweet, soul-stealing kiss.

He pulls back and grins my favorite lopsided smile. He looks like a little boy when he smiles like this. "I love it when you smile," I tell him.

"I love you," he counters.

"And I you. OK." I clap my hands together like a little kid. I'm suddenly very excited for him to see our journal. "On to the rest of your present! I know the blank piece of paper is overwhelming, but I did spend a little money on you," I kid.

"All right, what do we have here?" He takes out his journal and laughs. "It looks like the one I bought for you."

"Great minds…"

"Yep." He winks at me. "I love it."

"Well, there's a little more to it than the obvious." I flip it open to my first memory. I read the title of it aloud but let him read the memory for himself.

"Oh, baby," he whispers and flips through to glance at the ten or so memories written down. "This is unbelievable."

I feel a little self-conscious when he starts to read another one in earnest, so I place my hand over it and shake my head at him. "Save this for later."

"Argh…OK."

"I was hoping that you could journal on our memories as well. Let me see things through your lens. Wanna know how this came to be?" He nods his head at me.

I tell him how I came to find his cards and how the cashier told me he would be playing at Mona's that night. I tell him about how I went home that night reliving our past in my mind and how I saw it in a completely different light. I tell him that I felt the need, the drive to see him and make him mine and that I was completely overcome with longing for him. I tell him that I'd never felt that way about anything or anyone before in my life.

"And I finally faced the truth as to why I had denied you for all those years, why I had hidden my feelings from the both of us," I admit.

"Why's that?" His voice cracks a little.

I take a deep breath and finally acknowledge, "Because you were the best friend I'd ever had. Because your intensity scared me. Because I was so young and I wasn't ready...Because I was in love with you."

"Well, it's about time you owned up to that," he chuckles and kisses me again.

***

I find myself riding along the beach with the top off of the Jeep. I love the weather here. It's Christmas and it's seventy degrees at six o'clock in the evening. When Guns 'N' Roses' "Paradise City" comes on the radio, I crank it up and belt it out as loud as I can. Michael laughs at me and joins in. It makes me feel infinitely younger. I'm excited to see another part of Michael's routine, especially since he's assured me that it doesn't have any physical requirements like his tortuous outdoor habits.

I'm surprised when we pull in the Navy Retirement Home. I knew it existed, but I had never been here. "What are we going to do here? Do you have a family member here?"

"No, not really," he replies. "A while back, a friend of mine told me about his uncle being here and how it could be depressing, so I started coming here to play a little for his uncle every now and then. I enjoyed it so much that I started coming down once a week."

Will wonders never cease where he is concerned? It blows my mind how kind and considerate he is. He was always that way, but this is a whole new level of compassion. I'm incredibly moved. "That's really remarkable of you, you know that, right?"

He grimaces, "I think I get more out of it than they do."

Spoken like a true philanthropist. "You never could take compliments. You need to get that figured out because pretty soon the world is going to be paying you compliments," I chastise him.

"What?" He blanches.

"You're too amazing for me to be allowed to keep you all to myself," I predict. He just rolls his eyes at me. I can't resist leaning in and paying my respects with a lingering kiss.

And he is truly amazing. He picks his guitar and tells stories and listens to stories and weaves his songs in with the stories. If it is at all possible, I fall even more in love with him.

Chapter Twenty-three

Confessions

The next few days pass in a flurry of gigs, nightclubs, wonder, excitement, tenderness, journals, food, Mass. Every second that I'm away from Michael, I count down until we will be together again. He only leaves me when he has to work one of his many jobs. Fortunately, one of his jobs allows him to sit behind a counter so he can call me during that time. I'm able to squeeze a few visits in with Ginny while he's at work. I'm so tempted to tell her about him, but I'm just not ready for the interrogation. I want our relationship to remain as untainted as possible.

I make up for lost time with him by writing about our recent memories that we've made, which causes me to digress to memories of long ago. I treasure every moment I get to spend with Michael, knowing that our spell will be broken by secrets and miles soon enough. Michael has been so unexpected, refreshing. I've never met anyone so honest with himself and others. I hope to emulate him.

"Whatcha writing over there?" I'm pulled from memories of the last few days. I glance over and smile at him. We've been lounging on his balcony, enjoying the sounds of the waves and comfortable silence.

"I'm journaling about our last few days together," I reply. "What about you?" We've both been alternating between reading and writing. He's using the journal I gave him. So sweet!

Admittedly, it has been hard for me to concentrate, though. Every time I hear his calloused fingers scrapping across the turning pages, I imagine them on me.

"Right now, I'm working on some lyrics."

"Aah...I would love to hear them."

"You will when they're ready." He gives me his secret smile. Maybe they're about me, I muse. "Sit tight. I wanna show you something. I'll be right back."

"'K," I reply quickly as he has suddenly dashed into the apartment. I wonder what he's up to.

He returns with an old black and white marble composition book. "What's this?" I sit up a little so that I can examine it more closely and shift to give him room on the chaise.

"This," he says, framing the composition book in his hands playfully, "would be the play you wrote when we were in ninth grade English."

"Are you serious?" I gasp.

"Yep." He's glowing with excitement. He must get how much this means to me.

"Michael," I say his name and it's full of wonder, "how did you get this?"

"I quite artfully persuaded Mrs. Barfelt to give it to me after she graded it. It wasn't easy," he continues, "She really wanted to have it as an example of student work."

I open it up and read the title page, "The Diary of Anne Frank—In Action: A Play by Michael Bang, Kimberly Cline,

Lorraina Dabney, and Clinton Ross." I laugh as I remember us all getting together to plan our project. No one knew what to do because we'd never been given full creative license before this moment. It had been all worksheets and bookwork up until that point in our academic careers.

"I remember how you ever so democratically placed our names on it in alphabetical order even though you did most of the work. You surprised me so much with this," he tells me. "I was so used to you being so logical about everything. I'd never seen you really let go and be creative. And, then, BAM! Everyone in our group is floundering, wondering, arguing about what on earth we're going to do. You just wandered over to the window with your hands on your hips, looking out like you were studying the most complex of views. Then, you turned around and said, 'We're going to write a play based on Anne's diary.' It was genius. Your face lit up like Christmas. The imagination I saw dancin' in your eyes was magical. I fell in love with you all over again."

Tears have sprung to my eyes at his description of that moment. He's made it feel like it just happened yesterday. "I think you are remembering it with a biased slant. I don't know that it was all that dramatic," I kid.

"Oh, it was. Trust me."

"That's when I started writing in earnest," I remember. "I'd written a little over the years but just for me and only little snippets. After we performed that for the class and Mrs. Barfelt graded the hard copy, she pulled me aside and drilled me with questions."

"Like what?"

"She wanted to know how I went about writing it and stuff. I told her that Anne's diary is so vivid that I could just see it, ya know? Anyway, she seemed happy with my answer and told me that I was an excellent writer. I was so shocked. I figured out years later that there was already a published play version. I guess she was afraid that I'd copied it. Anyway, other than my singing, I don't think anyone had ever paid me a compliment like that one."

"You've barely let me hear you do anything more than hum," he complains.

"That's because I sound like a screeching, sopping wet cat compared to you," I tell him in all seriousness.

"Pssh…" he asserts and fiddles with the notebook, "So, did you start writing more after this?"

"Yes," I whisper. I am suddenly very sad. He must sense that because he puts his finger under my chin and tilts my head up for a light kiss.

"What did you write?" he questions against my lips.

Goosebumps make quick work of covering my body down and back up again. "Hmmm? Umm…poems and stuff." He places a kiss on each of my cheeks, on the tip of my nose, and then his lips find mine again for another feather light kiss.

"Why did you stop writing?"

His spell is broken. "How do you know I stopped?" I pull back and ask him.

He frowns and places his hands on the arms of the chaise, surrounding me. "I just know. So, why?" Crap. When Michael wants something or wants to know something, no pat answer will do. He's tenacious, gum on the bottom of my shoe.

"I just...did. I got busy and preoccupied with school. I will have basically finished two degrees, Summa Cum Laude, in four years, one of those degrees is even in English; and I work almost full time. There just weren't enough hours in the day."

"You know what I think?"

"What's that?"

"I think that's what you were born to do—write. You are gifted. Reading your memories back reminded me of what a great storyteller you are." My gaze has drifted down, and he pauses to bring it back to meet his. "Look at me," he demands and I immediately comply. "Not many people have this gift. You have to share it with the world. If not, withholding it is the most selfish thing you will ever do," he finishes passionately. Hmm...*Selfish begat selfish.*

"Thank you for believing in me," I mumble.

"Now, how do we get you to believe in yourself?" he wonders.

I swallow hard and tell him, "I've written more this last week than I have in years. We may be on our way there. Don't give up on me."

"Never," he promises.

I try to change gears in this suddenly serious conversation, "You know, I never did figure out how you managed to get classes with me that year. P.E. I could understand, but Advanced English I and Spanish. I would think for someone who failed the year before you would have been in less…challenging classes." He throws his head back with laughter. I laugh with him but smack him in the stomach with the notebook too. He's laughing at me. "What? Why are you laughing at me?" I grumble.

He barely pauses long enough to squeak out, "Did you just figure that out?"

I take in a deep, indignant breath. "No," I protest, "I just didn't want to give you the satisfaction of knowing that I wondered about it."

He makes a motion of chopping my nose off my face. "Nose to spite face!" He accuses.

"Yeah, yeah, I know!" I concede. "Anyway, now I want to know."

"I got my mom to take me up to registration early so that I could have some one-on-one time with my counselor. I assured her that the only way I would apply myself, as they had been asking me to do for years, was if I could be in advanced classes that year. I assured her that the only reason I failed the year before was because I wasn't academically challenged. She was putty in my proficient hands," he finishes maniacally.

"It's a good thing we went to a small school," I say. "Or it wouldn't have been quite that easy." I feel the need to take him down a peg or two.

"Oh, I would've found a way. I was highly motivated," he assures me with a glint in his eye.

***

Michael leaves to go get Chinese takeout. I remain sitting on the balcony, staring out at the waves and the vastness of the Gulf. It wasn't too long ago that I swore I would never be back to this area. That if I could get out, I would never return. I even dreamt of living in a well-visited, touristy area so that my family would come and see me; and I wouldn't even be required to visit them here. Now, look at me, contemplating a life here with Michael. It's crazy how quickly my life has changed. I thought I would never find anyone. I never really wanted to find anyone. I wanted to devote myself to my chosen career, have a nice house, have a few friends. That was going to be my life. All I can think of now, though, is having that career but devoting myself to my relationship with Michael. The career used to be the main course; but, now, it had been relegated to nothing more than a much ignored, yet required, side dish.

"That was delicious," I tell him as we finish our General Tso's Chicken. "So, anything planned for tonight?"

"No, not really. What would you like to do?"

"Well, I wouldn't really *like* to go visit my father, but I think that I *need* to."

190

"OK. Do you want to go alone or would you like me to go with you?"

I contemplate this a moment. "I think it would be good for you to go, but I have to warn you he was very angry with me the last time I saw him. I'm not really sure what to expect." That thought leads me to another. "Have you seen him lately?"

"No, he stays to himself since he got out."

"Aah…yes, his illustrious prison sabbatical," I say acerbically. He had been arrested and had served some time for assault and battery. "Nice."

"All right, I guess there's no time like the present. Ready?"

"As I'll ever be," I reply.

***

We pull up outside my dad's place, and I am astounded by how absolutely trashed my old homestead is. When I lived here, it was a real deal, living, breathing, working farm. Now, it was like a ghost town, and my dad was the only living occupant. Seeing it eases the ache I feel for my old way of life because nothing even resembling my childhood home still exists.

Michael kills the engine, and we sit in silence for a minute or two. Finally, I take a deep breath and release it. "I think it might be better if I go and judge what kind of mood he's in, OK?"

"Yeah, sure. I'll wait here. Let me know if or when you want me to join you."

I squeeze his hand and let it go quickly. If I don't move quickly, I may never have the courage. I make my way up to the porch and raise my hand to knock on the door. A snarl stops my hand mid-air. I turn my head to look at the mangiest pit bull I've ever seen. "Hi, puppy," I coo. "Aren't you a poor little thing?" I continue in my little singsong voice. I crouch down and let him sniff my folded hand. He immediately decides I'm not harmful and rests his head on his paws, keeping his eyes trained on me less I become a threat. I ease back up and rap on the door.

I hear a lot of grumbling and movement. I see the curtain move back and hear someone announce my presence. I push my hair back behind my ears, swallow the lump in my throat, and say a silent prayer. I repeat a calming mantra over and over as someone shouts, "Be right there."

Finally, the door swings open with a welcoming flourish as if I'm some kind of idiot who believes that everything going on in there is perfectly acceptable and normal. "Is my dad here?" I ask the woman with the crazy wide eyes whose name I can't remember.

"Yeah, he's coming. You wanna come in?"

"I'll just wait here if that's OK."

"Yeah, yeah. OK. He'll be right out."

I turn and stand on the edge of the porch, trying to focus on the beautiful man staring back at me. I give him a slight smile. He smiles back at me brilliantly. I wish I could be that optimistic. I'm lost in this thought until I hear a shuffling behind me. I start to turn around when I hear his gravel filled voice.

"Lorri," he snorts, "what are you doing here? You finally figure a way to have me arrested, or you wanna just hang me from that fucking tree over there?"

Oh, shit! Oh, shit! is all I can repeat in my head. My eyes fall on his face and I notice that he has a long, thick beard and scraggly salt and pepper hair that juts out in tangled clumps all over his head. He's so gaunt that his nose protrudes at an awkward angle from his face. My gaze travels down his shirtless form until it reaches his red clay covered pants. He's barefoot. My mouth drops open to try to respond; but when I make eye contact with him, I see the absolute absence of humanity in his stare and that scares the shit out of me. He barely had any before. Now, there was none.

I take a deep breath, shake my head, and turn to make my way back to the Jeep. My mind is reeling. There's no way I can talk to him. He's loaded or high or something. There is no dad here. Michael is looking at me with a look of utter astonishment. I turn my finger round and round. Start the car. Start the car. I will him. Thank God, he gets it. I hear the Jeep crank up.

I hear my dad behind me. I think he's still on the porch, though. Thank God! "It works both ways, Lorri!" he screams at me.

I don't think so! I spin around and point my finger at him. "You're *damn* right it does!" I counter. What has gotten into me? I've never raised my voice at either of my parents, especially not my psychotic one!

I jump in the Jeep. As I'm pulling my seat belt on, I glance up and see him running at me with his fist raised. Michael is turned around and starting to back out slowly and I chant lowly, "Go, go, go." as I watch my dad chase me out of his driveway. Michael floors it and backs all the way out to the road and spins his tires as he slams it into first so that we can get the hell away from him.

He stops a little ways down the road to pull me in for a hug. My violent sobs rack both of our frames. "Shh, shh, shh," he tells me. "It's gonna be OK." He rubs my back and my arms and my hair over and over until I calm down.

I choke back a sob and look at him. "I'm so sorry that you had to see that."

"What?! You have nothing to be sorry about." He frames my tear soaked face with his hands and looks me in the eye. "Nothing," he repeats more forcefully.

I sniffle a little more and take a few deep breaths. "Let's go home," I tell him.

"OK." Never letting go of my hand, he pulls back out onto the road and looks over at me. "You know, I forgot he calls you Lorri."

"Yeah, I still hate to be called by that name. It reminds me of him too much."

"Damn, I forgot what a crazy bastard he is too."

I laugh a little. "Have you ever seen him like that before?"

"Yep, once."

"Really? What happened?"

"He was high. He was riding one of the horses at the river, claiming to be an Indian. His face and chest were all painted up and he had feathers in his hair. It was pretty crazy."

"Yep," I released a long sigh, "it's pretty crazy."

He casts a sidelong glance at me. "You know it's pretty remarkable."

"What's that?"

"You've turned out pretty normal."

He has me laughing again. "I'm normal? I don't feel anything like normal."

"Relatively speaking," he adds and elicits a new round of laughter from the both of us.

***

He pampers me when we get back to the studio. I stand at his window, overlooking the Gulf. My soul feels as vast and as deep and as undiscovered. He makes me a glass of lemonade and massages my neck. I grab his hand and lead him outside. Somehow, I think what I have to do now will be easier accomplished if we're outside. A light drizzle has begun to fall. Normally, I would find this soothing. Garbage's lyrics buzz through my head. Am I sabotaging us on purpose? Why do I feel this need to come clean? I teeter for a moment and toy with the fact that I don't have to tell him; he doesn't ever have to know, but I know that's not right.

I sit him down on the chaise and lean back against the balcony rail. I forge on, knowing that I have to be completely honest. This is already killing me. I can't imagine living our entire lives keeping up this pretense. "Michael, I have to tell you something and it's not good," I preface. "There's a reason my dad acted that way other than the fact that he's probably high and most definitely insane. It's something I've been wanting to tell you about but I've been afraid. Very afraid. Afraid of what you'll think of me, afraid I'll lose you. But I have to tell you." I make an effort to still my hands.

"OK."

"And I need you to not interrupt me, OK?"

"I won't." He looks worried, and I have a moment of doubt that I have to push away very quickly.

"I'm going to start at the beginning, if that's OK?" At his nod, I tell him that it all started a few months before I graduated high school. I tell him that he'd been right about *him* all along. He was awful. He treated me horribly and didn't respect me. When he stole some of my graduation money to buy pot, I'd finally decided that I'd had enough.

I got accepted to Ole Miss and got a full academic scholarship. I'd decided that there was no place for him in my life; but for some bizarre reason, I continued to date *him* until a couple of weeks before graduation. It was then that I broke up with him. I tell him how angry he was and that he basically started stalking me, showing up everywhere I went and coming to my home. It was scary. My mom was so furious, I tell him.

"So, it was the week of graduation. I'd felt bad all week, but I chalked it up to nerves and trepidation. He couldn't seem to leave me alone. Graduation night I decided to drown my fears and problems with alcohol, and I got drunk for the first time in my life. I think it took all of three Purple Passion Everclears," I recall. Michael smiles at me. I wish he wouldn't.

"Anyway, my friends and I got drunk and I even smoked a little weed. I ended up passing out in our hotel room pretty early. The next day, I felt even worse. Instead of taking it easy, I decided to go clubbing with some older friends of a friend. I didn't want a repeat of the night before, so I avoided alcohol and weed." I take a deep breath and steel myself. I look over at him to assess his gaze. He smiles at me tenderly and my eyes fill again with tears. "In my infinite wisdom, I allowed myself to be talked into doing XTC." His expression changes to one of shock. "Yes, I know. Little ole me, trippin'. I had a blast that night. I didn't pass out. I felt great. It was scary how good I felt. I woke up the next day and felt absolutely horrible, though. I never remember feeling that awful my whole life. I made excuses to my mom and Joe and stayed in bed for a few days. I started remembering, however, that I had felt bad for a while. I also remembered that I hadn't had my monthly cycle." I wish I could've gotten away with leaving out that last part. It was mortifying but no more mortifying than what I was about to confess.

"I went to the doctor and she asked me if it was possible that I was pregnant. I told her I didn't think so because we had used protection, but she thought it would be better if we went ahead and did a test. Lo and behold, it was positive and she presented me with my options." I can't look at him now, not yet.

"I was reeling, so I went to his house under the guise of wanting to get back together. I gave him some hypotheticals. I asked what he would do if I were pregnant. He laughed in my face and told me that would be wonderful news because then 'my proud, stubborn ass would stay right here and marry him.' I told him that all my scenarios were tests and that I was glad that we'd broken up. I never spoke to him again until the other day."

"I went home and started thinking about my 'options.' Could I raise a child? What would my mamma say or do? Could I still go to college? Could I give it up for adoption? I'd never agreed with abortion, though; so I really wasn't considering it. But then I started thinking about the irresponsible way I'd spent that last week. I got really scared about what I'd done to the baby. Then, I started thinking about what a horrible parent he would be and who in the hell was I to have a baby! I was so fucked up myself."

"I went back to the doctor and asked her to explain abortion to me. She told me that the fetus was not really developed yet as I was only a few weeks along. I took some pamphlets to continue reading about what to do. I decided that I had to tell my mom because no matter what I wanted to do I was still seventeen. She was so pissed. She yelled at me. I don't think I'd ever heard her raise her voice before." I finally steal a glance at Michael. His eyes are closed and his breathing seems shallow.

"She wanted me to give it up for adoption and go on to school late. I told her that I would definitely lose my scholarship if I went late. She said I could deal with those consequences and take out loans. Then, I told her about my behavior the week of graduation. I told her I was afraid that I'd harmed the baby and that I thought it would be best to have an abortion. After a lot of screaming and crying, she agreed. At some point, she called my dad and told him everything, which is why he hates me. The last thing he said to me, before tonight's episode on his porch, was that he couldn't believe I'd turned out to be such a whore." I wince with that particular memory. I knew I wasn't a whore. I was just looking for love in the wrong kind of way with the wrong kind of person. Not exactly unheard of.

Michael still hasn't moved a muscle. If his eyes were open, maybe I could get a read on whether or not he understands or might be able to forgive me. I take a deep breath and continue, "When they numbed me, Michael, I was awake and fully aware; and I swear to you, as I felt my body go numb, I allowed the rest of me to go numb. When I left, I felt nothing—no sadness, no sorrow, NOTHING. I was…numb, and I stayed that way until I saw your cards at Mona's." I release a shaky breath.

"I never told anyone in all that time, but I did make a vow that I would NEVER put myself in that position again. I wouldn't date casually. I certainly wouldn't have sex. I hoped that one day I would meet someone; but after a couple of years, I'd decided that no matter who I met I'd never get over what I'd done and would never deserve the kind of happiness that love would bring me."

"Michael, your faith is so strong. I'm afraid that with that kind of faith you'll never be able to forgive me." He never opens his eyes even after I stop talking for a moment. I wait patiently, thinking he needs a moment to digest everything I've just said. His look is pure anguish. "Michael?" I call gently. No answer. I wait another few minutes, but he never moves an inch.

I walk back inside the apartment and stand there for a few minutes, not knowing what to do. Finally, I slowly gather my purse. I turn back and hear nothing from the balcony. I bite my lip to stop myself from crying out. I can't cry anymore tonight. I've cried enough over the last couple of weeks to make up for all my years of numbness. I walk outside and jog to my car. It is suddenly very chilly and starting to rain in earnest. I sit in my car for a few minutes, wondering why on earth I felt the need to be honest about this. I've obviously ruined any chance I had with him. Suddenly, I can't breathe. I roll my window down and pull the damp air into my lungs until I can't ignore the rain pelting me in the face anymore. I start getting choked up again. With a final glance at Michael's still closed door, I start my car and put it into gear so that I can head home.

Chapter Twenty-four
A Thorny Redemption

By the time I get on the road, it's really coming down; and between the rain and the tears, it's hard to see. At least it's so scary a drive that I'm unable to consider anything else. Finally, I make it home. As soon as I lay my head on my steering wheel, I am bombarded with emotions. Relief to have made it home and relief to have finally confessed to him. Fear because now I know for sure he will never forgive me. Gratefulness for having had these last couple of weeks at all. Anger for not being able to hold on to it for longer.

I can't even allow myself a glimmer of hope, can I? Michael is so good, so pure. I'm ruined for someone like him. I know he's not perfect, but his faults haven't killed anyone. Mine did.

The rain has slackened up a bit, and I decide that now would probably be a good time to get inside the house. I pray that my parents are already in bed.

I jog up to the steps, kick my shoes off, and then tiptoe up and across the porch to peer in the living room. It's very dark. At least someone is still listening to me. I ease the door open and quietly head down the hallway to the bathroom. I'm soaked through and need to get a towel before I try to go to bed. At the thought of doing something so mundane while my heart is in tatters, my stomach protests violently. I shove my fist in my mouth to keep from crying out.

I'm so consumed with this thought that I don't see the wall jump out into my path to greet me. I hit it—hard. Shit!

"Grace, that you?" Joe calls out. *Ha ha! Very funny,* I think.

"Yes, it's just me. I'm sorry," my voice cracks on the last word.

"You, OK?" my mom probes.

NO! "Yes, I'm fine. I just stubbed my toe. It hurts." I'm feeling the second worst pain I've ever felt! Of course, that has nothing to do with my coordination deficiency.

"Come on in," my mom beckons.

Great! I crack their door open and force a small smile to my face. Just the right size for my supposed toe injury, I figure. "Yes, ma'am?"

"I wanted to let you know that Ginny called earlier. She wants to get together again before you leave."

I eye my mom for a second to see if I'm busted. Did Ginny mention that we'd only gotten together a couple of times? Her face doesn't show any signs of suspicion. Good thing I didn't use Ginny for an excuse tonight. "OK. Thanks. I'll call her tomorrow."

"Good. You, OK?" She finally seems to notice my appearance. "You're soaked."

"Yeah, I'm fine. Got caught in a bad downpour. I just need to get cleaned up."

"OK. Good night."

"Night," I mumble.

My mom elbows Joe, "Good night, Lorraina," he replies automatically.

I pull their door to and cross the hall to the bathroom. That was uncomfortable, but at least I'm not busted. I don't even know if I could muster the strength to lie my way out of any accusations at present. As I towel dry my hair, my mind begins to whirl and show me possible solutions to my Michael dilemma.

It's obvious from his stoicism that he's not anywhere near ready to forgive me. Perhaps I could write him a long letter explaining in more detail my thought process behind my decision. Maybe, if I wait until tomorrow, I could go over; and he might be willing to talk to me. I could read him my journal entries that I wrote about all that had occurred. I could read some about how much I love him, and he would see that I can't give up on him, on us. If all else fails, I could integrate myself into his life and become friends with him again until he realizes that he can't live without me in any other capacity than girlfriend. I grimace with the thought of the "friend" label. That would entail him trying to date other girls while I calmly stand by and act cool with everything. *NOT gonna happen!* I scream in my head.

OK, so maybe I get in my car and head back to Oxford, bury myself in my studies, and forget these past two weeks even happened. I feel a sharp pain that works its way from my heart, into my throat, and comes out in a sharp gasp of air. I squeeze my eyes together and fresh tears roll down my face. Now that I've let myself feel again, I don't think I could ever go back to the way I was, especially where Michael is concerned.

I stare at my reflection in the mirror until I begin to feel dizzy and the face that stares back at me looks like a psychedelic poster. My image twists and curves into odd, deluded shapes. A hysterical laugh bubbles up from within me and bursts out before I can stop it. I close my eyes for a moment, shake it off, and will myself to go to my room.

I decide that I'll take a page out of Scarlett's Handbook for the Seriously Screwed Up Romantic: Tomorrow's another day. I need to go lie down for a little while and try to clear my mind before deciding anything.

I grab a fresh towel and start toward my room. I hear quiet snores coming from my parents' room. That was fast, I think. I ease my door closed behind me and rest my head on the door while I grope for the light switch. After several misses, my bedside lamp finally clicks on. Finally...

As soon as I turn around, I hear a light pelting on my window. Is it raining harder again? I pull back my covers and start to peel my shirt over my head. I hear the pelting again a little harder this time. *No way!*

Grasping my shirt around my middle, I slowly cross the room to my window. I'm afraid to get my hopes up. I pull my curtain back and sure enough. In a little pool of light, there's Michael, standing back a little ways with his hands on his hips. He looks...aggravated. I'll take aggravated.

I throw my window wide. "Hi," I call out softly, thanking God my room is the farthest from my parents.

"Hey, it took you long enough," he replies. "Can I come in?"

"Through the window?" He nods his head. "Yes, OK."

I look down to see how far it is from the ground and see that he has already pushed and stacked empty milk crates under my window. He climbs up; he takes the screen off; and, between the two of us pushing and pulling, he propels himself through my window. He collapses on me, winded from trying to be quiet and falling through my window. We scramble to our knees.

"Why are you here?" I ask in hushed tones. I waste no time. It's killing me. Is he here to say goodbye? To forgive me? To chastise me?

I try to pull myself and him to our feet; but all of the sudden, I feel myself being jerked into a bone-crushing hug. His hands and lips are everywhere. He rubs my head with his hands. Then, his lips follow suit. My face is showered with little kisses and my arms are warmed under the brisk movement of his hands—up and down, back and forth. This is not the smooth, delicate Michael that I've come to expect. He's rough and demanding and desperate.

It offers something that looks too much like hope. What is this? I have to know. I pull back as much as I am able and ask in my loudest whisper, "Am I forgiven? Are you saying goodbye? I don't understand, Michael. You just sat there. You said nothing. I waited and waited and you said nothing."

"Baby, I'm so sorry that I froze." Kiss. "I'm so sorry that you had that awful experience." Kiss. "I'm so sorry that you'll have to carry that with you for all of eternity." Kiss.

"If I had kicked the Child Molester's ass the day that I found out about you two, none of this would've ever happened." His whole body tremors with barely contained fury. "I abandoned you. I knew you needed me, needed help. But I let my pride get in the way. You lashed out at me with your words, and I let that rejection get in the way of my taking care of you. I knew better, and I just walked away; and I don't know how I'll ever forgive myself." He grasps my head with both of his hands and rests his forehead on mine. "Do you understand that? You have your guilt and regret just like me. We both made mistakes, but I will never abandon you again. We can work through them together, though."

Part of me, starts rejoicing as soon as I hear the words…*you needed me, don't know if I'll ever forgive myself*. No one uses those words if forgiveness isn't part of the deal, right? The logical part of my brain rears up and says, *No, no, he hasn't spoken words of forgiveness to you and those words you must hear to know you have a chance*.

"Michael, I was a big girl, making my own decisions. I stayed with him. I allowed him to treat me the way he did and take advantage of me. Then, I let fear control me. Weakness control me. Your faith is so strong, so steady. How could your faith ever allow you to forgive me?"

He leans back and fixes me with his gaze. "It's my faith that gives me the Grace to forgive, baby. 'Verily, I tell you, whatever you did for one of the least of these brothers and sisters of mine, you did for me.' That's what my faith allows me to know. It took me a long time to understand it, but I can help you with that. I don't hold it against you, though. I only feel anger and sorrow for what you went through." I'm astonished by his resolve and his words.

"When you told me what you went through, I just…froze. All I could think of was jumping up and going to kill him. Do you understand? I'm trying to change my ways, but every day is a struggle. I'm continuously waging wars against my anger, my impulsiveness, my addictions. I was sitting there, willing myself not to get up and go kill *him*. Then, I was afraid if I moved while I was that angry, you would think all that rage was directed at you, and I didn't want to scare you. So, I just sat there, talking myself down. When I finally got control over myself, I went inside to talk to you; but you were gone. I was so scared. I got over here as fast as I could. I was ditching my car on the side of the road when I saw you walk onto your porch. I came to your window and waited for you, but you took forever."

"I was in the bathroom, freaking out," I tell him. "You really don't hold this against me?" I ask disbelievingly.

"No, Lorraina, I couldn't even if I wanted to. These have been the best two weeks of my life, and I fell in love with you when I was only fifteen. Nothing is ever going to change that. You made a mistake, but you're still a good person—the best."

"Michael, I need you to understand something, though. I really feel like I did the best thing for the baby when I made my decision. I talked it over with the doctor a lot. She told me of all the awful side effects that the baby could experience because of my stupidity. I weighed my and his parenting possibilities and found them severely lacking. If I had to go back and make that decision again, I don't think I would make a different one."

"I can understand that. I know you, and I know that you wouldn't have made that decision lightly."

"And you still forgive me?"

"Yes, of course."

I exhale a long pent up breath and brave a small smile. It feels as though I've been holding that same breath for almost four years. Was this why he was brought back in to my life? To help me overcome, and come to terms, with my past? "Michael, you have no idea what that means to me."

He runs his hands up and down my arms. "You must be freezing. I've drenched you through and through," he says.

I grab my towel from the bed and dry us both, stealing a couple of kisses as I do. "Can you stay?"

"Mmm…I want to, but I don't want to get you in trouble."

"I need you to stay," I clarify.

"Yes, I'll stay." He collapses on the floor and pulls me down with him. I collapse half covering him and half covering the floor. "Ya know, I never understood your draw to him."

"That's easy. Classic daddy issues."

"Really?"

"Michael, I was so messed up from the divorce. Part of me was very happy that my dad gave my mom no other option but to divorce him, but another part of me was devastated because he completely dropped out of our lives. And no matter how flawed, he was still my dad, and I just wanted him to love me."

"So, when I met him, I thought here's someone I can respect and he'll respect me. He was mature enough that I could see starting my own family with him. I dreamed of being the center of his universe and having that unconditional love. Everything quickly spiraled out of control, though. He cheated on me, mistreated me, stole from me. He was an utter lie."

I hear him swallow hard and feel him shake his head. "I'm sorry that you had to go through that, baby."

"Me too. But it made me who I am today. I think I'm stronger for it, and I definitely know what I want out of life."

"What's that?"

"You," I tell him simply.

Michael draws us both back up to our knees. I frown at him. I was comfortable. He gives me a knowing look and overwhelms me with his proclamation. "Lorraina, I've known and loved you my whole life. The day I first saw you was the day my life began. I used to write you poem after poem about that, remember?" I nod my head, feeling guilty because that's exactly why I destroyed everything he gave me. I didn't get it, and it scared me.

"I began to see the world in a whole different light." He squints his eyes thoughtfully. "Like before I'd only been trying to survive this world; but when I saw you, I knew there was more for me. I knew that through your love I could make this world a beautiful place for us to be in. I lost sight of that for a while, but I've always known that you are the one for me. You're the reason I turned my life around and fought against my former self. I knew that if I could conquer my demons I could win you for myself."

"And you did. I'm not going anywhere, Michael. Consider me thoroughly won over."

"I've wanted to make you mine ever since you told me that this is forever. I want to share every single day with you. I want you to bear my name, bear my children."

I shake my head in disbelief, "Michael, I—"

"Don't tell me you don't deserve that. Don't tell me you don't deserve to be happy." He forces my head up and the sincerity in his eyes is my undoing. I'm weeping again. "I told you once you were the most deserving person I know, and I still believe that. I know you made a mistake. But that's what life is made of, baby—it's choices and mistakes and wrongs and rights. It doesn't mean that you're any less deserving of what our life together will offer you."

His tone softens, "Yeah, you messed up. You'll never forget it. You'll never let yourself forget it. But you will overcome it.

You will go on to live a happy, healthy, peaceful life. You'll be the fiercest mother on the planet because you'll spend the rest of your life making up for that wrong. You'll let it shape you until you're the best at everything. It will drive you to be the best, the most forgiving, the most loving." His words shake me to my core.

His voice rises again, winding upwards into a strong, steady presence. "Look at what you did for me the other night. You had no reason to trust in me, to love me, to forgive me but you did. That's who you are." His finger taps my heart with each syllable. "That's who your choices made you. You're more understanding, more willing to accept, more willing to forgive, more willing to love. Look at what we've come to mean to each other in this very short time. You would have none of that before. You didn't understand it. You didn't get it. It took something awful to wake you up to this, but you'll never turn your back on that lesson."

"Michael, I...I don't know what to say. I want to believe every word you've said, but I'm still scared. I'm scared of what forgiving myself will unleash. I'm scared that forgiving myself is what will make me a bad person." I take a deep breath and close my eyes, willing myself to believe. "I want all of these things with you, though; so I'm willing to try. I know that I'm gambling with my very soul, but I will do that for us."

"I want you to be my wife." He shakes his head at my sharp intake of breath. "I know we've only been together for a short time, but you're the only person I've ever loved, the only person I've ever wanted to be with. Why waste anymore time? I've been fighting the urge to ask you to marry me since Jason told me that a pretty little blonde was waiting for me to perform." Another sharp intake of breath. *He knew all along?!* "Will you do me the honor of becoming my wife?"

My head is cloudy with fear and proclamations and possibilities. Surely, I did not hear him correctly. I realize that my mouth is hanging open in a most unladylike manner. I close it and shake my head a little, trying to clear the fog.

"Is that a 'no'?" He asks worriedly.

"No! I mean no, it's not a no. It's an 'I can't believe you just asked me that.'"

He grins his lopsided smile. "So what's it gonna be then?"

"Yes, of course. Of course, I'll marry you." I'm rewarded with a face-splitting smile, the likes I don't think I've ever seen on his beautiful face. I loop my arms around his waist and lean in and place my head on his chest. I can hear his heartbeat thundering under my ear. "I love you so much," I tell him simply.

He gently brings my face back up until our lips touch ever so lightly. His full, soft lips move over mine, delicate and searching. I hear myself moan with abandon. I deepen the kiss until I urge his lips open and pour my very being into him. The blackness behind my eyelids turns to little blinding stars. It feels as though we share the same soul in this moment. I hope that feeling never relinquishes.

I find some of my brother's clothes from the laundry room for him and sneak back to the bathroom to change. When I come back, he is stretched out on my bed, looking uncharacteristically shy. I smile and lean on the back of my door and take in the sight of him. He's mine, truly mine. It's something I never even dreamed possible. It's funny how life does that to you. You have a plan and dreams and desires. Then, in a flash, all that can change. All that you thought you wanted dissipates and you're left with what you what you needed. Never knew you needed but, nonetheless, did. I pull myself from the door and crawl under the covers with him. We lie there for a while and just hold each other. We speak only a little until we lose ourselves in a cocoon of acceptance and love and promise.

Chapter Twenty-five

A Little Piece of Forever

"Hey, you gonna wake up? It's our last day together," he chides me. This is exactly why I don't want to pull myself out of his bed. These last few weeks have been amazing. "Come on. I've got a big day planned for us and you're messing it up." He snatches my pillow out from under my head, producing a new round of protests from me.

"Mmm...I don't want to get up," I whine. "If I stay in your bed, I won't have to go back to Oxford, right?" I crack one eye open and admire the sight of him. He looks like he's ready to take on the world.

He pulls me into a sitting position and crouches down in front me, placing my arms around his neck. "Unfortunately, that's not the way it works, babe. Time will move on with or without you. Now, we can either have some fun together or sleep our way through our last hours." He places playful little biting kisses up my arm, across my chest, and back down my arm as he massages my back lightly. This is not helping. All I want to do is put my hands in his hair and pull him back down in bed with me. Before I can make good on my thoughts, he's up, stuffing things into an overlarge bag.

"Hey," I call out to him, "Happy birthday, baby."

"You remembered," he replies, sounding surprised.

"Of course I did."

"Let's go! Up! You're not distracting me. As bad as I want to be distracted by you, it's not happening. We're going to spend an unforgettable day together."

"Ugh! Why do you have to be so logical right now? I'm supposed to be the logical one," I protest.

"That's right. So quit making me take up your slack."

"Yeah, yeah," I mumble and make my way to the bathroom. "So what are we doing today?" I mumble around my toothbrush.

"After Mass, we are meeting up with Josh, our drummer, and his girlfriend, who I know you will like, and going kayaking."

"What's kayaking?" I frown. This sounds like another of his torturous outdoor activities.

"Similar to canoeing," he answers absentmindedly. He seems to be trying to decide between two different, yet very similar looking, water bottles.

"Oh. It's winter! Isn't there some kinda law against being out on the water in cold weather?" My voice is full of thinly disguised panic. I hate canoeing! I always tip over! That's not sexy! I lean on the doorframe and cross my arms.

"Not when you live on the Coast and it's eighty degrees in January." He doesn't seem to notice my hesitation.

"Ha! True." I hope I don't make a fool of myself. My brain is starting to function now, and I'm wondering about this double date thing, too. "Anyway, I thought we agreed to keep our relationship quiet."

He saunters over to me, and I swear my body temperature rises with desire. Does he have any idea how sexy he is? "We can trust them. I told them we weren't making anything official until you graduated. Told them that we wanted to avoid any family drama." With each word, he gets closer and closer to me until I can feel his warm breath on my face. And even though it's warm, I shiver.

"Sounds plausible," I murmur.

He brushes my hair back and my skin burns where he's touched it. He leans in for a good morning kiss. I think he intends for it to be quick, but I'm having none of that. I quickly deepen the kiss. He even tastes like outdoors, woodsy and fresh. I groan with regret as he breaks the kiss. "Was that not good enough for you, ma'am?" He teases me.

"No," I pout. Abruptly, he picks me up, eliciting a shriek from me. I circle his neck with my arms, grab handfuls of his hair, and tug gently. *I won! I won! I rejoice.* His kiss overtakes me and all victory flees from my head as I lose myself in our kiss. He's unrelenting as he backs me up into the wall, and I wrap both of my legs around him, pulling him as close to my body as I can. I feel ourselves join and I yearn so badly for him to be inside of me that I cry out a little.

He breaks the kiss all too soon and leans his forehead on mine. Our breath is coming rapidly now, and we both take a deep breath to calm ourselves. "Well," his voice cracks and I hear him force a swallow, "was that better?" He's trying for a joke, but I think I see a chink in his armor. I affect him as much as he affects me. Good to know.

"Mmm hmm." is all I can muster.

He casts me a sly glance and, ever so gently, peels me off of him. "If you're not out in ten minutes, I'm coming in after you," he threatens.

"Promises, promises," I say to the now closed door.

***

"Kayaking is nothing like canoeing," I tell him joyfully. "We didn't tip over once."

"That's because you're with me," he boasts. "I wouldn't let you tip over. The water may not be freezing, but it's still too cold to immerse yourself in."

We were almost to the small island off the coast where, apparently, there were little campsites for our use. Michael and Josh plan on fishing and grilling their catch for us. I'm told that us girls are to relax and enjoy the view. Fine by me! I like Josh's girlfriend, Anita, and I really like the way Michael introduced me to her—his fiancée. My whole being filled instantly with love and desire so strong that I wanted to steal him away immediately and have my way with him. Unfortunately, my desire would have to wait as he has our day planned out to perfection. Of course, he wasn't forthcoming with many details, only telling me that I would love it and not regret leaving the apartment, which I had not so subtly hinted at.

We've made our way across the channel and around to the south side of Deer Island. My hands ache from gripping the paddle. Paddling wasn't very hard to do, but I realize now that I'd held a death grip on the paddle for some reason. As I flex my hands to regain some feeling, Michael pulls them into his own and massages them gently. He gives me a devastating smile that resonates to my core.

Michael and Josh ready their fishing poles while Anita and I make a pallet for us to lie down on. I've brought a book and my journal. Anita seems to have brought a book and a sketchpad. Good, I won't have to entertain her the entire time.

Anita and I make idle chitchat about school and the band and her work. She is an administrative assistant at a bank, but she wants to go to school for design and fashion. She even shows me a few sketches of her really cool rocker *chic* look. She wants to know the usual about me—what kind of law do I want to practice, am I sure that I want to go to school that long.

We sit in comfortable silence for a while. I'm reading. She's sketching. She politely asks about the book. I tell her it's one of my favorites—*The Great Gatsby*. She's astonished that I would read a book more than once. I assure her that certain books are so good that a reread is like the first time all over again. Much to my surprise, she hasn't read it the first time. I thought it was required reading for every high school junior. I delve into some of the details and focus on telling her about the love story in the book. I tell her all about Jay Gatsby and his plan to make enough money and raise his social standing in order to be good enough for his one true love—Daisy. I only give her enough detail so that her interest is piqued. I hope she reads it.

I ask her if she is sketching more for her rocker line, and she laughs and turns her book so that I can see she is sketching possible logos and designs for the guys' band. I tell her I'm insanely jealous of her ability. They look really good, and I think they will be impressed.

After a few moments, she breaks the silence again. "So, Mike, huh?" She ventures.

I was wondering when we would get around to that. I bite my lip a little and locate him on his kayak; he's casting his line. The sun seems to delight in dancing on his dark skin. I roll my eyes. No one has a right to be that beautiful. "Yeah, I know, right?"

"How'd that come about? I've never even known him to date anyone," she admits, seemingly astonished, "and now he's engaged. It definitely threw me for a loop."

"Well, we were best friends when we were in school," I tell her. "We lost touch over the years; but a few weeks ago, we found our way back to each other." This feels like a completely inept description of our reconnecting, saying anything close to what we've experienced, though, is way too personal to share with someone I've just met.

"High school sweethearts," she purrs. "I love it." She lays back on her folded elbow to rest her head on her upturned palm, giving me her undivided attention.

Her interest fuels my need to talk to someone about him. "Well, not exactly. It was unrequited love. Michael was two years older and obsessed with me," I admit on a laugh. "And I'm not just being arrogant about that. It was crazy, and it scared the hell out of me. I made him settle for friends. He was amazing as a friend, though. I wouldn't admit to wanting any more than that at the time even though we had a couple of close calls."

"Things seem to be working out now. He asked you to marry him, right?"

I glance back out at him and catch him staring at me. His gaze steals away whatever I had been about to say. I give him a little wave, which he returns along with a huge grin and an upheld whopper of a fish. I cup my hands around my mouth and yell, "Way to go, baby." I giggle at his obviously testosterone-induced reply. I barely make out, "man, meat, and woman."

"Sorry," I apologize half-heartedly. "I'm consumed by him."

"It definitely goes both ways."

"You think?" I hear the surprise in my voice. I've seen the evidence for myself, but I always wonder if my passion is as fervently reciprocated.

"Oh, yeah! I bet he's great in bed." My mouth drops; surely I didn't hear her right. Her next comment confirms the fact that my hearing is perfectly intact. "I mean, he's the strong, yet sensitive, type. Like, I bet he's totally in tune with your needs and desires," she finishes and looks back at me finally, taking in my surprised expression. "Oh, sorry," she mumbles.

I work my mouth closed and breathe a frustrated sigh. My initial shock over the turn of the conversation has abated. Maybe she can help me with my little problem. "Ya know…he won't," I hedge.

"He won't, what?"

"You know." I dip my head and raise my eyebrows at her.

She gasps, "What do you mean? Like at all?" I confirm with a nod of my head. "What's he waiting for?"

"This is between you and me, right?" I question and steal a glance at Michael like I'm afraid he can hear us. She nods her head. "He wants to wait until we're married so that we don't complicate our relationship with sex."

"Ugh," she replies indignantly.

"I know. I'm dying over here." I throw myself back dramatically on the ground. "I mean I think the no sex is complicating things worse than the act itself would!"

"Poor thing. I love Josh. We've been together forever, so I'm allowed to say this because we're perfectly secure in our relationship," she prefaces. "But Mike's hot and to have the feelings that you and him obviously have going on here and not be able to act on them, must be sheer freakin' torture. I mean, he's obviously got it bad it for you, girl, and you for him. And he's so…mmm."

I nod my head at her. "Well said."

***

Michael takes my hand and helps me up from our little picnic. His and Josh's feast was amazing even out on the little island. They caught plenty of redfish and even had grilled potatoes. We shared an easy conversation with them. It was nice. I could basically feel the sexual chemistry rolling off Josh and Anita and envied them immensely, for they were able to do something about it.

I'm jolted from my thoughts as Michael pulls me into an embrace a little distance from our campsite. He fists his hand in my hair and pulls my face up to meet his for a bone-melting kiss. I feel something at my back and realize that I'm backed up against a little tree. I throw myself into the kiss, but I break it this time. I'm very proud of myself.

"It's really not fair," I complain.

His eyelids stay closed as he murmurs, "Mmm...What's that?"

"You can kiss me like that and just walk away when all I really want is to pull you down on the ground and make love to you right here, right now." *Did I really just say that?*

His eyes fly open and they burn with passion as he narrows them at me. *Yep, I did.* "Is that what you think? That this is easy on me?"

I nod my head. "It seems that way."

His hands drop to hold mine by my side, and he threads his fingers through mine, holding them tight. "Oh, baby, I've never wanted anything, anyone more in my life. Do you have any idea how low my electricity bill will be this month?"

"Huh?"

"I've taken nothing but cold showers for the past few weeks," he explains.

I grin and bring my mouth to his neck. I caress him with my tongue and show him how amazing it would be if my tongue were allowed free rein. "Imagine my tongue running wild all over you. That's how good it's going to be between us, Michael."

"Damn, baby," he throws his head back and howls. When he looks back at me, my eyes gloss over as I see the love and desire reflected there in his own eyes.

"I'm sorry. I'll try to be good." I don't want to screw this up.

He leans and whispers, "And just for the record, when you wrapped your legs around me back at the studio, I almost lost it." My eyes widen as I realize exactly what he means by that. Damn is right.

"I wanna give you our present," he tells me.

"What?" His swift changing of gears has me reeling.

"You'll see. Wait here for a sec," he says with excitement bubbling in his eyes.

He jogs back over to the campsite and grabs an extra blanket. He starts to jog back to me, but he turns and jogs backwards, having a conversation with Josh. *Geez!* I gawk at his lithe body. In high school, Michael was still Michael. He was beautiful but not like this. He was kind of lanky in high school and a little self-conscious. Now, he looks so strong, so stable. I know that his confidence and self-assuredness plays a huge factor in that. He turns and catches me staring. I'm not sorry.

He doesn't slow as he reaches me and grabs my hand. I jog behind him to a more secluded part of the island. He spreads the blanket out on the grass and kisses me until I'm lying down. "Mmm…beautiful," he muses. I do feel beautiful when he looks at me like that. He takes his fingertip and runs it down my forehead, nose, and chin, creating a line of fire where his finger has touched me. Then, he uses both hands to run down my arms and picks back up at my thighs and runs his hands down the length of my body. I just lie there and try to focus on breathing. "Do you have any idea how alluring you are?" I cock my eyebrow at him. "No? Let me just say that every other girl that I've dated, or even considered dating, since I met you has had to compete with you."

I frown at him and mutter petulantly, "I don't like thinking about you with other girls."

"Trust me, baby. They didn't hold a candle to you." His look turns thoughtful. "Yep, I would always find ways they fell short of your measure. Her hair is not as long and thick as Lorraina's. She's not as tall as Lorraina. Too skinny—I like the way Lorraina has some meat on her bones. Lorraina's eyes are a deep green, almost emerald. That must be a rare feature, by the way. I've never seen another girl with your color eyes. I like the way Lorraina can tell me everything she is thinking with just one of her expressions. This girl's too hard to read. Lorraina would never play a game with me like this girl. She always tells me like it is."

"Wow! You've dated a lot of girls!" I giggle as his hands begin a ticklish assault on my body.

"It's been seven years. And some of them were lacking in more than one category."

"So how about our present?" I prompt.

"Well," he begins, taking a piece of paper from his pocket. "I've designed your tattoo for you." He shows me the tattoo as promised. There is a melancholy red rose and a joyful purple rose. He signed his name ever so elegantly.

"It's so pretty," I gasp. I sit up on my elbows. I'm fascinated, but I cringe a little. I've never liked pain. "Can we get it done today?" Even the brief thought of pain can't diminish my enthusiasm.

"Yes," he hesitates. "There's a catch, though."

"What's that?"

He licks his lips and swallows hard. "I need to draw this on your body for you."

"I don't understand. Do you want me to get the tattoo or not?"

"Oh, yes," he murmurs darkly, "I want to be permanently etched on your gorgeous body."

I purse my lips, still not understanding. "So what's the problem?"

"The problem is I want you to get it done at Moonlit Studio."

"And…"

He exhales hard and rubs the back of his neck rapidly. "And there are only guy artists there, and there's no way in hell that any guy is touching you that intimately for that long. If I draw it, all they have to do is ink it."

Oh! Possessive much? I love it! "Michael, they are professionals," I insist innocently. "They are not thinking about me like that. They tattoo hundreds of women!"

He shakes his head at me. "There you go lumping yourself into a category again. You're not just any woman. You're my woman," he asserts. I start to bristle at his calling me woman; but then he leans in and gives me a lingering kiss, forcing all thought from my head.

"OK." I relent. "But don't blame me if I can't keep my hands to myself while you're working!"

He grins. "If you don't want an amateur looking tattoo forever marring your delectable *derriere*, you'd better be good. By the way, you don't want it there, do you?" He frowns.

I shake my head and lie back down, not taking my eyes off of his, and unzip my jeans. His eyes are drawn to my movement, and then they shoot back up to mine and widen. He looks back down and watches as I fold and tuck my jeans under my underwear and point to the indention just inside my hipbone.

I hear his breath leave him in a whoosh. "Are you kidding me?" He marvels. I shake my head at him. "Yeah, I'm really glad I thought of this. It's going to be very hard to watch a guy touch you here for any length of time," he says as he runs his finger over the unexpectedly sensitive area. I'm on fire. He places a light kiss there, and I almost come undone once again.

226

He sets to work on our drawing. My skin tingles where he puts his mark on me. I look up at him and gaze at the determination marking his face. This is incredibly sexy. I don't think I can take it. I try to focus on something else but every thought leads back to him and his hands. Determinedly, I force myself to recall all the pertinent battles of every American war for the last four hundred years. I'm on the Mexican-American War when Michael sits up and tells me that both the roses are done.

"Yeah, about the rest of the tattoo," I begin, making a split second decision, "I'm not going to put your name on me just yet."

"What? Why not?" He doesn't hide his disappointment.

I throw my arm over my face. I'm suddenly very self-conscious. I've never made a demand like the one I'm about to make. I peek at him from under my folded arm. "I'm not going to put your name on my body until you either make love to me or marry me. Whichever comes first," I challenge him.

He frowns and mumbles, "That's not fair."

Hmm...Maybe this will get me my way sooner. "Sorry, babe. Who ever said life was fair?"

Chapter Twenty-six

Kiss Me Deadly

Getting my tattoo was one of the single most sensuous acts I've ever experienced. Through the pain, I felt great pleasure of marking myself for Michael, for us. All those years of flinging his art and his love back at him were quite simply erased at that moment. I hope he felt that too. If his heated stare was any indication, that was precisely how he felt; for he never took his eyes off of mine while the tattoo artist worked on me. He even had the happy rose added to his own tattoo so that ours would match almost exactly.

I'm jarred back to the present as Michael appears at my door to help me from the Jeep. "You OK? You seemed to drift off for a little while. Not having any regrets, are you?"

I reach up and wind my arms around his neck and stand on my tippy-toes to place a gentle kiss on his full lips. "Nope, not a one," I murmur against his lips.

He squeezes and lifts me up to give me a giant hug. "I'm going to miss you so much," he tells me. "I guess you need to get home, huh? Spend the last night with your family?"

I squeeze my eyes shut briefly and pull back to look at him. "I said my goodbyes yesterday. My parents think I left town then," I squeak out. He and I are both sick of lying.

He looks grim for a moment. He sets me on my feet. "I hate all these lies, but it won't have to be that way much longer."

"Nope," I agree. "Only a few months, which are going to drag by since I can't see you." I run my hands down his chest and circle his waist with my arms, laying my head on his chest. His heart beats so steady, so strong. How did I not know that he was all I ever needed?

"Mmm...I wish I didn't have to play tonight. I'd like nothing more than to curl up with you and let the world just melt away."

"That would be wonderful," I admit. "It will be cool, though, for our last night to mirror our first," I muse. This night will be a little different, I mentally amend, since I have a little birthday surprise for him.

"I didn't think of it like that. All right, let's go get ready then," he says reluctantly.

When he comes out of the bathroom, his hair is in disarray and he has a towel wrapped around his hips. It's low slung, showing off his impressive abs and indentations around his hipbones. I hear my sharp intake of breath and wonder if I will ever get used to looking at him like this. I hope not.

I make my way over to him and run my hands through his damp hair and comb it through with my fingers. Michael closes his eyes and a secret smile appears on his lips. "I hope I don't ever take for granted your touch," he whispers.

I feel my heart swell, and I place a kiss on each of his cheeks before he pulls me in for another one of his soul-stealing kisses. I'm breathless when he finally releases me. When I calm myself a bit, I remember that our kisses are numbered and our time together is finite. He has a way of making me forget those little details. This leaves me with a bitter taste in my mouth. *Focus on the time you have,* I chide myself. "Hey, music man," I perk up, "I have a special request for you tonight."

"You do? Well, what'll it be?" He smiles lovingly.

Sudden shyness causes me to blush; but I forge on and inquire, "Can you play 'Glycerin'?" Requesting it in front of everyone would have been even more embarrassing. Like I would have rendered myself transparent for everyone to see with just that one little song.

"By Bush?" He asks surprised. I nod my head. "Yeah, yeah. You like that song?" He asks surprised.

"Love it. I think it's one of the most beautiful, heart-wrenching songs I've ever heard. There's just something about it that throws me every time I hear it. Not many songs can do that, you know? Just reach in, grab hold of you, shake you, and make you look at things in a whole different light." These are all the reasons I'd tried to avoid listening to this song over the years. I couldn't face the effect it had on me.

"Mmm...Well, I better bring my electric guitar then. It wouldn't sound quite the same without it." I tremble in anticipation.

***

Mona's is pretty packed tonight, so I sit at the bar and make small talk with Jason. He's as gregarious as ever. I tell him that I'm leaving tomorrow, and he pats my hand and tells me that

Michael will be OK. I guess he interprets my frown as fear. I'm not scared for the reason he thinks I am, though. We've overcome distance before, and Jason probably thinks that I think Michael might cheat on me or something like that. No, he would never do that. I'm scared of what my life will be like without him there. When I imagine going back to school, the images are black and white and faded. Like I was before Michael. I'm scared to feel that way again. I never want that again. I look at Michael and see him in glorious Technicolor and that infuses the rest of my life.

I'm jerked from my musings as I hear the opening cords to the song I've requested. I grin as I let the song's lyrics take on a whole new meaning in my life. Before, the song portended sadness and misery for me. Now, I feel hope within the lines. And I pray it communicates meaning to him where my words have failed. It seems music has always been that magical portal for us. I hope he knows that I've gone head to head with my old friend fear where he is concerned, and I've conquered him.

***

We're halfway through the Big Bang Theory's gig. Typically, I would wait for Michael beside the stage, and we would get a drink and dance a little and make out a little before he goes on for his second set. Tonight, however, I've decided to do something completely out of character for me.

I'm standing off to the side of the stage a little where Michael can't see me. As I hear the final bars of "Simple Man" fading out, I watch Michael jump off the stage and look for me. I feel a sudden attack of nerves, but Josh makes eye contact and nods his head at me. I smile slightly and make my way center stage, and then I quickly try to channel my inner Lita. The hardest part of singing this song is that I have to start without a lead in. It serves my purposes so well, though, that I barely contain a laugh. Michael will have no warning for what's to come. I'd briefly considered doing my own rendition of the Stones' "Can't Get No Satisfaction," seeing as how all this abstaining was getting to me, but decided this one would be way sexier.

I take a deep breath and belt out the first line. Oh my…It has an immediate effect. Michael spins before I can finish it. It's one of the sexiest opening lines of a song ever. As soon as the band kicks in high gear, I'm off. My nerves and fear completely disintegrate. I sing to the crowd for a moment. When I hit the chorus, though, I focus everything I've got on Michael. His eyes are burning, and they penetrate mine. I smile around my mic and wonder if I'll get to have my way with him tonight. I parade around the stage, hoping against hope that I'm exuding sexuality.

T.J.'s guitar riff that will close out the song has barely begun when I feel the mic tugged from my hand, and I marvel as I watch it fly toward Josh, who deftly catches it and laughs with his whole body.

Michael is tugging me behind him toward backstage. As soon as we round the corner, I'm against the wall writhing under him as he kisses whatever breath I had left clear out of me. I feel his hand snake its way up the outside of my thigh, and I comply with his unspoken demand to wrap my leg around his. His other hand barely brushes my breast but then comes back and caresses it full on.

My hands make my way into his silky hair, and I force him even closer to me as he kisses me roughly. My eyes flutter open to catch him watching me. I groan into his mouth at the look in his eyes, and they go even more molten if at all possible. He pulls back a little, placing little nipping kisses on my lips. Both of his hands disappear from my body to lean on either side of my head on the wall.

I whisper against his lips, "Happy birthday, baby."

"Damn, baby, you are the hottest thing I've seen. I don't know how you pulled that off, looking hot and as cute as hell simultaneously, but damn!" He drops his head to lay it upon my rapidly beating heart. I drop my face into his neck and breath deeply. He smells so good—a lethal combination of Michael and sweat and arousal. My whole body tenses.

"I'm glad you enjoyed it."

"Hell, I loved it. I'll be relying on that memory for a long time to come."

I blush as I realize what that means, and the sheen of sweat that had crept over me during my performance causes me to shiver as I allow his words to wash over me. It really couldn't have gone better. Unfortunately, his kiss might just be the death of me as Lita's lyrics play out in my head because I know that's all I'll be getting from him tonight.

233

I slowly open my eyes and look lovingly around Michael's studio, memorizing all the little details so that when I'm back in my drab little dorm room I can properly imagine him here among his things. I shift slightly and bring my head up to rest on my folded elbow so that I can stare at him. He's still sleeping. The covers are resting just above his hips, and I can make out half of his crucifix.

I look back up at his head and begin to mentally sketch every detail. From his disheveled midnight hair to his thick eyebrows and even thicker eyelashes. I know that under those deep-set, slightly slanted lids are the brownest of eyes. Sometimes, they are so dark that I could barely discern his pupil. His high, wide cheekbones match the rest of his beautifully sculpted face from his straight nose to his angular jaw to his stubborn chin. I close my eyes and burn the image to the inside of my eyelids. Every time I close my eyes, that's what I want to see—Michael's beautiful face. I open my eyes to find him staring at me; a little smile plays at his lips.

"Whatcha doing?" he asks playfully as if he doesn't know the effect he has on me.

"Oh…Nothing. Just trying to memorize you," I admit without really thinking too much about it.

"I wouldn't think you would have to with all those pictures you took last night," he grumbles. Ah, yes. I must have taken around fifty pictures of him and us. I smile as I remember how fun it was to make him my model. Look this way and that—pouty face,

The Thinker, kissy face. He protested a little until I persuaded him as only a woman in love could. I had definitely misappropriated the use of the camera my mom bought me.

"That was fun," I tell him.

"For you maybe," he grimaces. "It's a good thing I don't believe that a picture steals your soul. As many as you took, I'd be completely bereft."

"Such a beautiful soul too," I whisper.

He brings himself up to my level and places a gentle kiss on my lips. "I tell you what. How about I make breakfast while you get ready? I want to make sure and satiate your hunger before you have to hit the road."

My eyes widen with pure lust as he uses these very sensuous words to describe the act of breakfast. "It's not fair for you to talk to me like that, ya know?" I feel things moving inside of me that, before him, I'd never before felt.

"Who said life's fair?" He throws my words back at me, so I smack him playfully with my pillow as I get up to take my own cold shower.

***

I get out of my car and walk back toward his Jeep. He's followed me to the edge of town and the road that will lead me away from him for the next several months. *Oh, God, months.* I cringe. He meets me in the middle and threads his fingers through mine. He brings my hands up to his mouth and places lingering, little kisses all along my palms and wrists. I am afraid to speak. If I open my mouth, I may start crying; and I don't want that to be our last memory together. So we just stare at each other and take each other in. I promise with my eyes that nothing will come between us, and he returns that promise with gusto.

Finally, he breaks the silence, "I love you, Lorraina. Forever. I'm so grateful that you walked back into my life. And as much as I hate your leaving, I'm grateful we had these last few weeks together."

"The bitter with the sweet, huh?"

"Yeah, the bitter really bites."

"It does indeed. I'll miss you so much," I tell him again. I lay my head on his chest and focus on the erratic beat of his heart for a moment. "I love you, Michael. Please take care of yourself for me, OK?"

"You got it," he replies gruffly.

He releases my hands to frame my face and pull it up to his. I see tears shimmering in his beautiful eyes; and, of course, I feel mine well up immediately. He closes his eyes and a single tear escapes to trace its way down his cheek. I kiss it away before he ever so gently slants his mouth over mine. His gentleness seems to seep into me and caresses me so lovingly, all the way to my toes. I feel myself relax and pour everything I feel and more into our goodbye kiss.

Neither of us says anything as we get back into our vehicles. I glance up at my rearview mirror and watch him dash away a few tears. I start my car up and a melancholy tune fills the air. I quickly locate a mind-numbing CD that somehow found its way into my collection. I've never felt so grateful for the existence of AC/DC.

I pull out onto the road and keep my eyes on my mirror as I watch Michael watch me. I see him wave, flash his lights, and turn off before I reach the highway. I quickly depress the accelerator as I merge with the traffic heading north.

I feel myself hiccup a little and quickly turn the music to blaring. I try to lose myself in "Back in Black". It reminds me that Michael wears mostly black and that he is indeed back. I skip to "Hell's Bells". There we go. That won't remind of him at all. I start to sing along with the song, thinking I've got a tenuous grip on this; but it is, nonetheless, a grip. Yeah, I'm not going to lose it. I murmur, "You got me ringing." I whisper, "hell's bells." Then, I'm choking. Finally, I'm sobbing. I turn the music off and let my cries fill the car.

Chapter Twenty-seven
My Most Miserable Existence

Getting back into the swing of things at school was one of the hardest things I've ever tried to do. When I wasn't talking to Michael, writing to Michael, or writing about Michael, I was daydreaming about Michael. I played and replayed all the memories we made. I imagined and reimagined what our life together would be like.

Fortunately for me, I'd saved some of my easiest classes for last semester, so they didn't require my full attention. I looked around at my life and wondered how I'd ever thought that academia and work would have completely fulfilled me. I still had my job, but barely. Elise was constantly getting on to me for being absentminded. She told me to be grateful that I'd been such a diligent employee for the last few years because if I hadn't have been she would certainly get rid of me. I think she was only half-serious. Surely, I hadn't gotten that bad.

I did, however, find time to talk to my local priest about joining the Catholic Church; and he referred me to a very nice and helpful lady who offered to privately walk me through the conversion classes. This, by far, has been one of the most interesting experiences of my life, but I've yet to share that with Michael.

I missed Michael so much that it physically hurt. Sleeping and eating were no longer necessities. If I slept, I didn't get to write to

Michael. If I ate, I didn't get to talk to Michael. Therefore, I did them only when I absolutely had to because passing out from exhaustion or lack of nutrition would also interfere with my Michael time.

Our conversations were amazing and reminiscent of our teenage years. We talked about everything and nothing and all that lies between. Sometimes, our conversations bordered on the explicit, which was quite shocking at first. Then, it was exhilarating. I guess I'm to blame for that. One night, when I was missing him particularly bad, I told him of my first dream that I'd had about him after seeing his work at Mona's. That led to him telling me some of his thoughts on the subject, and so on. Thank goodness I had a roommate who was practically never in our room.

I am daydreaming about one of these particular conversations when I hear the store phone ring. I move over to answer the phone, but it quits ringing rather abruptly. Hmm...

"Lorraina, phone!" Elise shouts. Elise never shouts. I turn to gape at her and her hand is over the mouthpiece. She has a scowl on her face, and she continues in a quieter voice, "I was in the middle of some trying figures, Lorraina, but had to stop and answer the phone on the sixth ring. And, lo and behold, it's for you."

I cringe under her unfamiliar use of sarcasm, and blush down to my roots. I'd done it again. "I'm so sorry, Elise. I didn't even hear it ring." I pick up the phone and wait for her to disconnect. "Hello? This is Lorraina."

"Hi there," replies the sexiest voice I've ever heard.

I smile, completely forgetting that I am in trouble yet again. "Hi," I respond. "What are you doing calling me at work? Is everything OK?" Michael never called me at work unless I gave him a certain time that assured Elise wouldn't be here.

"I'm sorry, but I couldn't wait to tell you."

"Tell me what?" I'm intrigued.

"That I managed to get a few days off in a row during your spring break."

I mentally clap my hands together and happy tears spring to my eyes. "Michael, that's great! Are you sure?"

"Yep, I've arranged for someone to cover for me where I would be missed and get out of some other things where I wouldn't; and because of the way my classes fell, I'll only miss one class. It's all settled."

"This is the best news I've ever heard," I gush.

"I've got a little money saved up so I was thinking I would get a hotel room, and you can come and spend as much time as possible with me. Maybe you could find some interesting things for us to do."

I could, in fact, think of some interesting things for us to do but nothing that he would deem appropriate. "Yeah, absolutely. I have to work some, though," I say on a frown. This job has just been getting in the way of everything lately!

"That's OK. I'll take whatever time I can get."

Michael and I continue to make plans for a couple more minutes. I can't believe it! Only eight more days and he would be here! I hang up and basically float up to Elise's office.

I knock lightly on her open door before poking my head in. I feel like I should've come with a white flag. "Ms. Elise, you got a minute?" I broach.

"Not right now, Lorraina," she mutters.

"Uh...OK. I'm sorry. I'll come back later." I turn to go.

I hear her sigh loudly. "Lorraina, it's OK. Come on in."

A huge smile overtakes my face, which I immediately try to rein in less she think I'm not contrite. I can't get it under control, so I give up. "Ms. Elise, I'm very sorry that I've been so distracted and careless. I promise that I will do better, though. I've just had some news that will set my mind at ease so that I can refocus on my job and my classes."

"Your classes are suffering too?" She asks with raised brows.

Ugh...Why did I say that? "Yes ma'am, a little."

"I've known you for a long time, young lady. This is not like you." Her voice is full of motherly admonishment and concern. How do moms manage that?

I take a deep breath. "I know. It's just..." I'm distracted by his beautiful face for a moment. Maybe if I tell her, he'll stop invading every single one of my would-be thoughts. "I met someone."

Elise's head snaps back as if I slapped her. "You what?"

"I'm in love," I whisper.

She shakes her head for a moment, closes her eyes, and takes her glasses off to bridge her nose with her thumb and her index finger, rubbing them up and down for a moment. She looks up at me and there are tears in her eyes, which cause me to frown.

"Aah, Lorraina. I'm so happy for you. You have no idea how worried I'd been about you. You seemed so cut-off, so distant. I prayed that you would meet someone who would cut through all of that, shake you out of it so to speak. I figured it would happen eventually. I just hoped it wouldn't be too long. I didn't want you to miss out because you were too old and cynical. Like a particular bookstore owner who you try to emulate."

Now, I'm the shocked one. Here I was thinking that I'd hidden all of this quite nicely. I'd hidden it well enough from myself for a while, so I figured others were clueless as well. "Ms. Elise, why didn't you ever say anything?"

"Well, I hinted at it here and there. But these things can't be rushed. Enough about the past, though." She waves an impatient hand. "Tell me all about him."

"Where to start?" I puzzle. "His name is Michael. He was one of my oldest and dearest friends. He professed his love for me a long time ago, but I was too scared to admit my own feelings. He had a rocky start to adulthood, but now he's in school. He's working really hard at building a good life for himself. Besides all that, he's so talented. I think he can play like five different instruments. He can draw and paint just about anything. He writes his own lyrics and poetry. And...he's amazing," I finish on a sigh.

242

She gives me a little grin and shakes her head at me. "He sounds amazing. I take it it's more than just friendship now?"

"Yes, he's asked me to marry him," I squeak out. I still can't believe this little fact. I pinch my lips together because I think my smile may look more like a homicidal maniac's than a woman in love.

"Oh, honey. That was fast. But when you know, you know I always say."

"I know. I still can't believe it. I went home sheathed in complete dread and stumbled upon the only guy I've ever loved. It's been crazy. I love him like crazy. Miss him like crazy." I shake myself from my little reverie. "Anyway, he's coming to see me during spring break. Can we rearrange the schedule a little so that I can have as much time as possible with him?" I cringe a little because I know I really don't deserve to ask for any special favors right now.

She smiles at me and laughs. "Absolutely, I don't even want to imagine how distracted you would be if you're working and he's right down the road waiting for you."

"Thanks, Ms. Elise. I can't wait for you to meet him. You're gonna love him," I promise her.

***

Only a few days to go, I muse. I try to refocus on my professor's lecture about preparing for our midterm, which is the day before break. He seems to make eye contact with me in particular when he stresses the need to prepare several thoughts on possible discussion questions and practice responding to them. I fidget in my seat a little.

When he releases us, I pack up slowly because I'm not looking forward to going to the library to study. His voice cuts through my procrastinating brain, "Miss Dabney, do you have a moment?"

"Of course, Dr. Richardson," I reply quickly. Shit! He's never asked to speak to me before, and I've had him for several classes. If he wanted to say something, he just said it. And he's called me Miss Dabney. I fear this conversation is going to go somewhat like the one I'd had with Ms. Elise. I move over to his desk as he packs up.

He pauses and looks up at me. "I'm going to cut right to the chase here, Miss Dabney. You're not doing well in my class or your others, for that matter. What do you plan to do to rectify that?"

"Oh...I'm going to take care of it, Dr. Richardson." I launch into an explanation of my plan to bring my grades back up, telling him that I will use extra time during spring break to get caught back up. I'm pretty impressed that I know exactly what I need to do in order to get caught up considering I haven't given it much thought.

He seems to believe that I have a sound plan. "That sounds good, Lorraina. Your situation is not dire; but as your advisor, it's my duty to make sure you stay on the right track, especially since you have been awarded a scholarship for law school. We can't send a less than excellently prepared candidate, you understand?"

"Yes, sir. I'll take care of it."

"Great. I hope everything is OK."

"Oh, yes. Everything is fine. I've just had a lot on my mind." I leave with another promise to do better. I really do have to get my stuff together. I'll worry about that after Michael's visit, though.

Chapter Twenty-eight

My Little Pearl

I pull into the hotel parking lot and kill my engine quickly. I grab the rearview mirror and tilt it so that I can smooth on my lip-gloss and twist the tendrils framing my face one more time. I smack my peony pink lips at myself and shiver as I anticipate where they will be landing in a matter of minutes. I grab my bag and jump out of the car. My new flirty skirt billows up a little, and I hurry to smooth it down. *Whoa, girl!*

I walk as briskly as I am able on my new heels without compromising my tenuous hold on coordination. As I reach the stairs that will lead up to his room, I throw my hand up on the hand rail and lift my leg to take the first step, shooting a glance upwards to my destination. When I do, my breath hitches in my throat. He's been waiting for me at the top of the stairs. He lays his book down and stands up. He has a brilliant smile on his face. He's cut his hair a little. I mentally frown—less for me to run my hands through. I thought I would always prefer him in black, but here he is in a plain white v-neck t-shirt that fits him rather snugly. He hasn't discarded my favorite pair of faded blue jeans or his black motorcycle boots, though.

I have frozen in place as I grin up at him like an idiot. I take another moment to admire him. I have a sudden flash of my favorite scene from *Up Close and Personal* where Redford stands at the bottom of the escalator staring up at Michelle Pfeiffer. I had always thought that was absolutely the sexiest thing I'd ever seen. Not anymore. I finally remember that I should move up the stairs. He starts down toward me so that we meet in the middle.

"Hi," I whisper.

"Hi yourself," he whispers back. I giggle at our anticlimactic beginning. "You look happy to see me," he surmises.

"So happy," I assure him.

"Me too." He reaches out and places his hand on top of mine on the railing and moves down to my stair. I turn until my back grazes the rail. The light touch of it and his hand and his breath have my body singing. My eyes widen and I swallow hard. I look up at him and am elated to see these same things reflected in his eyes. I give a shaky laugh. His other hand comes up to finger the little pewter cross at my neck.

"You're wearing my cross," he states. "I didn't think you had it anymore."

"I didn't get rid of everything. I'm so glad. This has come to mean so much to me." He leans his forehead on mine.

"Mmm...Lorraina," he murmurs. "This is crazy." He grasps the back of my head in his palm and pulls my forehead to his lips and kisses it, then my cheek, next my other cheek, finally my mouth. He slants his mouth over mine and moves his lips in a lazy, sinuous way. Like he has all day to stand there and kiss me. I stamp down my impatience to devour him and go with the flow.

After what seems like forever, he pulls back; grabs my hand; and leads me up to his room. After he lets me in, he leans back on the door and spins me in his arm so that I land on his chest with a quiet thump. His eyes are electric, and I attack him with all the pent up desire I've been feeling these past few months. We kiss and touch each other until my lips are swollen and my limbs are lethargic. At some point we find ourselves lying on the bed, staring at the ceiling. Only our labored breathing fills the otherwise silent room. Did I seriously think our reunion was anticlimactic?

Michael pulls himself up on his elbow and stares down at me. "By far my favorite hello ever," he decrees.

"I've had better," I kid him. "Why just last week, my linguistics professor welcomed me by—"

His lips cut me off as he begins another assault on my senses. He tastes so delicious that I never want to stop kissing him. He has other ideas, though, and he pulls back all too quickly. "God, I missed you."

I place my hand on his cheek and run my fingers through his hair. Still plenty of it there for my purposes, I muse. "I missed you too, Michael, so much." I pull him back down for another kiss.

I stretch and before I open my eyes I know that the sun has gone down and I've fallen asleep on Michael. I shouldn't be surprised; I haven't slept well in months. I hear him very lightly picking his guitar across the room. I pull myself up on my elbows and watch him play for a moment. After a few minutes of staring at him, I accuse, "You let me fall asleep."

"Oh…I couldn't help it. We both dozed off. I woke up before you and didn't have the heart to disturb you. You looked so peaceful. Anyway, I wanted you well-rested for tonight."

"Oh, yeah? What are we doing tonight?" I already have plans of my own for him.

"Dinner and talking," he says.

"That sounds ominous," I tell him.

"No, no." He shakes his head and grins. "It's nothing bad."

"OK. Let me go freshen up." I close the bathroom door and stare into the mirror and urge myself not to chicken out. I want Michael to make love to me tonight. No, scratch that, I need him to make love to me. I want to be his in every way possible and just can't imagine waiting anymore. I run through my plan once again. Look irresistible. Apparently check. Steamy make out session. Double check. Dinner so that I can ply him with wine and tell him of my hopes for us. Up next. Followed by a round of pool where I can bend this way and that in my cute skirt while consuming a couple of alcoholic beverages to bolster my courage. This should all result in Michael needing me as much as I need him. Finally, I can have my way with him. I give myself a huge grin and ignore the little voice inside my head that reminds me he really wants to wait.

***

He's taken me to a little Italian restaurant on the outskirts of town. I'm surprised that he knows about it, but he assures me that he's done his research so that we wouldn't waste any of our time

249

together on less than perfect moments. We're waiting for our food to arrive, so I figure now is the time for me to discuss my ideas for our future together. I take a long pull from my wine, and I began to shiver and blanche. It was a little drier than I expected. *So much for being seductive.*

Michael shoots me a knowing grin and asks, "You OK?" I nod at him, not yet ready to try to speak. "You gotta slow down with that. It's meant to be savored not chugged." He laughs a little.

"I need a little liquid courage," I admit.

"Oh, yeah. What's wrong?"

"Nothing is wrong exactly. I just want to talk to you about a couple of things," I hedge.

He just raises his eyebrows and nods his head at me.

He doesn't throw me a lifeline, forcing me to take an unassisted plunge. "Well, I wanted to talk to you about what's been keeping me so busy."

"You mean besides having hot phone sex with me?"

I feel a thrill shoot down my entire body and coil in one telling spot. Oh, how he gets to me. I feign irritation at his ploy to sidetrack me. "No, actually. This is the exact opposite of all that. I've been attending Mass here, and I've found a sponsor who volunteered to ready me for joining the Church."

He has the decency to look ashamed because of the different planes of thoughts. He recovers quite nicely. "Really? Why didn't you tell me?"

"Well, I wanted to be sure that it was going to work out at first. Then, I wanted it to be a surprise. Because I started back in January, I'll be able to take Holy Communion at the Easter Vigil."

He sits back and expels a breath, running his hands through his hair. He quickly sits back up and takes my hand in his. "Lorraina, you have no idea what this means to me. I'm just…I'm just blown away. I mean I know we talked about it, but I thought it would take you time to come to terms with everything and…now. Now, I just feel like my entire world shifted. Like I can very clearly see our whole lives together. If that makes any sense."

It does. I felt the same: as if before I was just imaging our life together, but now it is our reality. I'm taken aback that we both have that same feeling, but somehow I'm not completely surprised. We seem to truly mirror each other, and it's an amazing feeling.

"I started out doing this for you, for us; however, I very quickly realized that this is the most amazing thing I'll ever do for myself. I've come to realize so much about myself and my faith and how I want to live my life. It's hard to put into words, but it feels like coming home. It's a very similar feeling to what I have when I'm with you. It's just so…right."

He squeezes my hand tight and continues to hold it while he leans in and kisses me gently. I've never seen a couple sit next to each other in a restaurant like this. I promptly decide I will never sit across from him again. This position is quite convenient. "Babe, that's so cool. I remember what it felt like when I first recommitted myself. It was indescribable, so I can imagine what you're feeling."

I take a deep breath to fortify myself for my next admission. "Michael, I have something else to tell you that may be quite shocking. I hope...I think that you like it, though."

"Now who's making who nervous," he jokes.

I offer him a reassuring smile and squeeze his hand tight. "It's nothing to be nervous over. I promise. I've been writing more," I begin.

We relax our grip and he laces his fingers through mine. "That sounds like an excellent thing." His thumb scratches across my palm, drawing my attention to our hands. My mouth goes dry at this seemingly innocuous movement. I lick my lips and refocus my gaze on him. He is staring at me knowingly. I shake my head a little at him and roll my eyes, trying to dispel my wayward thoughts. He clears his throat and takes a drink, and I can tell he's trying to do the same. The server, thankfully, chooses that precise moment to deliver our food.

We're distracted for a few moments, enjoying our meal. After my initial hunger has been sated, I broach the subject again. "As I was saying, I've been writing again. A lot. I suddenly have a lot to say. It's crazy. I've also been thinking about what you told me about having a gift and needing to pursue it." I take a deep breath and release it. "So I've applied to a creative writing program, and I know you were thinking about that route. Does that bother you?"

He gives me a half grin and shakes his head. "I think that's perfect. I think it's what you were meant to do."

"I'm nervous. It's unchartered territory for me, but I just feel…driven to do it. Like once I started writing again, I couldn't stop. I have to write."

"That's how I feel about my art. I guess that's why I have a notebook full of napkins and matchbooks and old envelopes. When it takes over, there's no stopping it. As it should be when you discover your passion."

"That's how I feel about my life right now. It's as it should be. I've rediscovered my faith and it's grown exponentially, I've rediscovered you and my love has grown exponentially, and I've rediscovered creating and it's grown exponentially. It's all so amazing but overwhelming, too."

He nods his head seriously at me and concurs, "I get it."

"So, the shocking part. The creative writing program that I've applied to is a little ways from home."

He laughs. "I hate it there. Where are we going?"

"Just like that. You don't even know where and you agree to go with me?" I know my words and my eyes are full of wonder. I figured he would be offended that I didn't consult with him first. I should've known better. That wasn't Michael.

"Yep, it's just like that."

I thrill at his simple yet declarative words. "Are you at least curious as to where you've agreed to move?" I give him a little knowing smile.

He rolls his neck and shoulders and flexes his hands like he's getting ready for battle. "OK. I'm ready. Give it to me. Where're we headed?"

"New York City." My half grin turns into a full grin. I immediately bite my lip, trying in vain to suppress it.

He falls back against his chair. "Wow…I didn't see that coming." He falls forward and runs his hand through his hair. "I mean that's more than a little ways, babe."

My stomach drops. I can do no more than stare at him open-mouthed. Is he serious? I thought he might want a fresh start, but now I'm not so sure. "Michael—"

I think my tone and demeanor must clue him in to my distress because he immediately cuts me off with, "Baby, I'm kidding. I'd follow you anywhere. New York has been on my list of places to visit for quite some time. Now, we'll be living there, which is way cooler than visiting."

"Really?" I squeak out.

"Really," he affirms. "I was only kidding."

I playfully smack his arm. "Thanks a lot for scaring me. I want this so much. And how is it that something I'd never even dreamed possible is suddenly the thing I want most in the world?" I shake my head in amazement.

"I'm just glad you realized it before you were halfway though law school and bored out of your friggin' mind," he teases.

"I'm not just talking about school. I'm talking about it all. You, our life together, my faith, all of it. Now that that's my path, I can't imagine anything else. I know that I've never wanted anything like this in my whole life. I wanted my degrees, I wanted law school, and I wanted to help people. But this—I've never felt this…this burning desire before. It's so overwhelming, all-consuming even." I realize I've been talking with my hands as if they could communicate more than my actual words when they freeze in the air at the end of my rambling confession. I'm suddenly very embarrassed. I feel my face warm, and I drop my gaze. I feel his fingertips under my chin, and he pulls my gaze back up to his.

"Don't ever be ashamed of your enthusiasm," he whispers. "I love it. It makes my heart smile."

That's so sweet. "Thank you for saying that. I just felt a little self-conscious, gushing like that."

"I like you gushing. And typically I like you blushing, but not over something that you should be proud about. So, what school are you applying to?"

"NYU. They have one of the best programs, and they have generous scholarships for financially strapped, but completely dedicated, students like myself. Well, rededicated students. I'll be able to focus if you're not so far away from me. Anyway, I used to dream of running away to New York when I was a little girl."

"I remember. People always used to wonder how a little girl from Mississippi became a Yankees fan. You used to be so funny defending them to all those Braves fans," he remembers on a laugh. "I think me, you, and New York City would be awesome. I bet they even have yoga, and I've been dying to try it! And I have some friends living there. Been there about a year or so. I'll get with them about some prospects and start figuring out what I'll do there. I wanna continue with school, but I'm good with going part time and working full time until we get things situated. I've been thinking about what kind of degree I want. I have to say I'm kinda leaning toward music or art education. Would you mind being saddled with a poor, humble teacher?"

"I think that would be perfect for you, for us; but only if I can call you Professor Bang." He throws his head back in laughter.

"You can call me whatever your little heart desires, babe."

We spend the rest of dinner talking about all of the things we will see and do in New York. All of the typical touristy stuff until we have enough connections there to figure out what real New Yorkers do.

***

"How did you know about this place?" I ask him.

"Mmm…I have my ways," he teases me. *Mmm…he certainly does*. I told him I wanted to go play pool, which he said would be fun, but he had another idea. I'm very happy that I didn't argue my plan. This is much better.

"I've always loved it here. I usually bring a blanket out when it's nice and study on the far side of the lake where it's quiet. I never dreamed of experiencing it with you at night like this. It's breathtaking."

We fall into a companionable silence as Michael takes my hand and we make our way around the lake. Darting in and out of the trees and shrubs are little trails that are spectacularly lit up. I've taken my heels off and hold them in one hand while Michael holds my other. Every time that I come to a log, I feel the need to turn it in to my own personal balance beam. I don't know that I've ever felt this buoyant in my whole life. I keep looking at Michael, expecting him to evaporate before my very eyes. We only have a few days together, and that's the only thing keeping my feet on the ground right now. Otherwise, I'm pretty sure that I'd just float off into the great unknown.

I move to step off the log and suddenly Michael spins me around like we are dancing and pulls me in until I stumble into his chest. *So much for feeling graceful and weightless,* I think. "Hi," I whisper as I realize I'm only several centimeters from his face. I'm looking down at him slightly, and his look is serious as he forces me to drop my shoes, places my hands on his chest, and moves his hands into my hair, unclipping it. I close my eyes and tilt my head back as I revel in the feel of his hands gliding through my hair. He leans in and buries his nose in my hair. I feel and hear him breath deeply. My entire body quakes.

His hands run down my neck and back until they come to a rest on my hips. "Mmm…You have no idea how alluring you are, do you? My God, you are the most beautiful thing I've ever seen. That's what I thought the very first time I saw you. That's what I thought when I was fighting with you outside the restaurant. That's what I thought the first moment I saw you sitting at Mona's. It's as if I will never get used to how beautiful you are, inside and out. Just pure beauty."

His words cause something in me to splinter off and break free. I almost weep at his sincerity. What did I ever do to deserve this level of adoration? I don't get it; I just hope that I can live up to it.

We make our way around the lake, making small talk and enjoying each other. We reach the gazebo that juts out over the lake; it looks like something out of a fairy tale. It's completely lit up as well and is reflected in the lake, doubling the splendid luminosity.

Michael takes my shoes from me and kneels down before me to help me with them. I put my hands on his shoulders and swallow the lump in my throat as he looks up at me with what can only be described as the most beautiful gleam in the world. I only smile a little because it somehow breaks my heart at the same time.

"Lorraina, the night I proposed to you was one of the best nights of my life. Later, I thought about it and felt like I didn't do it justice, though."

I give him a worried frown and assure, "Your proposal was perfect. I wouldn't trade it for all the flowery language in *Othello*."

He snickers a little. "Well, it wasn't that it was bad per say. We were both reduced to blubbering idiots, and I never want you to question my hasty proposal or your yes because I've dreamt of being your husband my whole life. And I've never wanted anything more. And," he pauses, "I didn't have this." He pulls out a little box, which takes my breath away before he even opens it. My hands fly up to cover my open mouth. I figured with his current starving student status I would get a wedding band one day but not an engagement ring.

"Lorraina, you've made me the happiest person on earth these past few months. You're the best friend I've ever had. I've never imagined any moment more than this one. Except maybe the one where you walk down the aisle toward me and make me yours. Or the first time we make love. Or the moment when we have our own place together, and I make it beautiful so that every day when you wake up you smile at the ridiculous amount of happiness you feel just by walking around our little place cuz baby it will be little but we *will* be happy. Or maybe the one when we have our first child. A girl we call Rose who is as stunning as you inside and out and who has my tenacity for life. Or maybe when we have our little boy who we call Wyatt cuz that's the name of a little boy who is well loved yet dances with trouble just like his old man. I've imagined all these moments and then some; but they all begin with this one, which is why it is my favorite." He takes a deep, steadying breath while all I can do is stare at him adoringly. "Lorraina Marion, will you marry me? Will you be my love, my life for all eternity?" He cracks the little box open, and I see a little pearl waiting for me and my answer. I can't make out much more than that because tears have almost completely distorted my vision.

I drop to my knees and frame his face with my hands while I just stare at him and take him all in. I want to remember this perfect moment for the rest of my life, every little detail. The woodsy smell of him, the warm temperature, the little duck noises, the soft wind stirring my hair. The fact that I'm barefoot and looking at the most incredible man I've ever known and ever will know.

"I don't think I could ever doubt your intentions toward me, Michael, seeing as this is your third proposal." I watch his eyes brighten as he remembers our first conversation during which he told me that he was my future husband. I grin at him and answer, "I know I rebuffed your first proposal, or perhaps it was more of a declaration, but this will be my second yes, so never doubt it." I take a deep breath and confirm, "Yes, Michael Leon, I will marry you; and we will have the most amazing, most loving life together. I love you. So much."

We kiss forever as my tears spill over both of us. His wish for a blubber free proposal effectively ruined once again.

***

I stare at myself and will myself to move away from the mirror and into the room. Michael has no idea that I plan to seduce him tonight, and I'm suddenly a little nauseous. What if he turns me down? I don't know if I could take it. I need him so much. Now more than ever. I let my eyes trail down my nightgown. I tried to pick something sexy, but those outfits weren't me. I settled on an ivory gown that has soft, muted ribbons of color and lace around the neckline. The front is quite demure. When I turn around, though, that's a different story. I spin and take in the sight again. I've never worn anything this beautiful in all my life. I reach to tie the gown at the top with the thin ribbon and glimpse my pearl next to the fabric. The color is almost identical. I smile and let my gaze run over the open tear shape that leaves my back bare and rests just slightly above my bottom. I bite my lip and think here goes nothing.

I force myself to exit the bathroom, and my eyes search the room for Michael immediately. He's leaning over the TV wearing nothing but my favorite dark gray pajama bottoms. "I almost got it," he says, putting a movie in. "There we go. You ready—" His words stop abruptly as he turns and looks at me in my gown. OK. Maybe it's not that demure. I bite my bottom lip again, which is becoming an almost constant reaction with him around. I try to release it and end up running my tongue over it before biting it again. "If you had any idea what I want to do with that lip right now…" He leaves the threat/promise hanging in the air between us. It bolsters my courage.

I walk over to him and put my hands on his chest. "I know you want to wait, but Michael it just feels right. I need you so badly, and I know you need me too. Please don't say no to me, to us. I feel like we've waited long enough to be together, don't you?" I wait with bated breath.

He stares at me a moment and seems to come to some kind of decision. I can't tell which one, though. He leans in and kisses me tenderly. *No, no,* I cry in my head. He's going to tell me no. His reluctance is tangible. He pulls back a little to murmur, "I want to…so bad, but I don't have any protection." *Oh, thank God.*

My cheeks warm because he's about to realize this was all premeditated. "Umm…I've been on the pill for a few months now. I don't think we have to worry about the other stuff, seeing as we've both abstained for so long."

"Oh. Oh, good," he gets out before he begins to devour me with his hands and his kisses. I hear him groan as his hands brush my naked back. He slows down to pull back, and I see desire swimming in his eyes. I pray I'm good at this. I don't want to let him down. His look says he's about to get everything he's ever wanted. "Are you sure?" I nod my head enthusiastically. "Cuz I'm pretty sure I would die right here on this spot if you asked me to stop," he says on a grin. "I've wanted you all my life."

"I'm sure. I've never been more sure about anything or anyone," I tell him.

He smiles at me before he begins to kiss me, more tenderly this time. He pulls back to focus his kisses on my chin, my jaw, my neck. I'm lost as his kisses leave me hot but shivering. He chuckles against my throat at my reaction. I run my hands through his hair as I force him to apply more pressure to the kisses that are simultaneously feeding my need and driving me crazy.

His hands start moving again in tandem with his mouth. Where his hands go his mouth follows. When his hands trace my breasts, I know I'm in trouble. When his mouth brushes my satin-covered nipple, I almost come undone. But he extends that sweet cruelty rather than letting me dwell on it as he tastes and teases one while rubbing the other and then lavishes the other with his mouth, showing them both equal attention.

He breaks away from me and walks around me to remove my gown. I hear his sharp intake of breath as he glimpses my back. My eyes shoot up to the mirror on the bureau in front of me. Our eyes meet, and I almost buckle under the weight of his stare. I feel him trail his fingertips around the shape of the tear. I close my eyes and lose myself in his touch. It's delicate yet torturous. He places feather light kisses where his fingers have traced until he is on his knees, licking and teasing my tender flesh on my lower back.

He moves back to my neck and unties my little ribbon. I open my eyes to find his questioning mine in the mirror. I manage to give him a small smile. He uses his hands to push the silky gown down. Where it glides over my skin, I have goose bumps. I hope he can't see them. I've never felt so exposed in my entire life. He seems to like what he sees as I watch him, watch me. My eyes immediately look at my rounded stomach and my wide hips. I suddenly feel self-conscious. I try to close my eyes, but he gently tells me to open them back up. His voice leaves no room for questioning. So I do. I watch his hands move to massage my breasts as he kisses my neck and my shoulders. I move my eyes back up to find his watching his hands, and I've never been more turned on in my life.

He tilts my head back until his mouth finally moves back to mine, and he sears me with his kiss. When I'm so weak that I'm afraid I'm going to slide to the floor, I feel his arms snake under my knees to lift me and carry me to the bed. I turn effortlessly in his arms, and his lips never break from mine.

As he lays me down on the bed, I run my hands over his gorgeous chest, and place my lips on his heart tattoo with my name on it. "Mine," I whisper. "You're all mine."

"Always have been," he confirms. "Always will be."

I pull him in to seal his promise with a kiss. He moves down my body, kissing and teasing. I close my eyes tight when I feel him start to remove my underwear. When I feel his lips move over my own tattoo, I have the courage to look down at him. He gazes up at me with those piercing deep brown eyes and questions me, "Mmm…So I'm about to fulfill your ultimatum, Lorraina. When do I get my name right here?" His fingertips graze my beautiful roses.

"As soon as humanly possible," I tell him.

I gasp as I feel his finger make its way down to enter me. His tongue demands entry at my mouth almost simultaneously, and I lose myself in our kiss. I feel the vibrations of his moans as he works my body for what seems like hours. When he finally deems me ready and I'm about to explode with the need of him, he enters me smoothly. He pulls his head back and locks his eyes with mine.

"I love you, Lorraina," he tells me.

"I love you too, Michael."

I lie on the bed, trailing my hands across his chest in a swirling little pattern, staring at my beautiful ring. It's a gorgeous pearl. I never even knew I liked pearls until I saw this one. The band is made of silver or white gold. I'm not exactly sure. As the band sweeps up to join the pearl, it's divided into three little rows of tiny diamonds. It's simple. It's exquisite. It's him. It's me. It's perfect.

We've been very quiet. I wonder for a moment if he's asleep. I allow my brain to go back to our lovemaking. Mmm…I'm quite certain there's not an inch of my body that he didn't worship with some part of his own. I shiver again as I feel myself stirring with just the memory of it. I feel him chuckle beneath me.

I lean up on my elbow and take him in. He's beautiful. I tell him so. He chuckles again. I can't stop smiling. "I've never experienced anything like that," I confess.

"Yeah. Me either," he agrees.

"I don't really want to talk about our past experiences, but I have to say that I never knew sex could be like that."

"That's because we didn't have sex," he tells me.

I feel myself blushing. "Oh. Yeah, right, what I meant was I've never felt like that. So loved and so adored. And so…fulfilled. It was incredible." I stop short of asking him if he thinks every time will be like that. He'll think I'm an idiot.

"Me either," he says again. "I cared about the people I was with before, but it was just like it was something to do. I don't know. With you, I just had to show you how much I love you and care about you. I had to make sure that you absorbed every touch, every emotion."

My mouth has gone dry listening to him describe our lovemaking. I suddenly want to do it all over again and test my theory about it being incredible every single time.

My gaze goes back to my ring. "This is exquisite," I tell him.

"I'm glad you like it."

"I love it. It's unique. I've never seen anyone with a pearl engagement ring."

"I wanted something unique for us since our love is, ya know? Besides, I think you get the significance behind the pearl, right?"

"Yeah, purity, change, dignity...Something beautiful shaped by chance and mud and determination."

He picks up my hand and kisses my pearl. His other hand tucks my hair behind my ear and curls around my neck. "Something perfect, flawless made that way through transformation."

***

"Ms. Elise, this is Michael Bang. Michael, this is Ms. Elise Andrews." I step back and let them shake hands. I've refused to let go of one of them so he has to make do.

"Ms. Elise," I hear Michael say, "Lorraina has told me a lot about you and your business. I'm happy that she works for someone like you." *Oh, that's so sweet,* I think adoringly.

"Oh, honey. I'm the lucky one. This one has been a stellar employee," she tells him and winks at me. I thank her with my eyes since she omits the fact that I've been less than stellar lately. "Michael, Lorraina tells me that you're quite the musician. Come see our music selection and tell me how we measure up. " I watch as they make their way to the back of the store while I try to switch gears and get into work mode.

Later, as Ms. Elise leaves for the day, I hear Michael ask her permission to stay and study. He promises that he won't distract me. He just doesn't want to be too far away, he tells her. I smile to myself. I've watched them together for the last hour or so. I wonder if he knows she is putty in his capable hands. She assures him that it will be fine as we are a little slow because of the break.

As she passes by me, she pats my hand and tells me what I need to do for that night and that I did well choosing Michael. "Honey, that is one sweet boy," she tells me. "He loves you an awful lot."

"He told you that?" I gasp. I can't believe he would just come out with that. It seems so personal.

"Oh, no, not in so many words," she assures me. "But I know he does. Be careful with him. He's very sensitive."

My eyes widen. "I will be," I promise her. "I love him an awful lot, as well."

She pats my hand again. "Good night, honey."

"Night, Ms. Elise."

My eyes seek him out. His head is bent over his book. His hand rubs his neck. There's no one in the store but us, so I head over his way. He smiles up at me as I approach him. I move to stand behind him and massage his neck. I can't resist some small kisses on his neck as I rub. "I can't study when you're touching me," he admonishes me. "Besides, I promised Ms. Elise we would be good."

"I know, I know," I huff. "I just needed a minute."

I find myself suddenly sitting in his lap as he ravages me. I just as suddenly find myself standing upright as he tells me to get back to work. I frown at him over my shoulder as I return to not doing a whole lot of anything except thinking about him.

We close up the store and decide to go for drinks and pool at a nearby pub before heading back to the hotel. I don't have on my skirt anymore but these jeans are pretty tight, so I'm hoping for a repeat of last night and this morning and later this morning.

We've been shooting pool for quite some time. Long enough for me to have a couple of drinks and for him to have a few beers before cutting himself off since he's driving us. My drink is empty; and since it's Michael's shot, I make my way to the bar to get another. I'm leaning over the bar to yell my order to the bartender when I feel someone slap my ass. My mind immediately goes to Michael, but I dismiss that thought, knowing it's not him. He would never do that, not in public anyway. My body freezes for a moment, considering how to best handle this.

I spin around to defend myself from any more advances and realize I'm too late because Michael has already cornered the guy. Before I can gather my wits, he has his hand around his neck and is choking him.

I rush over, yelling for him to stop. He doesn't seem to hear me at all, though. I get up in his face and scream for him to stop it. The guy seems like he can't breathe. I'm petrified but determined to make him stop. I put my hands on Michael and push him as hard as I can. He doesn't even budge. I'm pretty sure I'm shrieking now and begging him to stop, but he just won't. I look back at the guy and his eyes are closed and his features are slack. I don't think anymore. I just rear my hand back and slap Michael across the face. His eyes fly to mine, and I start crying as he drops the guy onto the floor. I drop to my knees and reach out to check his pulse.

The guy's eyes fly open, and he yells at me to get away from him before I even touch him. I take this as a good sign and breathe a sigh of relief. He jumps up and tells Michael that he's fucking crazy.

My eyes fly up to Michael's, and I see something twist in them. I don't get it. We were having a wonderful time and, snap, just like that he tries to kill this guy. If I think that I've seen the worst of it, I've got another thing coming.

He pulls me to my feet and backs me against the wall where he's just held the guy up and scared the shit out of me. He releases me quickly but fixes me with his glare. "What? Did you like it? Is that why you took up for him?" He stuns me with his questions.

Before I can answer, he continues, "I knew you were a tease in school, but still, really?" He snarls at me. "I had no idea. I wish I had, though."

Copious tears spring to my eyes immediately. I don't even know what to say to these accusations. He is so far off base and so not my Michael that I'm completely caught off guard. I don't know how to react.

Michael spins around on his heel and takes off out the front door. I stand there for a minute or two, collecting my obliterated thoughts and wiping the tears from my face.

I run up to the bar, pay for the drinks, and apologize for Michael's behavior. She seems completely oblivious to what's just transpired.

I look across the bar at the guy. He and his friends are kidding around. No harm, no foul. I guess.

When I get out to his Jeep, I find him hunched over it. I cross my arms over my middle, and I move very slowly toward the passenger side. "I'd like to go now, please," I tell him.

He nods his head, not even looking at me. I just want to bawl my face off. I don't quite know what to do or say. Was he so blinded by anger that he wasn't aware of what he was saying, or was he able to say what he really felt because his guard was down? I think of the Michael of last night who so sweetly proposed to me and so tenderly loved me. I can't reconcile him with tonight's Michael.

Our ride back to the hotel is silent. When he kills the engine, I put my hand on the handle to get out; but his quiet sob stops me. Thoughtless, I reach across the Jeep quickly and gather him in my arms. I kiss him all over his head and rub his back, trying to offer some measure of consolation for all that he's feeling. All that I don't understand.

He grabs me hard and holds on to me as though his life depends on it. "Ah...God. I'm so sorry, Lorraina. So sorry," he mumbles over and over again.

"Shh," I tell him. "It's going to be OK. Whatever that was. It's going to be OK."

He pulls back and gazes at me. "How can you say that after what I said to you? After I fucking choked that guy for touching you?"

My pulse quickens as I remember how scary that was. "I'll admit. It was a little extreme. Have you ever done that before? Lost it like that?"

"Yes."

"I take it that the fight with *him* was like that."

"Yes, that was the last time."

"Great, so all your anger revolves around me," I mutter petulantly.

"Huh? I never thought about it like that, but you're not the only reason I've snapped. Please don't think that. It's definitely my problem. Not yours."

"Ours," I state. He looks at me questioningly. "*Our* problem. We'll figure it out. I'll admit that was pretty scary, but that's not who you are, Michael."

"I just kept waiting for you to turn around and smack that guy. When you didn't, I just got so mad. I was across the room before I even realized it."

"Well, I kinda froze. For a moment, I thought it was you. Then, I was like what the hell do I do about this. When I turned around to defend myself, it was too late. I'm sorry that you misunderstood."

"Please don't apologize to me. You didn't do anything wrong."

I run my fingertips over his tear-softened lashes, trying to dry his eyes and fulfill the desire I've had since the very beginning. I love that I can touch him so freely. "Have you ever tried to get help for your anger, Michael?"

"No, not really. I thought I had it under control."

"Well, I think you need help dealing with it. Do you think you could ask Father Patty about how to go about getting some help? I know you trust him."

"Yeah, I think so." He loses himself in thought for a moment. "Ya know, I've very effectively avoided the source of my anger for so long that I really didn't think that would happen again."

"Your dad?" I guess.

"Yep, I can't even talk to him anymore. When I see him, we argue automatically. Now that I'm grown, our fights aren't pretty, so I stay away. I visit my mom when I know he won't be there, or only when others will be around to take the sting out of his comments."

"I'm so sorry, Michael. I wish he could see what I see," I whisper.

His voice comes out at barely a whisper when he admits, "I think he does. I think that's why he hates me. He thinks I'm weak."

I'm across the car and in his lap before he can protest. I throw my leg over his and catch his face with my hands and kiss him into what I hope is complete and utter oblivion. I know I'm thinking of nothing but how good he tastes, how good he smells, how good he is.

I wrap my arms around his head and kiss him harder and faster until I'm completely lost. I feel his hands come around my bottom as he pulls me into him. I get immediate confirmation that my attempts to distract him have been successful. I pull my lips back slightly and against his murmur, "Take me upstairs to your bed, please."

He groans and slides down from his Jeep with me attached to his front. I wrap my legs around him as he carries me toward the hotel. I glance around and assure we are alone. I tighten my legs around him. He groans again. "See how strong you are," I tell him. "You're the strongest person I know."

***

My three days were up so fast. Other than our little blip our second night, it was perfection. It's just how I imagine our life together: simple, sweet, wonderful. Saying goodbye to him hurt so badly. I hated it. I never want to have to say goodbye to him again. These next two months were going to kill us.

Chapter Twenty-nine

Regaining My Tomorrow

I pull into my parents' front yard and kill my engine. I would've driven straight to his apartment, but it's thirty miles further and I'm practically running on fumes with no money to rectify that little inconvenience. Furthermore, I'm a little nervous to see him. I haven't spoken to him in almost two weeks and that's got me really freaked out. I think I may have screwed things up between us, but then I remind myself that I was meant to be with him, made to be with him. We've just hit a rough patch because of school, but everything is going to be fine.

I survey the yard and realize that all the vehicles are absent and the porch light is on. I guess my family is out. I was really hoping to get some money from Joe for gas and head to Michael's. I guess that will have to wait.

I pull myself out of my car. I'm exhausted, and I need a shower. My euphoria over graduating has finally passed, leaving me completely drained. I smile as I remember Ms. Elise giving me grief over not walking, but if Michael couldn't be there what was the point? More importantly, it got me home five days earlier.

I throw my stuff on the floor and myself on the bed, kicking my shoes off as I stretch out for a minute. I pick up my phone to call him again, but my fingers hesitate over the buttons. I let the receiver drop on my chest for a minute and recall our last conversation and the many messages I'd left him since. We didn't really have a fight per say, but it was awkward. I'd had to make him understand how important my last few weeks of school were. I was struggling to maintain my GPA. It had dropped as a direct result of the amount of time I spent daydreaming over him, which was in direct correlation to the amount of time I spent talking to him.

I asked him if we could set up times to talk so that I could try to refocus. I joked that it would be reminiscent of when we were back in school and our talks were forbidden. I knew he wasn't crazy about it, but he acted like it was fine and that he understood. When I called for our first scheduled talk, he didn't answer. I'd left so many messages since then, each one increasing in desperation. I was completely freaked out by the time it was time to head home. I kept reassuring myself that we didn't come this far to lose each other over something so trivial.

I hear the incessant blaring of the phone being off the hook and realize I never did dial a number. I hang it up for a second and dial Ginny's number instead. I've been so tempted to call and tell her all about Michael. Now that I need her advice, I realize that's exactly what I should do. I need someone to confide in.

I get her on the phone immediately. I take this as an auspicious sign. "I need to talk to you about Michael Bang," I blurt out almost immediately.

"Oh, I know. I'm so glad you called," she inserts.

"Is everything OK?" She sounds weird. My problems fly out of my head.

276

"Well, I wanted to call you as soon as I'd heard but figured it would probably be better if we didn't talk about it while you were trying to finish up classes." I've never heard her sound so flustered before. *Heard what?*

"Ginny, what did you hear? You sound weird."

"Well, I just don't want to upset you because I could tell you cared about him and all; but I'm glad you want to talk about it."

It? Michael? Does she already know about me and Michael? From what I understand there are only three people who know all about us and none of them interact with anyone I know. "Talk about what exactly?" I ask still confused.

"Well, Mike, sweetie," she says almost impatiently.

I sigh. "You do know? I'm sorry that I wasn't the one to tell you."

"It's OK. I only heard about it a few days ago. I couldn't believe it. So young and so tragic."

My entire body tenses. I sit up abruptly. "What do mean by that, Ginny?" My voice sounds sharp.

"I just mean it's such a shame. He seemed to be getting his life together from everything I've heard, and it's just so unfair. And the way his parents treated the whole thing. Hardly even telling anyone and all. I know you saw his cards at Mona's, but did you ever catch up with him while you were home last?"

My mind is completely blank so that I can't really focus on what she's saying, but I know it's important. "Ginny, I don't have a clue what you're talking about." I start shaking my head and realize that I'm biting my lip so hard it hurts. *Is he hurt or in jail or what?*

"What?! Lorraina, did you not hear about Mike? Mike Bang, sweetie. Your friend..." I say nothing and she continues even though something screams inside of me to tell her to shut up. "He died."

A slight moan escapes me. "No, no." I'm back to shaking my head and biting my lip.

"Oh, Lorraina. I'm sorry. I had no idea you hadn't heard. What did you want to talk about him for then?"

"What happened?" I ask automatically, ignoring her question.

"Well, from what I've heard, something went down at his parents' house and Mike left upset. He lost control of his car just a mile from their home and died on impact."

My room suddenly feels vacuous. I hear her talking but can't make out any of the words. I open my mouth to speak, to say anything. Nothing comes out. After a minute of her rambling, I cut in, "I have to go. I'll call you later." I hang up, not even sure if she said goodbye.

Oh my God...Oh my God. There has to be some mistake. I look around my room for some indication that this isn't real, and I barely even recognize where I am. It all seems...foreign. A moment ago it was like I was in a vast tunnel. Now, I feel the room constricting upon me and I can't breathe.

Nope, no, no. There's no way he's gone, I tell myself. It has to be some kind of mistake. Ginny seemed sure, though. I stand up woodenly and grab my keys. I walk out to my car and move to get in it. As my hand reaches for the door, I remember I don't have any gas. I chunk my keys at the door. I hear a shriek and realize that I'm pulling at my hair. I have to get out of here. I have to figure out what's going on.

I look around wildly for some means of escape. Nothing. I turn from my car and start walking. Then I'm running. I run through our yard and throw myself over the fence and take off through the pasture. When I reach the other side, I bend to cut through the barbed wire fence. As I do, I feel the welcome pain of the pointed metal scraping down my back. It doesn't slow me down.

When I reach the edge of the woods, I dart in the trees and rest my hands on my knees, trying to catch my breath. I feel myself gagging, and I succumb to wracking dry heaves. I wish I could throw up. Maybe I would feel better.

I have to…I have to…I need someone to talk to about this. I need to figure out what happened. I grab for some brush to steady myself and end up shredding it with my hands. I scream and howl. I did this to myself. I have no one. No one. I try to calm myself. There has to be a better way.

When my breathing finally slows, I realize that I'm crying profusely. It feels as though my entire body is sobbing, so I just sink. Sink to the ground. Sink into madness. Sink into sweet oblivion.

***

I open my eyes and am greeted by the darkest of night. I blink hard and look around for a moment, trying to figure out where I am. Oh. Yeah, I'm in our woods. I roll onto my back and will myself to get up. I can't lie out here all night. I need to find out exactly what is happening with Michael. I bring my hands up to rub some warmth into my face and arms. It's cold out here, which is weird. I hear a distorted, distant laugh. *Why am I thinking about the weather?*

I pull myself up and start walking. I realize very quickly that I don't have on any shoes because my feet are stinging. *Damn! That hurts!* I love it. It forces me to consider what is happening right now instead of focusing on...I can't even think it. My path back to the house is much slower than the one to the woods.

I walk up the little sidewalk in front of our house and glance up at the moon. It's almost midnight and my family still isn't home.

After I get into the bathroom, I flip the light switch and lean back against the door. *OK, I tell myself, you need a plan. Get a shower, get some money, go find out what's happening with Michael. OK.* I blow out a breath and look down to take off my clothes. I'm covered in dirt. My mom's gonna freak if I get this all over the place. I laugh again at the absurdity of thinking that thought at this precise moment. I feel my face distort with pain, and I throw my hand over my mouth and taste dirt. I throw my arm around my middle to try to hold in the gut-wrenching sobs I feel about to spill out of me and feel immense pain. My crazy laugh turns into a little squeal and erupts from my mouth.

I turn and glance in the mirror and gasp. I don't recognize the person staring back at me. Her hair is matted together in dirty clumps and her face is streaked with dirt and dried blood. Why was I bleeding? I lean in closer to get a better look. I have scratch marks down my face. I have a brief memory of myself pulling at my hair and scratching at my face. I can't believe that was even me.

I jump as I hear the front door slam. Someone knocks on the bathroom door, and I open my mouth to say I'll be right out. Fire burns a path up my throat and nothing comes out. I reach over and turn the water on in the bath. That should help them figure out I'm in here.

I try to speak quietly to myself. Nothing. The image of me shrieking and cursing and babbling jolts me. I'm back in the woods freaking out.

I close my eyes and try to dislodge the memory from my brain by shaking my head side to side. One step at a time, I remind myself.

***

After my shower, I'm feeling more humanlike. I test my voice and some harsh, discordant sounds make their way out. I walk into my room. Before I can shut the door, Jerome is there.

"Hey, what's up?" He asks. I turn and face him." You look like shit," he states matter-of-factly.

Never one to beat around the bush. "Thanks. I feel like it." I manage.

"Damn. You sound like shit too. Are you sick?"

"Yes, I'm coming down with something," I tell him.

"Oh, well, it's good to have you home. You here for the summer?" I nod my head. "All right. Well, you should get some rest. I can't believe you drove home that sick. Let me know if you need anything. Mom and Joe won't be home till later. Went dancing after the drawdown." He wiggles his brows suggestively. I laugh a little. It sounds forced and weird. "Night, Nay Nay."

I don't want to ask him, but I have to know if it's really true. "Jerome, did you hear about Michael Bang?"

He turns back around and leans on my doorframe. "Yeah, I'm sorry about that. I know ya'll were friends."

I nod my head. "It's true then," I mumble. Jerome goes blurry and I close my eyes.

I feel his hand pat my hand. "Hey, hey, now. It's going to be OK," he tells me.

"I just found out," I confess.

"What? What do you mean you just found out?"

"I mean I just found out that he…he's gone like," I glance at my clock, "like four hours ago."

His face tightens. "No one called you?"

"No, no one called me because I have no one *to* call me."

"You're not making any sense. What do you mean?"

282

I sit down dramatically on my bed, feeling every bit the petulant child. "I mean I have no one who thinks enough about me to call me and tell me that...one of my oldest friends died." I wish he were only one of my oldest friends. I wish I didn't feel the sharp pain thinking about every other role he'd played in life as of late. No, that's no true. To take that pain away, I'd have to give up all the joy he'd brought to my life.

"Well, to be honest, we just found out a few days ago. It was kept real quiet for some reason. I'm sorry you didn't know sooner. I would've called you if I'd known."

"Do you know any details?"

"Not really. Only that he crashed near his parents' place and died instantly, which is a good thing if you're gonna go. He'd been buried a week before I'd even heard."

I close my eyes and nod my head. He'd heard it too, so it had to be true. *Is there some measure of consolation in the fact that he hadn't suffered?* "I'm gonna get some sleep now, OK?"

"I'm sorry about your friend. You gonna be OK?" I nod my head at him as fresh tears stream down my face. "OK. Let me know if you need anything. Night."

I lie down and roll over on my bed and face the wall. I don't even know what to do with all this. I close my eyes and run over our plans in my head. I weep gently as I think of all that we won't experience. We were going to have our marriage counseling classes with Father Patty and get married in a private ceremony at the end of the summer before we left for New York. I was still waiting on my acceptance, but we'd pretty much decided we wanted to go there no matter what. Sometime before all of that we were going to let our family in on our plans.

I jerk abruptly with a sudden thought. I throw my covers off and spring from my bed. I dig through my purse and find my little box. My hands shake as I slide our ring onto my finger. I'd taken it off before I'd gotten here so my parents wouldn't question it. I wish more than anything, well almost anything, I'd never removed it. He'd put it there.

***

The next month is a blur. Time marched on somehow; but, for me, it felt frozen. I didn't really know what to do with myself. Other than the mindless summer work, I didn't do much of anything. I sat in front of the TV. I sat on the porch. I walked around our property. I saw Michael in everything around me, so it was hard to focus on anything for a length of time. I couldn't journal. I couldn't write. When I tried, all I wanted to do was write *Michael, Michael, Michael, Michael, Michael, Michael* until his name covered one page and then the one after that.

I'm not ready to go to our church yet, so I attend Mass near my parents' house. I pray every single day that God will help me see a way out of this. In fact, my faith is what is helping my heart heal. I just wish it would communicate with my head a little more because I still just don't get it. I've prayed so much that I don't even need my little pamphlet on how to pray my rosary anymore.

I know I need time to grieve, but I know I need to move on. How can I do that, though, when I spend all of my time reliving every single moment I had with Michael, when I spend every moment I'm alone listening to our songs, when I stare at my little secret shrine to him? It's amazing our six months together generated so few physical reminders. I'm sure he has tons more as he was the more productive out of the two of us, but my attempt at getting into his apartment was thwarted when his landlord told me that someone had long ago cleaned his place out.

I know that I need to put our plans into action, but I'm not sure how to go about doing that. I know that I will. If not for myself, for Michael. I could never disappoint him by giving up on everything, which is what my baser instincts tell me to do right now.

Of course, all of this must be hidden away from those around me because what would I say? *Yeah, so I finally opened myself up again, and you'll never believe it. It was to a boy I'd loved almost my whole life, but then he died.* That doesn't even compute for me. How would I make someone else understand it? So I try to pretend like everything's OK. I can tell that I'm not doing a very good job by the odd looks my family gives me. When I catch those, I'll automatically be overly enthusiastic about something, which is not me either and only invites more strange looks.

My mom constantly asks me why I'm not spending my summer hanging out with Ginny or doing other crap people my age should be doing. It's then I realize I don't know any people my age. I'm sure there are people out there like me who've lived shit lives and feel older than anyone else around them. I know there are people who have loved and lost just like I have, but I don't know any of them or how they get on with their lives. So I just make up different answers. They're so lame that I don't even remember which ones I've used. I have spoken to Ginny twice since that night. I was so tempted to tell her everything, but part of me feels like I deserve to suffer in abject silence.

This thought hits home with me. I'm handling this much like my first self-imposed mental exile. That wasn't me anymore, but I wasn't quite sure what to do to change that right this moment.

I'm sitting on the couch one afternoon pondering my favorite Michael memory when Jerome plops down beside me. It takes me a minute to realize that he's waving something in my face. "Oh, hey. What's that?" I ask, feigning enthusiasm.

"Hey now. Calm down," he replies dryly. My feigning really does need some work.

"I don't know, but it's thick and it's from NYU."

"Really?!" That almost sounded like real enthusiasm. "Hey, you can't say anything to mom. I applied there, though."

"Yeah, I kinda figured that part out. You gonna open it or not?" He waggles it over my head playfully.

I grab for it and he jerks it farther out of my reach quickly. My momentum is such that we both tumble to the floor. I laugh hard from the impact and silliness of it, but laughter soon turns into sobs. He slaps me in the face with the packet. "Stop it," he commands me.

"I know," I murmur as I dry my face. It's like my brother knows that something's eating its way through me; but, thankfully, he doesn't probe. "OK. I'm good. Give it here," I demand.

He hands it to me and I rip it open. A couple of brochures fall out as I focus on the cover letter. I hold it up over our heads, and our heads knock as we maneuver to read it. I laugh a little more. *Hey! I didn't have a complete meltdown that time, I muse.* This is both good and bad news.

"'We are pleased to inform you of your acceptance to New York University's prestigious College of Arts,'" I read aloud.

"Wow. That's cool. New York."

I sit up and shake my head. He sits up with me, watching my face. "You're not going."

"What? I didn't say that."

"You didn't have to. You're an idiot if you don't go."

"How can I? How can I do this on my own I mean? In theory it sounded great, but I'm not so sure now."

"What's changed?"

Every-freaking-thing, but I can't tell him that. Maybe one day but not today. "I guess I was just feeling particularly brave when I applied. I don't know how I feel now."

He turns to look at the wall and says nothing for a minute. I move to get up off the floor, but his words stop me. "What if I went with you?"

"Huh? You wanna go to New York? With me?" My voice rises with every question.

"I gotta get out of here, Nay. I don't know…I just…I gotta go. I never considered New York, but if you'll be there we can lean on each other. And it's about to get real crowded around here with Weldon and his new family moving in."

Our parents had agreed to let Weldon and Mariah move in here. They're gonna help with the baby while they finish school. Of course, they had to agree to get married. So it would be crowded. Nevertheless, I can't picture Jerome living in New York but if that's what he wanted, I will not stand in his way. "I think it would be very cool. I wouldn't be as apprehensive if you were there with me."

"There's a shutdown crew that I know of that works out of New York, so I wouldn't be in your hair too much."

"Let's do it," I tell him. I could do this.

"All right then," he replies on a smile.

***

As summer starts hedging toward an end, my outlook is much better. In only a couple weeks, it would be time to put this place behind me for a little while. My world is starting to feel real again. Like when he first passed, it felt so artificial. Part of me thinks it wasn't real. Like he's still out there somewhere, but we just can't be together. Like before, only this time is more permanent. It doesn't suck any less, but it makes the pain more palatable when I imagine it that way.

My motivating factor—I want to make him proud. He had such great faith, and I was fortunate enough to be included in that if only for a little while. So I can and will do this. I will live my very best life even though it can't be with him.

I'm in my room organizing things to bring, things to leave behind when a knock at my door breaks me from my reverie. I'm kind of relieved to have the distraction, so I bound to the door quickly. I throw it open, and a handsome young man greets me. He's unexpected. The only people that ever come around here are old horse-traders and old farmers. Keyword there is old.

I blink my eyes a couple of times and prompt him, "Yes?"

He stares at me for what feels like a full minute. "Hey. My name is Jamie Jones. Um...You, uh, we've never met, but I'm Mike's brother."

I feel my whole world shift. I knew he had one out there, but I'd never even seen him. I think we exchanged pleasantries a couple of times over the phone when Michael lived with him back in ninth grade, though. I finally remember that I should say something. "Um...Hi, I...Do you want to come in?" I finally manage a coherent utterance.

"Yeah, yeah. That'd be great." He smiles a little, looking slightly relieved.

I watch him walk in, and I'm just utterly and completely stunned. He has dirty blond hair similar to mine, and it's cut real short. He's very tall and broad compared to Michael. He carries himself nothing like him either. Maybe he's just nervous.

Then, the questions start bombarding me. First, how did he know about me? Second, why did he come to see me? Third, how is that he looks the exact opposite of Michael? I don't want to formulate my other question into actual words. I have to talk myself down to keep myself from badgering him.

I guide him to the living room. I want to ply him with my questions but don't want to overwhelm him. Fortunately, he makes it a little easier on me.

"I know you're wondering what I'm doing here. I hope that it's OK that I'm here." I nod my head fervently. Anything. I'll take any little piece of Michael. "Oh, good. Well, when I cleaned Mike's place up a couple of months ago, I kinda just put it all in boxes and stared at it for a while. When I finally got the gumption to look through his things," he pauses to release a shaky breath, "I quickly realized that he had a lot of secrets. And a great many of them had to do with you."

I just nod my head. I'm not sure what he knows, what he wants to know, or what I should tell him.

"One thing was very clear. He sure loved you."

I close my eyes and revel in that for a moment. I finally open them. "I love him too. I can't believe…"

"I know. Me either. He was my little brother, ya know?" I give him a tentative smile.

"He really looked up to you, loved you." I tell him. "I'm so sorry for your loss."

"Yeah, thanks."

"I wish we'd met before…"

"Yeah, me too. I had to do some detective work to figure out who you were and where you were. You weren't easy to find."

"So, you didn't know about me before the funeral?" I figured not, but I had to ask.

"No, I wish I would've, though."

"Me too. I don't even know where he's buried."

He expels a pent up breath and tells me, "He's buried in a family plot about an hour from here where his dad and our mom grew up. I'll write it down for you before I go."

"Good. I'd like that. You know we've been friends since school, right?"

He blushes a little and replies sheepishly, "Yeah, I know a lot about you now. I've been reading his journals, including one that I'm guessing you started for him."

Aah, my Christmas present. "Really? You have them. That's wonderful. I bet you've gotten a lot of insight into his life."

"I have. It's been…very cool. To know he was that happy before…"

"I'm so happy he was happy," I gush. I know he's gone, but I try to focus on what we had before he left and how good it was for the oh-so-brief time we had together.

"I'd…uh…like to hear your take on things if you don't mind," he requests.

I launch into every detail I can. I'm so thrilled to be talking to someone about him, especially someone who loved him and knew him. Jamie really seems to enjoy hearing my story, so I hardly leave any details out. When I tell him we had planned to get married this summer, he wipes a few tears from his eyes. When I tell him he'd already named our children, he loses it for a few minutes. I rub his arm as I wait for his tears to subside. All too soon my time with him is up. He leaves me the information for the cemetery.

As he opens the door, a question flies out of me that I don't even remember mentally posing. "Jamie, was Michael buried by a Catholic priest?"

He turns to look at me, shakes his head, and says with regret, "No, no, he wasn't. His parents haven't practiced in years. We didn't even realize Mike was attending church or anything." He wrinkles his forehead at me. "I keep noticing you call him Michael. Our mom's the only other person who called him by his given name."

I nod my head and my gears start turning. Michael was living a dual life for sure. I'm so glad that Jamie found his things and me. I hope he realizes all that Michael was, and that given more time, he would've reconciled these two distinct parts of himself. "I love his name, so I started out calling him by it. Then, Michael wouldn't let me call him Mike. He liked that I was the only one who called him that." I grin thinking about the few times I used his nickname. He would get so pissed.

"Hey, I'll be right back," he says. "I got something for you."

"OK." I watch him walk out to his truck and again marvel at how different Michael and his brother are from one another.

He bounds back up my steps with a rather large box. "I wasn't sure if I wanted to part with this stuff, but I know you'll take care of it. I kept some things, of course. I think these things will mean a lot more to you, though."

"Oh, Jamie," I start and my voice cracks. He has no idea how I hate the fact that I have very few physical reminders of Michael. "Thank you, thank you so much. I'll treasure them always." I don't know what's in the box and I don't care. The fact that they were Michael's things is all I need to know.

"You want me to bring it in for you?"

"Oh, no, I'll manage." I grab the box and turn to open the door. He shuffles around me and pulls it open for me. "Jamie, thank you so much for coming here. You have no idea how much all of this meant to me."

He smiles and I see a little of Michael in him when he does. Instant tears spring to my eyes. "I think I have an idea. Your visit did a lot for me too."

"Jamie, I'm so sorry to ask but I have to know. What happened to Michael that night?"

He runs his hands over his face before he replies tersely, "We don't really know. One minute Michael was there, hanging out. The next he was gone. Everyone is messed up over it, but our mom, especially, is real tore up over it."

"I'm so sorry for your family's loss," I tell him.

"Thanks. Well, you take care."

"Thanks. You too. Bye, Jamie."

"Bye bye, Lorraina."

I make it back to my room without toppling my box over. I close the door and lock it even though no one will be home for quite some time. I steeple my hands under my chin and try to gather some strength. I think this will be good for me; however, it's also going to hurt like hell.

Chapter Thirty

The Art of Memorializing

By the time I'm halfway through the box, I have more questions than ever. Michael sketched some beautiful pictures of me. Most of them were of my face. A couple of them were nudes. You couldn't really see anything, but it doesn't take much imagination to figure out that I'd posed for him that way. I blush as I think of Michael's brother looking at them, but I have to say it's astounding to see how Michael saw me. My flaws were still there: rounded belly, flared hips, chubby toes. However, he saw the beauty even in my imperfections and managed to convey that through his work.

I found several different poems that spoke of love and loss and described perfectly how I've been feeling all summer, but I wonder if he wrote them recently or if they were older. Were they inspired by me or by fear of us ending? I hope he didn't feel this way about our future. Most of me leans toward thinking they are older poems.

The journals. These slay me. Over and over. They're beautiful but haunting. I love reading about us from his perspective. It is absolutely incredible yet absolutely terrifying. I've never hurt so bad other than the night I found out he was gone. I sob for what seems like hours. One particular entry really cuts deep. The night that I sought him out at Mona's. Our first night; it held so much promise. I can hear him thinking these thoughts in his sexy baritone. All that confidence with an underlying layer of vulnerability.

***

I make my way to the stage and begin setting up. Jason told me that there's a pretty little blonde over on one of the couches waiting for me to play. It was everything I could do not to tear over there, jerk her up, and kiss her until she was a writhing mass in my arms. It had to be her. It had to be Lorraina. Any other girl wanting to see me would have wasted no time in making herself known. I know I have to put the ball in her court, though. Whatever she came here for, she would have to make that known. After the way she tortured me for all those years, I'm not gonna make it easy on her.

I get ready to get going and mentally chuck my entire set list. I'm gonna have some fun with this. I know what she likes. I know what will get her going. Even if it's not her, it'll be fun pretending, though. I shake that thought. It's her. It has to be. Now that it's a possibility, I won't survive, otherwise.

I kick it off with a popular, catchy song with suggestive lyrics that reminds me so much of her. My good girl with a hidden desire for bad boys like me. She's gonna have to face up to that real soon. Although in my case, I guess I would be considered a reformed bad boy.

Damn, I'm having a hard time concentrating on my performance. What is she doing here? What does she want from me? All this shit I've gone through to make myself better for her and I still don't feel ready to take her on. Fuck that! I'm ready. I mentally kick myself. I'll have to quit cursing again, damn it!

I play a couple of her favorite songs, and I sneak in one I wrote for her after our stupid fight. The fight that got me to wizen up a little too late. Thank you, God, for that fight and for that stubborn girl.

All right, I've had about enough of this shit, Lorraina. Come on baby. Is that you? How 'bout this one? I transition into "Jealous Guy." This one pretty much sums up our entire relationship. Damn! She's still as stubborn as ever.

It takes me two more songs to get her to turn around. When she does, it's a sucker punch to my gut. She's more beautiful than ever. And the way she's looking at me. I feel a slow burn move over my entire body that turns into rapid-fire movement. I need a minute to collect myself, so I motion Jason over to her. I hope he gets my drift.

I wrap up that song, and she just looks way too comfortable over there. I launch into "Every Rose Has Its Thorn." It was the first song I'd ever shared with her. It has the desired effect. She looks like she wants to kill me and kiss me at the same time. Woman, you don't even know the half of it, I think. You don't stand a chance.

***

When I finally come to, I hear my family stirring. I figure I'd better go make myself presentable before dinner. I surreptitiously try to make my way to the bathroom. When I reach the door handle, my mom is suddenly standing beside me. I try to hurry it along and avoid her seeing me like this. I've scared my own self with my look after suffering the blissful torment that is Michael's journal.

"Lorraina, look at me," she demands, leaving no room for hesitation. My head flies up of its own volition. I hear her sharp intake of breath. She grabs my hand and propels me into her room before slamming and locking the door. "What is going on with you, young lady? And no more lies."

"I..." I don't know what to say. My mom has never confronted me like this, so it is hard for me to think on my feet. I release a long pent up breath and try to take another one to calm myself, but before I can I burst into tears. My mom just pulls me over to the bed and allows me to put my head in her lap. I hear her shushing me while her hand moves over my hair. I let it all go. It feels so good. When my head begins to throb, I figure now's a good time to stop crying.

I sit up, and she just stares at me expectantly. "I have some things to tell you. I don't know how you're going to feel about them, but I want you to know that I'm going to be OK." She nods her head at me encouragingly. Of my three confessions, I'm not sure which one she will find more shocking or which one she will be more disappointed in, but there's no time like the present. "Mamma, I have some things to tell you. I hope you'll let me explain everything before you rush to judgment."

"Lorraina, I just want you better. You have not been yourself all summer. You know, you haven't been yourself for a long time, but these past few months have just been pure torture."

"I'm sorry, Mamma," I tell her. "I'm getting better I think, though." Here goes nothing. I decide a head first plunge is my best bet. "First, I'm Catholic now." Furrowed brow. "Second, I'm moving to New York to get my MFA in creative writing." Squinty, angry eyes. "Third, I fell absolutely and indelibly in love but he…" my voice falters here, but I forge on muttering words I'd only said aloud to myself, "he died." Utter astonishment.

"Wh…What? What are talking about? I don't understand."

I launch into a retelling of my past several months. I leave no details untold. Well, almost none. I don't go into great detail on Michael's visit to Oxford. Only the pertinent information is necessary there. I pull the pewter cross from my shirt and show her our engagement ring that is hanging from the necklace. She gasps and oohs and ahhs. She cries when I tell her how I found out about Michael's passing, and she wishes that she could've gotten to know him better. She tells me she was so preoccupied when we were hanging out in school that she barely remembers him. I go and get her pictures of him to jog her memory. I show her some of the drawings that he did of me and various other things. I can't help but get worked up over how amazing his work is. I can tell I'm not just biased either. My mom thinks he's phenomenal as well.

"So Michael is responsible for your writing again and your attending church again?" She asks disbelievingly.

"Yes, Mamma. He...he reawakened me. I was sleep walking through my life before. As a matter of fact, I had no life. I had one friend left over from high school, and that was only from force of habit. We didn't have a real relationship. I didn't confide in her and share my life with her. I hung out with her when I came home. I was merely functioning, and Michael snapped me out of all of that."

"I'm so happy that you're writing again. You know I think your writing is beautiful. I'd always hoped you would do something with it. Does it have to be New York, though? It's so far."

"I know, but it's my dream. I am going to do something with it. I want to write stories. I want to write stories about people who live their lives on the fringes of society. You know...outcasts and bad decision makers like Michael and me. People who have something to say and something meaningful to pass on. Law was something I was interested in, but I've found that this is my passion. This is what I was called to do."

"Well," she sighs and smiles slightly, "I've always wanted to go to New York. I think it's wonderful, Lorraina. I couldn't be happier for you. I've always wanted you to be happy. You deserve that, honey."

"Thank you, Mamma."

I'm back to hugging her tightly again when I hear her murmur, "Catholic, huh?"

I sit back and start gushing about how I found my way to the Catholic Church.

***

Now that I've gotten myself together a little, I know what I have to do. I call and make an appointment with Father Patty. When I show up, he gives me a vigorous hug and tells me he's so sorry for my loss.

"Thank you, Father. I'm sorry I haven't been by to see you sooner, but I just needed some time." I tell him about Michael's brother coming to see me and how I found out that he didn't have a Catholic burial. "Is there something you can do about that?"

"Oh yes, of course," he reassures me. I'm so relieved. That had become the most important thing to me all of the sudden.

"Thank you so much, Father."

"Of course, of course. You had to be so shocked, Lorraina, as I was so shocked about it all. He was doing so well. But only God knows our plan and our fate. We have to believe that He knows best even in these unbelievably tragic situations like Michael's."

"Yes, Father. I hope one day I can understand that, but I have to admit I'm not there just yet." He gives me a knowing smile. "Will you pray with me?"

"Of course," he says as he invokes the Trinity and offers me words of wisdom and comfort.

***

After Father leaves Michael's graveside, I just stare at it in a strange state of peace and disbelief. Father's words were so beautiful, and I feel so blessed to have realized that Michael and I needed that.

I sit down on the grass beside his grave and start running through it all. Reliving my pain, my guilt, my mourning. Part of me feels like I don't have the right to grieve because I wasn't there for him in the end. I tell that part to shut up.

I end up lying down beside him and am surprised to see stars shining back at me. It hurts to experience that beauty without him. I need to go soon, but I'm just not ready yet.

My voice startles me after so much quiet for so long. "Michael, Michael. I miss you so much. Can you see me? Do you know how much you are loved and missed? I'm sorry, Michael. I'm so sorry. I wasted so much time that we could've had together." A twisted laugh escapes me as I consider where my thoughts are headed. "Michael, you remember Heathcliff? I get it now. Really get it. I thought I got it before; but, no, I was clueless. I would give my very soul if you would haunt me for all eternity. Anything to have you near even if only in my twisted and damned psyche." I shake my head a little and relinquish that insane thought. "That's not true, Michael. I wouldn't give up my soul for that because then I wouldn't get to be in Heaven with you. My time here is limited, and it will be over before I know it. I want eternal life with you. So, as hard it will be, I'm going to live a good life on this earth, trying every single day to be an amazing person, the person you saw in me so that God will see fit for us to spend eternity together."

I tear up and wipe them away quickly. I feel like I've cried enough tears to last me a lifetime. Instead, I start to filter through all of my memories of us, of him, of his beauty, of his flaws, of his goodness.

I wake with a jolt. Disoriented for a moment, I blink rapidly. I slap myself on my forehead and start laughing uncontrollably. "Oh my…" I tsk. "Michael, you've turned me into Poe." I wipe tears of laughter from my face and giggle anew as I imagine Michael and I laughing together one day over the fact that I'd fallen asleep next to his grave just like Poe used to do for his Virginia. Our time in Heaven was going to be amazing.

***

Today's the day. The day I uphold my end of the bargain in more than one way. I open the door to the tattoo parlor and am assaulted by a bevy of emotions, most of them sensual in nature.

"Hey. What's up?" One of the artists asks me.

"Hi. I've got an appointment with Brody," I tell him.

"All right, he'll be right with you."

I nod and take my paper from my purse and smooth it out. I hope he can do what I want since my paper is so crinkled. Chad did a great job with my roses, but I want Michael's usual artist to put his name on me.

A very tall, very bald, very tattooed gentleman greets me, "Lorraina? Brody. How's it going?" Brody thrusts his hand at me.

"It's going well," I tell him. I can hear the nerves in my voice. When I was here with Michael, it was like a dream. I barely even remember the pain. Now, I think, all I will remember is the pain.

"So whatcha got in mind?" He asks as I get seated in his chair. I hand him the paper and tell him that Chad did the roses for me already, but I need the name added to it.

"We can do that," he assures me.

Before I know it, I'm done. It wasn't even that painful. Brody hands me a mirror to see it from his perspective. I smile broadly. Michael's neat little signature is forever etched on my body, and I just love it.

"You like?" He says as he cleans me up and bandages me.

"Definitely. How much do I owe you?" I ask as he moves to clean up, and I pull my stretchy skirt back over my hip.

"This one's on the house, girl."

"What do you mean? Why would you do that?" I laugh nervously.

"You're Mike Bang's Lorraina, right?"

My heart plummets and I close my eyes tight, willing myself not to get too emotional over those most beautiful of words. "Um…yeah," I finally respond.

"Yeah, well, Mike and me go way back; so it's the least I could do for his girl."

"How…how did you know?" He chuckles and suddenly I realize how incredibly attractive he is. He's not Michael beautiful, but really, who is? That thought is immediately followed by the

304

thought that, for the rest of my life, I will probably compare every single male I meet to Michael.

"It may have had something to do with the fact that I had to stare at your face for about three hours when I inked his last tattoo." At my confused look, he continues. "You know? When he had that sketch of you inked on his thigh." I gasp and stare at him open-mouthed. "You didn't know," he states.

"No, I didn't know." I close my eyes for a minute and let that image sink in. Michael sitting here, getting my face inked on his thigh. "What did it look like?" I finally manage to ask.

"You're looking right at him with your hands folded under your cheek like you're lying down about to go to sleep." I nod my head up and down. I think I know the drawing. It was in the box. "Anyway, I have a picture of it. Besides his Mary, it was one of my favorite profiles that I've done. Wanna see it?"

All I can do is nod my head again. Would he ever stop gifting me with beautiful memories? Brody comes back over with a book open to many tattoos. My eyes seek out my profile. They land on it pretty quickly. I look so beautiful on Michael's copper skin. I'm inked in all black except for my eyes. My emerald eyes stare out at me. It looks like a more beautiful version of me. "Wow! I look beautiful!" I exclaim without thinking as I run my fingers over his thigh and my face.

"Yeah. He's one talented mother—" He breaks off and blushes a little when my eyes shoot up to his. "Uh...sorry. I tried to get him to go into the business, but he had other plans."

"Thank you for sharing that with me." I reluctantly draw my fingers away from the picture.

"Hey, you want this copy?"

"Really?"

"Yeah, I can get another one printed. No problem."

"Thank you so much," I gush.

I hold the picture to my chest as I say my goodbyes and make my way out to my car. I lay my head down on my steering wheel and just focus on breathing. Shit! I was suddenly so torn over leaving this town. What if there were more memories of Michael just waiting for me to discover them. Suddenly, my thought about Michael haunting me didn't seem so crazy.

I stare at myself on his thigh and imagine him lying down to go to sleep at night and caressing my face while we were apart. Staring at me while he talked to me on the phone. I shiver and try to rub away the sudden onslaught of goose bumps covering my flesh. I try to focus on what I need to do now.

I take the picture and place it in my visor next to my absolute favorite rose that he sketched for me...well, one of my favorites...and a couple of candid shots of him and us. Those pictures would make for some interesting conversation for Jerome and me on our way to New York.

***

I watch as the last rays of the sun snake out over the Gulf. I have never seen a sunset like the ones I've seen here. They are absolutely breathtaking. I'd come here to make my peace with my

Point Cadet Michael and reminisce over the spectacular memories we made here. It was where we'd spent our first quasi-perpetual night.

I'm puzzled over the fact that I'm a little torn up to be leaving this place this time. I've never had a problem going after what I've wanted even if that led me away from here, but I feel as if I've made peace with so many things and people that had me dreading this place. I almost don't want to go, but I know this is what Michael would want for me, and I want it for myself so much.

I close my eyes for a moment and whisper some words to him. I walk closer to the water for a second and crane my neck to see the remnant rays. Satisfied that I had, in fact, viewed my last sunset here for a while, I start toward my car and pause by our little oak tree that I so adored. I don't know what it is about this little tree that I so connect with. Oak and beach just don't seem to go together, but it just works here.

My eyes widen with disbelief as I catch a glimpse of a carving. I squint and move in closer, struggling to make out the carving on the tree. Unbelievable! There he goes again. Carved on the little tree are our initials. I run my finger over the design. The raised oak makes up a combination of our initials. In the middle is an M. On one side is a backwards L conjoined with the M and on the other side of the M is a forward facing L. He had made our initials mirror images of one another. I marvel at them until I can barely see them.

The sudden darkness surrounding me prompts me to dash to get my car and dig my camera out of one of my already packed bags. I sprint back and snap several pictures of the carving. It looks like behind the initials is a setting sun with all its rays surrounding it. I decide that it will be my next tattoo. I guess what they say is true. Tattoos really are addictive. My ink from my last isn't even dry yet.

I head back to my car and shift my box of Michael's things to the backseat so that my brother and I will both fit up front. For some crazy reason, he wants to drive through the night. I glance up at the impromptu collage that covers my visor and sigh. I'm happy that my brother is going with me. He's so excited, but I would give anything if it were Michael.

As I pull out onto the highway, I smile as I feel the burn of the addition to my Michael tattoo; and I grin even bigger when I anticipate the sting of my future Michael tattoo. I frown a little as I realize that I'm sure, eventually, I'll find someone to love and someone who loves me. I'm not naïve enough to believe that I can spend the rest of my life alone as much as the thought of being with anyone repulses me. I grin again, though, as I realize that whoever loves me will have to love my Michael too because he will be with me in almost every way possible—forever.

###

In Loving and Precious Memory of

Michael Leon Bang

This book is dedicated to Michael's memory. Some events were inspired by real events; and, of course, I named my main character after his inspiration. But my Michael is a work of fiction and my imagination.

To my soul mate best friend, Bobbie Myers, without your encouragement and enthusiasm, this wouldn't have been near as exciting to write. You were with me every joyful and frustrating step of the way. Your belief in my abilities kept me from succumbing to self-doubt and writer's block. And thank you for writing my biography!

To my husband and best friend, Sean, thank you so much for always believing in me. No matter what crazy ideas I've come up with over the years, you've always been the first on board and the most encouraging.

To my sons, Austin and Nolan, you inspire me every day to be my best and do my best. Nothing in this world has made me prouder than calling myself your mama.

I love ya'll so much!

Many members of my family inspire me on a daily basis, but none more than my momma, Marie McAdams. I'm so grateful for your love, support, and respect. I hope I made you proud. I love you.

Finally, to my many students over the years who've supported me and inspired me, when I think of you, tears brimming with gratefulness; love; and respect spring to my eyes. I'm so proud to call myself your teacher, and I'll always call you my student. A special shout out to BHS Class of 2017!

About the author

For as long as she can remember, Lynetta Halat has lived to read and has written countless stories and plays since she was a young girl. A teacher by day and an avid reader and closet writer by night, she has always dreamt of penning books that people could connect with and remember; and her first novel, *Every Rose*, is the perfect catalyst to launch her into the world of publishing. Her love of the English language prompted her to pursue a master's degree in English from Old Dominion University in Virginia. A self-proclaimed "Coast Girl," she lives in Mississippi with her adorable husband, two amazing sons, and two loveable dogs. She is currently at work on her second book.

Connect with Lynetta

Smashwords author page
Twitter: @LynettaHalat
Facebook: Lynetta Halat Author
Goodreads author page

Made in the USA
Charleston, SC
17 June 2013